[Handwritten: To: A... ... ... With ... Whitney]

This book is a work of complete fiction. Any names, places, incidents, characters are products of the author's imagination and creativity or used fictitiously. Any resemblance to actual events or locales or persons, living or dead, is fully coincidental.

All rights reserved, including the right to reproduce this book or any portion thereof in any form whatsoever in any country whatsoever is forbidden.

www.whitneysweetwrites.com

Inn Love

First Publication in 2019
An eRed Sage Publication All Rights Reserved
Copyright © 2019

ISBN: 9781603100984; 1603100989 Inn Love eBook version
Published by arrangement with the authors and copyright holders of the individual works as follows:
Inn Love © 2019 by Whitney Sweet

Re-publication by Whitney Sweet
All Rights Reserved Copyright © 2020 by Whitney Sweet

ISBN: located on barcode.

Cover Art purchased from Canva. www.canva.com

[Signature: Sweet 2020]

For Mom, Jaclyn, and Paul for your love and your support. For everyone else who helped me along the way, too.

1

It was nearly eight in the morning, in a little café in the centre of town. Jane Michaels prepared to greet commuters on their way to work. She moaned as she pulled a tray of muffins out of the oven. Up since five a.m. she felt weary and was ready for another cup of tea, which she would have, just as soon as her baking was done for the day. She opened the café eight years ago with the life insurance money left over after she buried her husband Tom. Alone, with their three-year-old, special-needs daughter, she packed up their house, broken hearted and grieving, taking only what they needed and moved back to town to live with her mother Fae. Eventually the idea of opening the café arose. Fae thought it was a great way to get her daughter out of the house after her granddaughter, Ellie, started school.

At the time, Jane spent all her spare moments worrying about how Ellie would fare at school as a spirited and strong girl, even if she was born with cerebral palsy. The girl loved learning and looked forward to going to class each day. The café helped to ease Jane's worry, at least about Ellie, but Jane only transferred the worry into the café once she knew her daughter would be alright.

As time passed, with them barely making ends meet from the profits made with baked goods, meals, and coffee, Jane's worries resurfaced anew. Her daughter was getting big now and needed a larger electric wheelchair. Jane wasn't sure how this was going to happen, despite subsidies that were available to her and the bit of money she'd managed to secure from local charities. She just didn't have enough to make up the difference. There were always online fund-raising pages, she supposed. That seemed complicated and unfair to others. Everyone's life was difficult in one way or another, why should she ask strangers to help her through a hard time when they had hard times of their own?

Sighing again, she slid in two trays of chocolate chip cookies and put on the timer and tried to put her worries away for now. The door chimed, and Jane felt happy because she knew it would be her daughter, Ellie, followed by Fae, her mother; two of her favourite people in the world.

"Morning, Mom!" Ellie called.

"Morning," Jane called back across the pass-through window which looked out into the café. Ellie rolled her wheelchair over the threshold with her grandmother behind, who toted a knapsack and a stack of mail from yesterday.

"Hi, sweetie," Jane said leaning down to kiss her daughter on the cheek. "Want a muffin? Orange cranberry just cooled enough to eat."

"Can I have butter and honey on it?"

"Butter and honey coming right up." Jane busied herself with buttering and poured a glass of milk to go along with the muffin then took the meal over to the table where Ellie came to rest by the window. Sitting next to her, Fae opened the mail. Mostly bills for the café. Fae's face fell a little when she opened an unfamiliar manila coloured envelope. Jane shot her normally poised-looking mother a glance of concern over Ellie's head. Fae cocked an eyebrow letting her daughter know she'd tell her later. Jane picked up a serviette and laid it next to Ellie's plate. Ellie ate slowly, picking up morsels of muffin, depositing them on her tongue with her right hand. Her left hand, the weak one, rested on her lap. Jane sat on a stool on the other side of her daughter.

"Did you remember to bring your notes for your presentation?" she asked her daughter, resisting the urge to wipe honey from the girl's bottom lip.

"Yup. They're in my knapsack," Ellie responded, mouth filled with muffin.

"Want to practice some of it with me? I have a few minutes until the cookies are done," Jane said.

Ellie was always eager to share what she had learned at school. Today she was doing a presentation on Komodo dragons. Jane's enthusiastic and smart daughter launched into everything she knew about the large lizards. Fae put down the mail and listened. Jane soon heard the oven timer buzzing. "Keep going, I'm listening. Just speak loudly," she said as she went across the dining area, behind the counter and into the kitchen. The smell of melting chocolate and vanilla wafted toward her as she covered her hands with mitts and opened the oven. Another whoosh of hot air drowned out some of what Ellie was saying.

"Speak up, honey, the oven is loud," Jane called. Ellie shouted a little, yelling facts in her mother's direction.

"The Komodo dragon can only see colours, they only have cones in their eyes. They cannot see well in the dark. Also, they don't hear as well as humans. They can't hear high pitched voices or low rumbling noises," Ellie's voice was shrill with the strain of yelling.

"Eyes with only cones, that's interesting," Jane yelled back while she slid the cookies onto the cooling rack. The doorbell rang. Jane looked out through the pass. "Good morning Ed," she said while she waved an oven mitt at the round-faced bus driver who took Ellie to school on the accessible school bus each morning.

"Good morning, Jane. And good morning, Ellie, Fae," he said, nodding to each one, removing his ball cap, as usual, when he looked at Fae. Jane felt a pang of loneliness as she watched. The sixty something, slightly balding gentleman grinned at her mother, obviously taken with the woman's striking green eyes enhanced by her thick, wavy, closely cropped white hair that was once as bright orange as a pumpkin. Her mother's skin still bore a healthy sprinkling of light brown freckles, though some were hidden in amongst some well-earned and dignified wrinkles around the thin woman's eyes. Jane inherited her mother's freckles but got her round build, dark hair and eyes from her father, who had passed away eleven years ago. The same year Ellie was born. Jane knew her mother would never admit it, maybe even didn't realize it, but this daughter knew her mother well enough to see she enjoyed the attention she was getting from the bus driver. It had been so long since any man had noticed Jane she wondered if she would even realize if a man was flirting with her – not that she necessarily wanted one to. After losing Tom, she swore to herself she was better off alone with Ellie. No men, no one to depend upon but herself. She'd never allow a man to take away her control. Losing a husband so young, just when her life was starting to build itself, was almost more than Jane had been able to bear. To have it happen again was her worst fear. She was better off alone, just with her daughter and mother to be there to support one another. Falling in love was too hard on her heart when the result might be loss and sadness.

> "Good morning, Ed," her mother replied, seemingly oblivious to his infatuation. "Would you like one of Ellie's special creation cookies from yesterday?"

"Of course," Ed said enthusiastically, as usual. He ate one of Ellie's special creation cookies every day. "What flavour did you come up with yesterday?" he asked Ellie.

"Pineapple and maraschino cherry, with vanilla frosting," she replied, predictably excited that Ed was remaining faithful to his support of her creations. Fae placed the elaborately decorated palm sized cookie into a small white box. The cookie itself was comprised of crushed pineapple and chopped dried cherries. The frosting was vanilla but dyed to a light pink hue by a splash of the cherry juice. The whole thing was topped off with a glistening electric red candied cherry. Undaunted by the wild-looking baked good, Ed lifted the cookie from the box and took a bite; chewed, and swallowed, and declared the cookie delicious, just the same as he declared every single one of Ellie's cookie creations delicious every single day. He put the cookie back in the box and closed the lid.

"I'll save the rest to have with my lunch," he promised. Jane had to give him credit, he always ate those cookies, even when the flavours were wild and, like this one, so sweet it hurt her teeth when she'd eaten one. It put her in mind of the baked hams her mother used to serve at dinner parties, gleaming and bedecked with rings of canned pineapple and sickly-sweet red cherries.

"Before you leave for school," Jane said, standing poised by the green chalkboard bearing the title *Ellie's Creations!* written in block letters at the top, "what's today's special cookie?" Jane wanted Ellie to be part of the café that she and her mother owned and operated. Her wheelchair and weak hand made it difficult for her to help much with any of the cooking or serving customers, so they found other ways to have her involved. One was her special cookie creations. Ellie responded right away.

"Cinnamon peanut butter twists topped with a chocolate covered mini pretzel."

"Cinnamon peanut butter twists, topped with a chocolate covered mini pretzel it is," Jane said as she wrote it on the board. She didn't know how her daughter dreamed up these flavors, though Ellie had a Pinterest page now, so maybe she was inspired by one of the thousands of recipes Jane knew were floating around on the website. Ellie passed her empty plate and glass to her grandmother and wiped her hand and mouth on the serviette. Pressing the joystick controller of her wheelchair she moved toward the door.

"Wait, you forgot your bag," Fae called after her as Ellie passed through the doorway.

"I'll take it," Ed offered.

"Thank you." Fae handed it to him.

"No trouble at all," he said, smiling at her. There was a pleasantly awkward moment between them. Jane grinned and resisted the urge to laugh, while inside, she fought that pang of loneliness again.

"Come on, Ed!" Ellie yelled from where she waited next to the electric lift door at the side of the bus.

"Coming," he called back. "I'll see you this afternoon," he said to Fae and left quickly, hanging the bag on the back of Ellie's chair from the straps before he pressed the button to open the door. She rolled in and he pressed the button again and she disappeared up into the bus. The women left behind in the café waved from the window. They heard the back-door open and close and Iris, Jane's kitchen assistant, came around the corner to the front to check out the board.

"Cinnamon peanut butter twist with a chocolate covered mini pretzel. Wow." She shook her head and chuckled. "I'll get to work on the batter," she said and returned to the kitchen. They had a few minutes before the café opened so mother and daughter sat in the window to discuss the mysterious manila envelope.

"What was in the letter, Mom?" Jane asked.

"Read it yourself." She passed the envelope over and then headed behind the counter to start the first of many pots of coffee for the day. She checked the clock and wrote the time, 7:55 a.m. in white grease pencil on the carafe and hit start to send the hot water through the drip filter. Jane read:

Dear Ms. Michaels, we are pleased to inform you that the building which you currently rent as the premises for your business Cutie Pie's Café, was purchased by Brookstone Holdings Limited near the end of the previous month. Your new landlords will be in touch with you very shortly to set up a visit and thorough inspection of the property.
If you should have any questions in the interim, please feel free to contact us via the contact information provided below.
Sincerely,
Amy Ping
Executive Assistant of Correspondence for Mr. Blair Brookstone
Senior Vice President and CEO of Brookstone Holdings Limited.

Jane looked up from the letter and felt her heart sink, instinctively knowing this wasn't going to be good.

2

Anders Brookstone sat in the sleek, black, exquisitely uncomfortable leather chair in his father's office. The chair was designed to make any visitors feel inferior, and it succeeded because Anders felt awkward and annoyed, just like he always felt when he was in his father's office. The chair had a low-slung seat that slid back at an angle so that his knees ended up being nearly level with his shoulders if he leaned backwards. The office was cold, in temperature and colour; all grays, chrome, steel and glass, designed to look efficient and important. Anders hated it. His own office down the hall was warmer with wood and books and comfortably designed chairs for guests, plush and soft, in friendly tones of rust and terra cotta.

"Anders." His father came striding through the door, looking much like his office, in a charcoal double-breasted suit, slicked down graying black hair, and shining black shoes. "Don't get up." He said as he walked past, sitting at his acrylic and chrome desk across from Anders.

"I couldn't if I wanted to, Dad," Anders said. "These chairs are torture devices.

"Never let anyone who comes into your office forget who is in charge." Blair Brookstone gestured to the portrait hanging on the wall behind him, a younger but equally handsome image of the man obsessed with wealth and power. "Be like this portrait, always watching, always powerful, always well put together."

Anders had heard this speech before, more times than he could count. He, himself, didn't believe power was made only by looking tall and wealthy.

"So, why did you call me here, Dad?" he asked, feeling a little impatient as his left buttock grew numb.

"I need you to drive out to—" he paused, flipping a cream-coloured file folder open to check the name of the place, "Millvale, to check out a new property the firm just acquired. It's a nothing little town but the property is overlooking a river. I'm thinking condos. There are a few businesses already in the building and I need to know if they might be worth trying to keep, or if we should just hike the rent and get

them out so I can send in the wrecking ball."
Blair slid the folder across to Anders, who heaved himself out of the chair, glad to feel blood flowing into his lower extremities again.

"Got it. I'll make an appointment with the tenants and head out there by the end of the week."

"Good. I'd like a report on my desk by the end of the month," Blair said, then picked up the phone and beeped his secretary. "Amy, coffee please, and get me one of those grilled cheese sandwiches for lunch." He hung up, looking up to see Anders still there. "That's all. You can go." Anders turned to leave. "Oh, your mother wants to know if you'll be bringing anyone to dinner on Sunday. I told her you'd be bringing that girl of yours."

"Yes, that girl's name is Meredith." Anders said, incredulous of his parents seeming oblivious attitude to his existence.

"Meredith, yes, of course. I know. Lovely girl. Beautiful. I'll tell your mother. See you Sunday." Blair never looked up from his desk. Anders stalked out of the office, glad to remove himself from the chill.

As he retreated down the hall, Anders considered Meredith. She was smart, funny in her own way, and pretty, if you liked a woman with dark hair, somewhat distant eyes the colour of limestone and a face with the bone structure of a humming bird, which Anders did of course. Meredith was just the kind of woman he'd always imagined he would marry. She was somewhat aloof and efficient; a woman who looked good in well-lit rooms. She was like a fine piece of pottery, perfectly smooth and a joy to admire. In fact, he was considering proposing to her soon, when he found the right ring. The timing was perfect. She'd just settled into a new job working at the local funeral home as a mortuary assistant and he was well established, just having purchased a large two-bedroom condo in one of the company's buildings near the office. It wasn't ideal, but a good place to start. He preferred to look up at trees, instead of down at their canopies, but it was close to work, and affordable since his father hadn't seen fit to give him a raise any time recently. He dreamed of one day owning a nice home in the country with lots of land for dogs and kids. For a fleeting moment he wondered if Meredith would like that too. He'd never thought to ask her.

    When he returned to the comfort of his own desk, he opened the file and telephoned the first business on the list. Cutie Pies Café.

    "Hello, Cutie Pies," a woman's voice answered.

    "Hello, this is Anders Brookstone, from Brookstone Holdings. Is this the owner of the establishment?"

    "Yes," the voice said.

    "You may have received a letter in the mail informing you that we are now in possession of your lease."

"Yes," the voice said again.

"Well, I'd like to make an appointment to come and inspect the property." He pulled his calendar closer to look at his week. "Would Thursday afternoon around two o'clock be alright?"

"One sec," the voice said and muffled the receiver. He could hear voices speaking in a heated way but couldn't hear what they were saying. "That would be fine, but please be prompt," the voice said.

"Absolutely," he replied, making a note on his calendar. "I'll see you on Thursday at two o'clock."

"Bye," the voice said and hung up.

Anders had spoken to a lot of business owners but had never experienced such a short conversation. He hoped the meeting would go as smoothly and as quickly.

3

On Thursday afternoon, Anders drove his Jeep out of the city and onto the highway toward Millvale. The town was just over an hour away from his office, a drive that became more enjoyable the further he got away from the city. As the tall glass towers turned into low rise buildings, then townhomes, then subdivisions, and finally, farmer's fields filled with winter wheat or cows, he felt the ever-present knot between his shoulder blades release. He rolled down his windows and breathed deeply. Unfortunately, his nostrils filled with the pungent aroma of manure, and Anders coughed at the unexpected scent. He quickly rolled up the windows and realized that as the odor lingered, he really didn't mind. It was a fresh, country smell that he should get used to if he wanted to move out here one day.

His research on Millvale revealed that it was a very small town, more like a village in fact. There was an equestrian park, a church, and a gas station. That was besides what was in the building the company had just purchased which held a bakery-café called Cutie Pies, a travel agent, a variety store, and a high-end beauty salon and spa. Based upon the map he'd seen, there was a river running near the back of the property and a large pond down the street. The town might be pretty, but Anders wasn't sure why his father had purchased this building. This didn't seem like the kind of place where a condo development would be of benefit or of interest. In the back of his mind, Anders thought that perhaps a cozy inn would be the right thing for the area. A beautiful country setting, well-appointed rooms, a hideaway from bustling city life, horses, nature, a river that probably offered good fishing in the back yard and maybe a nice restaurant where couples could come for romantic dinners. It was bound to be successful. He doubted his father would agree with his plan, but Anders would figure out how to sell it to him later, provided this place was as picturesque as Anders hoped it would be.

He parked on a narrow two-lane road outside the building. It looked a bit shabby from the outside, but clean. The tenants obviously took pride in their businesses since the sidewalk was neatly swept and the flowerboxes bloomed abundantly. He'd managed to make appointments with all the tenants for that day which had been a tricky bit of scheduling. Driving all the way out here more than once for an inspection would be impractical, regardless of how beautiful the drive had been. His father abhorred impracticality and Anders knew better than to push it with his father.

His first stop was the café, but before he went inside, he did a loop around the building. The foundation was in fairly good shape, though there was a crack here and there that needed patching. The brick had seen better days and would benefit from painting, if they decided to keep the building at all. Windows were due for replacing and the roof needed to be re-shingled before the end of next year. He made notes on his tablet and then went inside.

    The door chimed as he walked through. The café was painted in a soft yellow with slate floors and a long front counter with display cases featuring mouthwatering desserts. There were several trays of cookies displayed, and next to that there were brownies with thick chocolate icing cut into large squares. Equally large were the date squares, lemon bars, and raspberry cheesecake bars. Next to those was a rotating display case of pies, banana cream with a heavenly cloud of whipped cream called to him. He felt his mouth water and realized he hadn't had lunch before he left. He smelled something spicy, laden with garlic floating in the air. He looked at his watch and saw he was twenty minutes early for his appointment and figured he would have something to eat before doing business. No better way to understand if this place was worth saving.

    When his turn came, he ordered a slice of the banana cream pie, and a large coffee with cream, intending to only have a piece of the delectable looking confection. The smell of something tasty cooking tempted him to add to his order. "I'd also like whatever smells so delicious that you're cooking right now please," he said and licked his lips.

The woman behind the counter said, "That's the soup of the day, hot pepper gumbo. It comes with a slice of maple corn bread topped with melted butter." He noticed how lovely her slender hand was as it hovered above the cash register. He was also struck by how beautiful she seemed. Her face was round and friendly, peppered with freckles and she had large brown eyes. He suspected her hair was long, though it was hard to tell since she'd wrapped it up in a bun on the top of her head, but what he could see of it was a warm chestnut colour that he thought pretty. While her hands were slender, the rest of her was nearly the complete opposite. She had a solid frame, round and sturdy, but attractive. He liked her instantly and looked forward to watching her work as he ate.

"Sounds delicious," he replied. The corners of her mouth lifted only a little in response and he felt disappointed.

"That'll be fourteen eighty-seven," she said. He pulled out his wallet and grabbed a twenty. As he handed it to her, he saw a small sign next to the register that read *Try Ellie's Creation!*

Intrigued he asked, "What is an *Ellie's Creation*?"

The woman's face lit up and he was happy he asked. "It's a cookie," she said. "Invented by my daughter. She comes up with a new flavour every day. Today's is a mud puddle cookie." She grinned at him and her eyes shone. She gestured toward a display case on her right. He followed the pretty digits with his eyes, coming to rest on an elevated glass cake plate with a glass cover, where lumps of melted then cooled chocolate bedecked with gummy worms and chocolate cookie crumbs were stacked upon one another. They looked crazy, but also charming in a strange way he couldn't explain. He decided he would try one.

"I'll take one of those too please," he said feeling satisfied when the woman seemed to bob her head in a little happy dance. She re-tabulated his bill.

"Seventeen eighty-seven, please. Take a seat and your food will be right out." She took his twenty and handed him some change. He dropped the change in a tip jar next to the cash register and headed for a table near the window while she disappeared behind a wall into the kitchen. Anders thought that three dollars for a cookie seemed a little steep and he hoped it would taste better than it looked.

A few moments later a younger woman with dark skin and curls popping out from under a kerchief arrived and placed his meal in front of him. The coffee was strong but nice and hot and the gumbo was spicy as advertised. However, the sweet cornbread cut the heat and he appreciated the thought that must have gone into the pairing. The banana cream pie was heavenly.

He knew that whoever made it was very talented. He saved the mud puddle cookie for last, figuring that if it was disgusting, he had already enjoyed all the rest of his meal and felt happy and satisfied. When he bit into the strange creation, he found it surprisingly tasty. The chocolate had a hint of coffee in it which made it delightfully bitter. The creamy texture played nicely with the crunchy and sweet cookie crumbs and the gummy worm. While he at first thought it was going to be just plain old weird to eat, it was fun and didn't taste strange at all. It also appealed to the little kid who still lived inside him. The one who used to like to catch frogs and getting the knees of his jeans muddy and grass stained, playing in the park with his younger brother and nanny.

    The woman with the kerchief reappeared to collect his dirty plates.

    "How was everything?" she asked.

    "Delicious!" he said enthusiastically, and she laughed.

    "I'm glad you liked it. Can I get you anything else?" she asked, poised to leave.

    "I'm here for a meeting with a Jane Michaels, would that be you by chance?"

    "No, I'm Iris," she said, looking at him skeptically. "I'll get her for you." Iris disappeared with his plates and a few moments later the woman with the lovely hands appeared next to the table.

"You must be Anders Brookstone," she said frowning, wiping her hand on her apron before she stuck it out to shake his.

4

Anders stood and shook Jane's hand. She was pleasantly surprised that he didn't crush it in his grasp like some men did, especially men who held the power in any given situation. He owned their building and he oversaw her future. She felt her stomach flip at the thought of what that might mean, but then Anders said he was happy to meet her and for some reason she believed him. He had a kind looking face, if you focused on his eyes. His jaw was square and important looking, and his hair was a midnight black, cropped closely at the back and sides that showed off the brilliant blue of his eyes, which, she noticed now, were gazing at her intently. She swallowed before she spoke.

"I hope it will be nice to meet you as well, Mr. Brookstone," she said, keeping her voice inscrutable. He gestured to her to take a seat across from him and she did. From the corner of her eye she saw Iris' head bobbing in the pass through trying to get a look at what was happening.

When she'd come back to the kitchen with the man's dirty plates, she had nearly dropped them because she was in such a flap. "He's going to raise the rent! I just know it!" She was practically frantic. This, of course, had been Jane's worst fear, too, but she wasn't about to let herself admit that out loud, or to her employee. She wished her mother was here for support, but Ellie needed to go to the doctor and Fae volunteered to take her this time, so Jane would be facing their future. Alone. As usual.

"Well, Mrs. Michaels, that was a delicious lunch I just ate. You are a very talented cook," he said, a satisfied look on his face. She figured it was probably the sugar rush he was feeling after eating a piece of pie and a mud puddle cookie all at once. She kept her gaze aloof trying to look placid. He seemed uncomfortable in the shade her eyes were casting his direction. Good.

"Thank you, Mr. Brookstone, I'm happy you enjoyed it. Now, what else can I do for you? As you'll recall I'm under a bit of a time crunch." Her gaze went from shade to frost, forcing him to break eye contact. He covered this by looking down at his tablet where he'd made some notes.

"I'm here to get to know you, and the other tenants of the building, and see how our new investment is doing. Brookstone Holdings likes to be hands-on in their investments so, I'm making myself available for anything you might need regarding the building and the property in general. I've looked around outside and I can see that it is in fairly good shape, and now I'd like to have a tour of your establishment, so I can ascertain if there are any urgent matters needing attention to keep your business up and running. As your new landlord, it is important to us that you succeed." He looked up at her again and she felt her pulse increase a little and it forced her to look away, just momentarily. He swallowed when she reconnected their eye contact.

"And lastly," he continued hurriedly looking back at his notes, "I will need to see your business records to ensure that your establishment is a profitable and solid business for our company to keep as a tenant in our property." He looked up again, and this time she didn't flinch, though inside she chanted an oath, hoping that when he looked over the books, he'd be good enough to keep them here in business.

"Alright, that's no trouble. Can I send you an email with my records? I'm really in a bit of a hurry, Mr. Brookstone, and I don't have time to go over them with you right now." She looked at her watch to emphasize the point.

"Yes, an email would be fine for your financial breakdowns, but I'd also like to have a tour of the building. I won't trouble you to show me around, you go about your day and if I have any questions I'll just ask."

They agreed to this plan which Jane found to be a relief, and terrifying, simultaneously. She anxiously went about cleaning tables and serving customers while the man who held her future snooped around. Iris appeared by her side several times and hissed in her ear a play by play of the man's actions. She surreptitiously watched him as he opened cupboards, moved the fridge away from the wall, lifted garbage can lids, and even inspected the employee washroom.

Nothing was off limits to this guy. Jane fought the urge to grab him by the collar and throw him out the back door. This, of course, wouldn't be as difficult for her as it might be for other women because of her Amazonian frame, but nevertheless, this Anders Brookstone was still taller and more strapping than she. Maybe she could risk it, see if she took him off guard and shoved him through the door if he would turn around and run back to the city? Probably not. He seemed self-assured enough to defend himself from her sneak attack. While she contemplated an alternate plan, she got a glimpse of his behind. Not bad, if she were into checking out prospective partners, which she wasn't. She had to admit though that the man was in fine shape, even if he was the enemy.

The bell on the door rang out and Jane glanced at her watch before she looked up and saw Ellie and her mother come through the door. Just about on time. Jane let out a sigh to relieve some of her anxiety surrounding the day. It only partially worked. Now to hear about her daughter's appointment, one she hoped wouldn't result in any huge bills.

5

He stood in the storage room inspecting a stain on the ceiling tiles adding that to the tally of repairs that the restaurant would require to continue running as it currently was. When Mrs. Michaels emailed the financial documents, he would assess if it was worth doing any of these repairs. He suspected not, unfortunately. If it were up to him, he'd help every small and struggling business he came across, help them grow into something bigger and better, and most importantly, more profitable. Just because his name was Brookstone, it didn't mean he had any real say in anything. He worked for his father because it was a secure job, and he'd never done anything else. His father sent him to university for business and hired him the day after he graduated. Anders never wanted to look elsewhere for work because he liked the stability of his paycheck, and liked pleasing his father, even if he often disagreed with the man's decisions. His younger brother Alec had been the wild one. He went travelling through Europe after graduating high school and didn't come back for five years. This broke his mother's heart, his father's too, Anders assumed, though Blair would never admit such a thing. Anders was the stable one, the reliable one, the predictable one. All the Brookstones liked it that way.

Leaving the storage room, he headed back out toward the dining area where he was met with a somewhat unexpected sight. There, sitting by the window was Jane, and next to her was an older woman, whom he assumed was her mother, judging by the freckles speckling the woman's skin. Between them sat a little girl in a wheelchair. He stood where he was, watching them interact. The girl was very animated and looked happy, though he couldn't hear what they were saying. Jane looked concerned but was smiling, her mother held her face in a similar way. He stayed, observing the trio for a while when the woman with the dark curly hair glided up next to him.

"That's Ellie," she said tilting her head toward the girl. "She's Jane's daughter, and the one who made up that mud puddle cookie recipe."

"That was a good cookie," he said, meaning it.

They were both quiet for a moment, then Iris spoke to him without turning to face him, "Try not to close this place down, please. I like working here. Besides," she tilted her head again toward Jane and Ellie, "Jane needs this place. She's a widow, she needs it to look after Ellie."

"I—" He tried to speak but couldn't find his voice. He knew from the amount of information he had already gathered about this business that his father would more than likely want it closed. He would want to tear down the building and put up his beloved condos. Anders just didn't think there would be any way to convince him otherwise. Iris shrugged when Anders failed to continue his sentence and walked back to her side of the kitchen.

"Who's that?" He turned when he heard the girl's voice from across the dining room in his direction.

"That's Mr. Brookstone," Jane said, "he's here to look at the building and to see if it needs fixing. He's our new landlord."

"Hi, Mr. Brookstone!" the girl said enthusiastically as she zoomed toward him in her motorized chair.

"Hello," he said cautiously. He'd never met a disabled child before and was not sure what to do exactly.

"I'm Ellie," she spoke clearly, then held out her good hand. He was surprised by the girl's manners and confidence.

"I'm Anders Brookstone." He shook her hand. "Pleased to meet you." There was a moment of silence amongst the group until Fae introduced herself. Ellie looked much like her grandmother, she had her fierce eyes and similarly cropped hair, though it was more of a strawberry blond shade. The girl's build was also slight, much like Fae's, who was currently eyeing Anders in a manner which made his shirt collar feel tight. "You created the mud puddle cookie I ate, right?" he asked, trying to distract the two older women from piercing his soul with their laser death-ray eyes.

"Yup. Did you like it?" Ellie asked excitedly. Jane shook her head in a gesture which indicated to Anders that Ellie relished any feedback on her creations.

"I did. It was tasty. Where did you come up with such a great idea?" He spoke gently to her but tried not to appear to be talking down to the girl. *Be normal* he told himself, don't make this situation any worse than it will already be for these women.

"I dreamt it," she said.

"Ellie has always been very creative when it comes to her cookie creations, haven't you sweetie?" Jane stood behind her daughter and absent mindedly stroked the girl's hair.

"Mom!" Ellie spoke harshly, "don't mess up my hair!" Anders could see the girl was quickly becoming a "tween" a fact that was amplified by what seemed to him as evidence she'd just finished having a growth spurt. Her pants looked a couple inches too short and her knees were bent up at an angle slightly higher than ninety degrees. He realized that they would soon need a new chair for her. He wondered how they would pay for such an item. Surely the café couldn't provide such a necessity as that?

"Sorry," Jane said, glancing sheepishly up at him, her lovely eyes hooded in dark lashes. She ended the gesture by rolling her eyes as if to say, "kids these days."

"I'm all done here," he cut in, wanting to make his escape before he found out any more information that might make his life difficult. He just wanted to do his job, not ruin the lives of people who had a tough go already. He handed Jane a card as he got to the door. "Email those financial figures to me as soon as possible, please, and I'll get back to you about the list of repairs I will make."

"Will do," she said, looking distractedly back over her shoulder toward her daughter.

"Nice to meet you." He shook her hand and then waved to the other women. "All of you." He nodded to Iris' bobbing head in the pass-through window. "I'll be in touch." With that, he hastily retreated from the café, feeling somewhere between bewitched and horribly sad.

6

Later that night, after Ellie had gone to her room to do her homework, Jane and Fae sat at the kitchen table with cups of tea and discussed the doctor's appointment.

"The doctor recommends we get her a new wheelchair in the next six months or so. She'll be too tall for this one by then," the older woman said and lifted a steaming mug to her lips.

"Well it's May now, so, that'll be…?" Jane stopped and counted the months on her fingers. "November. Maybe we could push it an extra month? A new chair for Christmas? Do you think that Santa will bring it for us?" She frowned. Her mother gave her a half grimace in return.

"She keeps growing and getting stronger Jane, that's good. Remember how scared you and Tom were when she was born? Look at her now." Fae reached across the table for her daughter's hand and looked at her, misty eyed.

"I know." Jane sighed and clasped her mom's fingers lightly then retracted her hand to pick up her mug. "It's just, I wish there was a way I could get her everything she needs. I'm so proud of how confident and smart she is, I just want to keep her there in that place forever." Her mother nodded with emphasis to indicate her understanding.

"We'll find a way. We always do, right?" Fae spoke quietly.

"Yes, we always do," Jane whispered, her eyes worried and her brow furrowed. She picked up the pen and a stack of lined note paper she'd left lying on the table. She wrote out the remaining instructions for Ellie's cookie of the day and put the sheet into a large lime green three-ringed binder her daughter had decorated with glitter glue pens and butterfly stickers. Jane had kept every one of Ellie's creations since she started coming up with recipes. This was their third binder and it was almost time for a new one.

"Remind me to buy a new binder this weekend please, Mom," Jane said as she closed the front flap and slid the binder to the back of the table stacking the paper and pen on top.

"Today's cookie was a good one. Ed likes chocolate, so I put two in the box for him. Hope you don't mind." Fae chuckled to herself a little.

"Oh no, that's fine." Jane took a drink from her mug to cover the grin that was growing across her face. "Mom?" She was cautiously moving forward now. "Have you ever thought of talking to Ed outside the café, like maybe you two could go out together or something?"

"Heaven's no!" Her mother's green eyes turned an interesting shade of turquoise and Jane knew her mother was lying.

"Really, Mom, it seems like you two get along and Ed is a nice guy. He's pretty good looking too," Jane said, hiding her mouth behind her mug again.

"Yes, well," Fae responded, holding her mug with both hands, "he is a fine man. Truth be told, he has asked me out to dinner a couple of times. But I said no."

"What!" Jane was incredulous. She couldn't believe her mother hadn't told her this. "Why don't you go out with him? You like him, Mom, I can tell. And he really likes you."

"Well, honey," her mother was silent for a moment. "I'm just not ready, I guess. Your father…" She let the rest of her words die.

"I know, but he's been gone for a long time, Mom. Maybe you should try going on a date and see how it feels? It doesn't mean you can't still love and miss Dad, but it means you are living your new life without him."

"I don't see you living a new life," Fae said. Jane was hurt but knew her mother was not trying to be mean.

"I have Ellie to worry about. I don't want to date anyone right now. I'm happy alone." Her freckles grew a little darker from the effort it took to say that.

"No one is happy alone sweetheart," Fae offered. "Perhaps it is time for both of us to consider new things."

Jane didn't respond but found her mind drifting to earlier that afternoon and watching Anders Brookstone talking to her daughter. She had seen the look of shock on his face, and then the look of sympathy, pity, and something else she couldn't pinpoint. Guilt? Maybe, or dread, or some sort of combination. She was certain there was a shadow of some sort that had flashed through his blue eyes like a cloud over a calm lake. Their little family had become accustomed to the looks they received whenever they left the house. Tom, she remembered, used to be furious at the parents whose children gawked at his own, the ones who would shush and drag their children away from a grocery store aisle at the slightest question or lingering stare. Perhaps worse were the parents who did nothing and just let their children yell out "What's wrong with that girl?" and they never answered the question. She knew that it was hard for him to accept that there was anything wrong with their daughter. She was perfect in their eyes, though in her heart Jane always knew that life would be a struggle, not just for them, but for Ellie. She had thousands of questions that filled her mind after Tom's death. What would happen to Ellie if she died too? Would Ellie make it to college one day? What would she do for a living? Living life confined mostly to a wheelchair was difficult, very difficult. The world was not designed to help people who were different. Jane wanted nothing more than happiness for her only daughter and she would do anything to guarantee that for her. Unfortunately, the café, while popular and a great place to work, left very little at the end of the month that she could put away for Ellie in case of a rainy day, or, as was the current situation, in case of the necessity for a new wheelchair. The look on Anders Brookstone's face reinforced this to her. They were soon going to be in trouble. And it wasn't just going to be a little bit.

Jane looked at her mother. "I just wish I knew what the future holds, Mom."

"We all do, Janie." The older woman nodded, sadly.

7

Looking in the mirror Anders worked on tying the double Windsor knot in the blue tie Meredith had picked out for dinner with his family.

"Matches your eyes," she'd said, in her way, which was always calm and serene. Absent-mindedly he wondered if they taught morticians to be calm sorts of people since working with dead bodies was admittedly creepy. You certainly wouldn't want any sudden movements around the embalming room if you could help it. Meredith sat on the edge of his bed waiting for him, picking invisible bits of lint from her grey skirt. Her light eyes looked even paler in the light from the window. Contrasted with the nearly blue-black of her angular bob he thought she looked absolutely striking. The picture of a future Brookstone woman.

He had again been contemplating the perfect ring for her. Tiffany's was the customary choice of the Brookstone men. One carat, platinum, knife-edge band, princess cut diamond. Traditional, but flashy. While he knew Meredith would most likely love this type of ring, he wasn't sure it was right for her. Something was holding him back and he just couldn't figure out what it was.

"Darling, are you having trouble with your tie?" Meredith walked up behind him and looked at his face reflected in the mirror.

"No, no. I've got it," he said and finished, though the tie ended up a bit crooked.

"Are you alright? You seem a bit distracted. Here—" She turned him toward her and fixed his tie.

"Oh, just dinner with my parents. You know." He cocked his mouth, then turned back to the mirror, careful not to look directly at her for fear his thoughts on the engagement ring may be visible in his face. "Better, thanks." Anders donned his suit jacket, in a charcoal that accentuated his own dark hair and they rode down in the elevator silently. Meredith kept her hands folded in front of her body, even when Anders grazed a hand down her back to feel closer to her. He knew she was on the reluctant side of the affection scale but hoped that the more he reached out to her the more willing she would become to express her feelings. They had been together for some time and things never seemed to warm up, leaving Anders feeling lonely many times when they were together. He loved Meredith and wanted to show her his affection. Riding alone in an elevator seemed like the perfect opportunity, but Meredith evidently felt differently about the situation. Anders sighed and attempted to release the feeling of loneliness and focus his mind on dinner with his family, realizing he often felt alone with his family too.

Leaving the elevator, they hailed a taxi and rode to his parents' place across the city in the same direction as he had driven the day before to visit the café. The image of the little girl in the wheelchair—Ellie—stuck in his mind. Guilty bile began to rise in his chest, and he coughed.

"Are you alright?" Meredith reached toward him and took his hand a gesture Anders was glad to accept.

Anders cleared his throat. "Yes, yes." He held her chilly hand in his, hoping his warmth would transfer to her. "Have you ever met a child in a wheelchair?" he asked, trying to seem nonchalant.

"What a peculiar question," Meredith said and looked at him, thoughtful for a few moments. Anders waited for her response and ran his thumb back and forth over her knuckles using friction to warm her skin. "No, I haven't met a child, or really anyone for that matter, who was in a wheelchair. I had a friend in elementary school, Gloria, who had a prosthetic arm. Why do you ask?" She pulled her hand away and folded her fingers in her lap, looking at him with her eerie eyes.

"Yesterday, when I went to check out the new property Dad bought, I met a young girl in a wheelchair. I was thrown, I didn't know how to talk to her. I felt so awkward." Anders was embarrassed by his confession and hoped Meredith wouldn't think less of him.

"Whatever for?"

"I didn't want to say anything that might have been offensive," he said, not entirely meeting her eyes. Meredith was a very practical straightforward woman. Thoughts like these would most likely, never cross her mind.

"What did you say to her?"

"I said hello, tried to act as normal as possible. I told her the cookie recipe she invented was good." He looked at Meredith with pleading eyes hoping he'd done alright.

"That seems fine, Anders. I think the most important thing is that you acknowledged her. She is a person, just like everyone else, regardless if she is in a wheelchair."

Anders knew that she was right. He took her hand and grasped it. She patted his hand and then removed both of hers back to her lap. Anders didn't tell Meredith how he was going to be responsible for closing her mother's business and leaving her without an adequate wheelchair in the very near future.

When they arrived at his parents, his mother greeted them at the door, dressed in a crisp mint green skirt suit with her pale blond hair curled elegantly around her ears. She had an enormous grin on her face. Anders figured something must be up since he never got such a happy greeting from his mother. They moved into the house and found his father in the den smoking a cigar and talking with someone who had his back to the door. It was his brother Alec.

Back from another stay in Europe. This time, Alec had been studying working with marble, so he could install beautiful marble floors in his father's condos.

"Alec!" Anders grabbed his younger brother in a bear hug. Alec's build was slightly more muscular than Anders, slightly taller, and slightly blonder too. He had the same eyes, his father's eyes, though his face was somewhat rounder, like his mother's. "When did you get back?"

"Last night," Alec said jovially, slapping his brother on the back. "There's someone I'd like you to meet." He swept his hand across the room toward a woman who stood silhouetted in the window. "I'd like to introduce you to my wife, Valentina."

Anders wasn't sure if he'd ever been flabbergasted before, but this for sure, would be the time to try it out. Valentina was a striking woman. Tall, curvaceous, with a bright face and long brown wavy hair. Her outfit was a riot of colour. She had a free spirit aura about her. Happiness and a welcoming energy radiated from her being.

"Hello, it is so wonderful to meet you," she said, sticking out her hand.

"You too," Anders replied, stunned.

"I've heard so many wonderful things about you, all of you!" Valentina turned her gaze upon each of the Brookstones and Meredith in turn.

"Hello," Meredith said, shaking the woman's hand. They made a funny pair, tall and small, curvy and straight, serious and colourful.

"Yes, you are Meredith, Anders' love," Valentina offered.

"I'm his girlfriend, yes," Meredith agreed.

"So, what the heck, little bro. When did you meet Valentina?" Anders needed more details, immediately.

Alec looked upon his wife with a gaze that sparkled from a thousand feet away. It was the type of gaze that made people who weren't in love feel queasy. Anders was, of course, in love so it had no effect on him whatsoever.

"We met in Tuscany," Valentina chimed in. "In Carrara. My father runs a marble mine. Alec came for a tour one day and, well, as they say, the rest is history."

"It's all true," Alec agreed, fawning over Valentina a little.

"Tell us, where did you get married?" Mrs. Brookstone jumped in over sips of her drink.

"We got married in a little church in Tuscany," Alec began telling the story. For a guy who didn't talk much and wanted to keep a low profile for most of his life, this might be the most exciting thing he had ever done.

"The priest was a funny little man," Valentina regaled them. Her voice was melodious, delightfully accented and peppered with Italian phrases. She was easy to like, so charming, and lovely. Anders could see why his brother hand chosen her to be his wife.

"Afterward, we ate a feast of grilled octopus, and freshly baked bread with olive oil," Alec beamed. "We took lots of pictures. I'm sorry you all weren't there but, I just couldn't wait to make this woman my wife."

"It is a whirlwind romance," Valentina said, laughing.

"I know, my head is spinning," Anders grumbled under his breath.

8

On Monday morning Anders went in early to the office. He had a lot of things to think about. The shock of his brother getting married was the main thing that kept him from sleeping in past four o'clock, that and the thundering storm rattling outside his bedroom window. He couldn't believe it. For his brother to marry someone he only just met. It was so unexpected. Anders couldn't imagine doing such a thing. Though he genuinely liked Valentina and looked forward to getting to know her, the thought of not planning out a life step as large and important as who to marry was mind boggling. Anders liked to plot, to be sure, to do what was right for the big picture. What if Valentina turned out to be the wrong choice.? What then? Anders pushed that aside. His brother knew what he was doing, he hoped.

Anders, he had other things on his mind too that had gotten him out of bed early. Namely Cutie Pie's Café, along with Ellie and her striking mother. The other businesses in the building were also on his mind. The spa was doing well, better than he'd expected, but it wasn't enough to leave the property running as it was. He'd finish his report for his father this morning. In his gut, he wanted to save the businesses, especially the café. The look on Jane Michaels' face stuck in his mind. When he read her email and reviewed her financial documents his heart sank. They were just barely making the rent every month. He had hoped for better and wondered if there was something more, he could do to help save the business, but in his post little-brother- got-married haze he could think of nothing. He finished writing the report and walked down the hall to his father's office and deposited the folder on his desk.

Looking down at him from the portrait high up on the wall was his father's face. Even if he weren't aided by the dim light in the hall that shone through the door, Anders could feel the superiority oozing from his father's gaze. Anders felt a rise of bitterness in his throat. He turned and left the office quickly and walked back to his desk where he sat with his head in his hands.

His brother eloped and his parents, by some miracle, were happy about it. It must have been because Alec had been gone for so long when he lived in Europe the first time that they were just happy to have him home and safe. Anders had never been brave enough to do anything, of which, his parents did not approve. He was the good one, the sturdy, dependable, responsible, obedient older brother. At thirty-four, he had never imagined falling out of line with the Blair Brookstone way. Alec had always been braver, more adventurous. Three years younger and full of fire, their parents had never known how to deal with the towheaded wanderer. Just to now have him settle down, work for Brookstone Holdings and live in the same city as the rest of the family, had them head over heels trying to keep him home.

Anders suddenly felt overcome with exhaustion. He sat and laid his head on his forearms. Thoughts of jealousy and bitterness swirled in his mind surrounding his brother's marriage and his parent's lack of enthusiasm for his own relationship with Meredith. He tried to push them aside. Why couldn't they see Meredith, acknowledge her presence, her dependability, her beautiful, if not a little startling, figure and see that he would be proposing shortly to the woman, a woman who might give them their first grandchild, very soon. Instead they gave his brother all the leeway possible, freedom, and no expectations, and were thrilled to just have Alec in their lives. Why couldn't they feel the same way about him? He'd always done everything they wanted or asked of him, while Alec had never done anything they'd asked.

Anders adjusted his head on his arms to prevent his ear from being smashed, closed his eyes, and took some deep breaths to push the bile back down his esophagus, and thought about the report he'd just left on his father's desk. He'd suggested keeping the building and transforming it into a hotel. He'd run the numbers, tourism was a good idea for the area and he knew that he'd be able to keep the businesses already in the building, maybe even give the café a bigger spot in the building. Make it a full restaurant, with a nice big kitchen where Jane Michaels could do more of her fantastic cooking. He knew it would work; he'd just have to convince his father of the idea.

* * * *

Somewhere between his deep breathing, the gently pattering rain hitting the window, and thoughts of slender fingers handing him a plate full of freshly baked cookies, Anders had fallen asleep. He was startled awake by his office phone. When he lifted his head, he found his neck had a terrible crick and that it was just barely light out. He glanced at his watch and saw it was a few minutes after six and wondered who would be calling at such an early hour.

"Hello," he said, pulling his head away from the receiver to clear a frog from his throat. "Anders Brookstone, Brookstone Holdings."

"Mr. Brookstone?" said a familiar female voice in a tone that was very keyed up. He couldn't place who it was with his sleep addled mind.

"Yes," he said cautiously.

"This is Jane Michaels, I wasn't expecting to catch you in the office at such an early hour." The voice sounded confused now and he pictured the tall woman looking befuddled, her pretty hand wrapped around the phone, pressing it to her ear. "We have a problem," the woman went on, sounding less confused, concern creeping into her speech. "There's a leak, a huge, enormous leak in the café and I can't stop it. It's probably the roof. All the rain overnight—" She let the sentence die.

"I'll be right up to take a look," he found himself saying to her.

"You will?" she said, sounding surprised. In fact, they were both surprised by what he'd said, since, he hadn't intended to offer to drive all the way out to her so soon after having seen the property, particularly when he could have just sent one of the many contractors they employed to look.

"Absolutely," he said, somewhat in disbelief at his own words. They hung up the phone and Anders immediately picked up the receiver to dial his brother. Anders knew how to handle real estate, but roofs were another matter. He was going to need Alec's help. He hoped the newlyweds didn't mind being awoken this early in the morning.

9

Half an hour later they were on the road to Millvale from the city. He, Alec, and Valentina were all crammed into the front seat of Alec's pick up.

"I want to see my husband at work," Valentina had declared when Anders expressed his surprise at her coming along for the drive. She was dressed for work to boot, in a pair of cut off overalls that he recognized were once Alec's, a red plaid shirt tied around the waist to make them fit more snugly. Underneath she wore a bright yellow tank top and had sensibly placed her long hair in pigtails wrapped up neatly on the sides of her head. She even wore a pair of old sneakers that were flecked with paint, indicating to Anders that she liked to get right into projects and didn't mind getting messy. Out of the three of them, Anders looked totally out of place in his navy slacks and crisp white button-down shirt. He was dressed for the office while his brother and sister-in-law were better prepared to handle whatever crisis they were headed into.

When they arrived, they found a pale looking Jane staring out the bay window of the café. Her mother Fae stood next to Ellie who was waiting for the school bus under a rainbow coloured umbrella that was fastened to the back of her wheelchair.

"Mr. Brookstone!" Ellie called him when she saw him get out of the truck. She waved enthusiastically at him. He waved back, happy that she would remember him. He certainly remembered her and had been thinking about her and her mother a lot lately. He was happy now that he'd made the decision to come out here himself.

The three Brookstones scooted across the street and stood under shelter of a nearby tree branch.

"Good morning, Ellie," Anders said. "You as well, Mrs. Michaels."

"Call me Fae," the silver-haired woman said, and shook his hand.

"Please, call me Anders," he said taking her hand. "You can call me that too," he said and winked at Ellie.

"Are you here to fix the leak?" Ellie asked her eyes traveling past him to his brother and sister-in-law. "Wow, you're pretty," she added when she saw Valentina.

"You are very pretty yourself miss," Valentina rolled her tongue around the letters in the words, making each syllable sound special in her Italian accent. "I very much like your umbrella."

"Ellie." Anders filled in the name for her and introduced his crew and the elder Michael's family member.

"Jane is waiting for you inside," Fae said and the three trooped off hopeful they could fix the problem without too much trouble.

Jane now stood in the centre of the café staring up at the ceiling. The bell on the door rang announcing their arrival. She didn't even turn around when they walked in.

"It's sagging," she said, her voice filled with dread. Jane resisted the urge to pop the bubble like an enormous zit.

"Don't stand under there," Alec snapped. Jane turned to face him.

"And just what do you know?" she snapped back.

"This is my brother Alec." Anders stepped in. "He works in construction." Jane's eyes flipped to Valentina and he could have sworn he saw a moment of jealousy in her eyes. But then Alec placed his arm around her, and it vanished. It was probably nothing. She was under a lot of stress and looking for a place to let it out. "Mrs. Michaels, please, it's not safe to stand there. The ceiling might collapse."

"Jane. Just call me Jane. I have you here at the crack of dawn, no need to be formal," she said with a wince on her face. There was a giant silver cooking pot placed beneath the ceiling bulge catching drips that were coming furiously from a pinprick hole in the centre. Valentina stepped forward and took her hand.

"We brought some tarps and plastic storage bins. Why don't we try to save your equipment and some of your baking while the men look after the leak?" Her suggestion was well received, judging by the look of relief that Anders saw on Jane's face.

They broke up into teams, the men heading up the back stair to the roof while the women tarped off what they could and packed up what could be saved. They loaded the back of the truck with the smaller pieces of restaurant equipment and bins of baked goods. Jane knew they could no longer be sold, but at least they might be able to be eaten by friends and family, so it wouldn't be a complete waste.

Anders and Alec inspected the roof and found that a large section of shingles had blown off in the storm.

"Dry rot," Alec said over the rain. "This whole roof needs to come off, the entire building. Needs new sheeting, tar paper, and shingles. New eaves, downspouts, the works. And don't get me started on the cracked foundation, which I know we weren't here to inspect but I noticed anyway."

They spread a couple of tarps over the section missing shingles in a futile attempt to save the roof. At least it would save some of things the people had inside the building, so they could take it with them when their businesses were forced to move, Anders thought to himself in between the bouts of dread he felt.

"How much?" Anders said, imagining his proposal to his father crumbling along with the walls of the café.

"Thirty grand, easy," Alec said. "Probably more once we get into the foundation work."

Anders swore to himself under his breath, wishing he'd been smart enough to bring a contractor along with him for the property inspection. He wanted to be efficient, please his father by saving money but instead he was going to cost everyone much more, especially the tenants of the building. Guilt rose inside him when he suddenly thought of Ellie in her almost too small wheelchair. "Is there anything we can do?" he said, hoping his baby brother had the magic answer.

"Tear it down. That would be the best idea, cheapest, easiest," Alec said. He watched as his brother's face sank. Anders ran a hand through his dark hair and looked like their father, only soaking wet. "What is it?"

"Nothing, I just wanted to save this place. There's something different about it," Anders said.

"Like the woman inside?" Alec said, picking up quickly, as usual, what his brother wasn't saying beneath what he had said.

"Not just her. All the other tenants too. And the girl we met outside. She's Jane's daughter," Anders said.

"Jane is some good-looking woman. If I weren't a happily married man, I'd ask her out."

Alec smirked, knowing he was getting his brother's goat. Anders rolled his eyes.

"You didn't do too badly in terms of wives," he shot back, thinking of the very shapely Valentina. The men climbed down from the roof and stood inside the backdoor drip-drying off a bit.

"I don't get it," Alec said looking like a blond reflection of his brother, "you're with Meredith, what gives with this woman? She's not anything like your girlfriend."

"It's not like I want to marry her," Anders heard himself saying, "In fact, I want to marry Meredith. I just want to help Jane and her daughter because they need it. Ellie has C.P. and they have extra expenses. It's the right thing to do."

"And as usual, you're always doing the right thing," Alec said.

"Yes, I guess so," Anders returned, feeling somewhat disappointed in himself for being so predictable.

"And did I just hear you say you want to marry Meredith?" Alec said, delight creeping into his voice.

"Yeah, you did," Anders said and blushed. He'd never said those words out loud to anyone.

"Well, congratulations big brother," Alec said, enthusiastically pumping his brother's hand, then grabbing him for a hug, sending wet spray off his shirt with his gruff back slapping.

"She's a mortician, right? That's kinda weird, but if you don't mind it then I wish you all the happiness in the world."

Anders didn't mind the fact that Meredith was a mortician. Not at all. But something about this was bothering him. He just wasn't sure what.

"Alec?" Valentina's musical voice drifted from the dining area.

"We're back," he called to his wife. The men started back to meet up with the women.

"How bad is it?" Jane asked into the empty space in the doorway where the men appeared in a mere moment. Her breath was sucked out of her chest when she saw Anders standing there, sturdy and dependable looking, large shouldered, with dripping wet jet-black hair and a now transparent white shirt grabbing onto his torso. "Whoa," she said quietly to herself, but Valentina heard her and smirked a bit.

"I'm sorry to say it's very bad," Anders said, focused on the floor to prevent himself from slipping in one of the gathered puddles on the slate tile. He looked up toward Jane and was momentarily struck dumb by how good she looked, her long chestnut hair hanging wet around her face and shoulders, her pale blue blouse clinging to all the right places.

For an instant time seemed to stop while Jane and Anders looked stupefied at one another. The newlyweds recognized that look, sharing a knowing glance past the awestruck heads. *Amore*, Valentina was sure of it. Back home, she had set up some of her sisters with their husbands. She knew a good match when spotted one.

Snapping back to reality, Jane started off toward the men. "Just how bad is very bad?" she asked, not paying attention, slipping in a puddle and went down, cracking her head on the counter.

As if in slow motion, Anders watched her drop. He took off across the wet floor, completely heedless of his own safety. Just as he passed beneath the bubble in the ceiling a ripping sound cut through the room and the sheetrock collapsed on top of him.

10

Jane woke up on her mother's chesterfield to the sound of Ellie laughing in the other room. She was cold, despite the blanket draped over her, she realized she was still wearing the wet clothes she'd had on at the café. Attempting to sit up was immediately regretted as her hand rushed to her skull to keep her brain inside.

"Ouch," she moaned as she felt a large goose egg on the right side of her head.

"That was a nasty spill you took," Anders said as he came toward her. When she looked up, she saw that he was dressed in one of Tom's worn out T-shirts. It was a bit snug, but she didn't mind the fit, only the fact it wasn't in the drawer where she'd put it after Tom passed.

"Who gave you that shirt?" she said feeling as prickly as she sounded. She stopped looking at him and closed her eyes, leaning her head back against the pillow, hoping the spinning would stop.

"Ellie loaned it to me, and one to Alec, to wear until our shirts dry out. She said no one was using them." He sat down in front of her on the floor and waited for her to open her eyes again.

"They were my husband's," she said a little more gently. "Please be careful with them."

"Of course," he said. Being in possession of clothing left behind by a deceased loved one was a funny thing. Either you got rid of them to eliminate a painful reminder of their death or kept them trying to hang onto something which once housed their body. When his grandmother passed the first thing his father had done was give away all her clothing. Anders had felt that this was wrong somehow, not that he'd known what to do with the dresses and hats that filled her closet. He hadn't wanted to get rid of them. It made it all too final in some inexplicable way. "How are you feeling?"

"Not good," she moaned again as she turned to look at him. He was back lit with light from the window, making him harder to look at. "Shift down toward my feet would you please. The light is too bright behind you. And, this way I won't have to turn my head so much to see your face." She leaned back against the pillow again and waited for him to settle because watching him move was too hard, both because her eyes were having trouble focusing and because seeing the T-shirt brought to life again was too much to deal with right now.

"How bad was the roof?" she said when she stopped hearing him moving around.

"Let's not worry about that right now. You have a head injury," Anders said, trying to be firm and gentle at the same time.

"I'm fine," Jane said sternly, and looked at him fighting the urge to hold the side of her head again against the swimming world floating around her.

"No, you're not," he said more seriously this time. "We can talk about it after you get back from the hospital."

"I don't need to go to the hospital. I just need to rest," Jane said and found the pillow once more behind her throbbing skull.

"You're going." Fae stepped into the room with some frozen peas wrapped in a checked tea towel. "Put this on your head. You probably have a concussion." Jane did as she was told, in too much pain to argue.

"Yeah, Mom, you need to go to the hospital. A concussion is serious. You could like, die, if you don't go to the hospital." Ellie came into the room, using her walker. She sometimes used her walker around the house when she felt strong enough. Jane thought maybe Ellie was showing off for all the company they currently had, which was somewhat of a rarity around this house.

"Your mother is not going to die," Valentina piped up from somewhere behind Jane's head. "She is a strong woman, and strong women do not just give up like that." She snapped her fingers.

"Here, Mom," Ellie said, holding out a bottle of painkillers.

"Thank you, sweetie," she said and took the bottle. When she looked at Ellie, she noticed her daughter's nails were colourfully painted. "Wow look at your nails. Who did that for you?"

"Valentina, she's really good at nails. And Alec fixed the funny wheel on my walker." Ellie sat down on the cushion next to her mom and Jane snuggled her tight.

"Just a loose bolt and locking nut," he said from somewhere behind her head next to the spot where Valentina's voice originated.

"You didn't have to do that," Jane said. "We would have managed."

"It was no trouble at all," Alec said, and his voice seemed genuine which made Jane relax a bit.

"Well, thank you," she said and hugged Ellie again.

"How long have I been out of it?" Jane asked and looked at Anders, whom she was now noticing had a white film covering his hair.

"About a half hour," he said.

"How did I get here?" she asked him.

"Valentina saw your mother's telephone number next to the phone, we called her, and she came to get you. We followed behind in the truck," he responded.

"After we got the ceiling off of Anders that is," Alec said with laughter in his voice.

"The ceiling?" Jane said, realizing the film in Anders hair looked like plaster dust.

"He's making it sound more dramatic than it was," Anders said trying to sound nonchalant while simultaneously shooting a dirty look toward his brother. "The part of the ceiling where the bubble was fell in on me. It hit me mostly on the leg. Just a couple of scratches."

"I got him bandages when they came in Mom," Ellie said, obviously proud to be able to help.

"You did, wow," Jane tried to sound impressed to cover up the worry she felt at the thought her daughter had taken on too much today.

"She was an excellent nurse," Anders said, and Jane saw how genuine his words were. He sat smiling at her daughter. Something deep in her core felt warmer and she shifted because it made her uncomfortable.

"Are you alright?" Fae asked, tuning into something in her daughter she couldn't remember seeing before but was somehow familiar.

"Yes, I'm alright, except for my head," Jane said, avoiding her mother's all too powerful gaze. "These peas are helping." Jane tried to look happy. "But maybe we should get to the hospital now. Ellie, go get ready for the trip."

"I'm staying here, Mom," Ellie said.

"You can't stay here alone honey," Jane said, a little surprised because Ellie had never asked to stay alone before.

"She won't be alone." Fae stepped in with a tone that told Jane she'd better not argue. "Anders, Alec, and Valentina offered to stay with her until we get back. Isn't that nice?" Her tone suggested that Jane was to agree that it was nice of them, and since her head hurt so much and she was so tired after dealing with the flood, she chose to bite her tongue and keep her fears that they were leaving her only daughter, her special-needs daughter, all alone with practical strangers. She hugged her daughter again, for what she hoped wouldn't be the last time, and climbed into the car with her mother. Though she felt somewhat worried, deep down she knew she could trust the Brookstones with the most precious things in her life. Her daughter, and her café, which she desperately hoped was not beyond repair.

11

While they waited in E.R. triage, Jane worked up the courage to ask her mother about the café and what she'd seen or heard when she'd come to pick her up. The painkillers and peas had helped, and she felt a little more like herself now, ready and capable to handle any bad news that was coming her way. Nothing could be as bad as when Tom had died. Anything that might be coming now would be easy to handle compared to that.

"Well, honey," Fae began after Jane asked the question that was sitting in her stomach like a burning lump. "It looked pretty bad. I think you should be prepared that we might not be able to keep the café in that building any more, or even at all if we can't find a place with rent that is the same or cheaper than that location. Judging by the looks on the Brookstones' faces it will not be good news." Fae reached over and patted her daughter's hand for good measure, a gesture that told Jane that her mother was there for her, as always, but also that things might not be looking so great for their future. And for not being able to buy Ellie a new wheelchair.

"Maybe Brookstone Holdings will just rebuild?" Jane tried to sound hopeful, though it was ringing false to her own ears.

"Maybe?" Fae said. "They seem like really nice people. They did come to help you at the near crack of dawn, stayed for hours trying to find a way to save your business, got you help when you hit your head, and are now babysitting your daughter for you."

"Yes, you're right. They do seem really nice. Especially Anders." Jane had a grin on her face that Fae was pretty sure she didn't realize was there. *Interesting*, the older woman thought. Jane groaned as quickly as she had looked merry and said, "Let's change the subject. Let's talk about anything else, please."

"Alright," Fae said, figuring now was as good as any other time to tell her daughter the news. "I'm going on a date with Ed."

"You're what?" Jane was so shocked she forgot momentarily that her head was hurting.

"Calm down, it's nothing." Fae tried to play it off as casual, but she failed miserably. A grin spread across her face. "He's taking me to dinner."

"Oh really." Jane laughed a little. "What made you suddenly decide you wanted to go out with him?"

"I always wanted to go out with him, it's just, well…" The older woman searched for the words necessary to express what she was feeling, which was rarely ever an easy task. "I just wasn't ready I suppose. But I thought about what you said, and you were right, I shouldn't just sit around all alone. Your father wouldn't want that."

"You're right, Mom, he'd want you to be happy." Jane squeezed her mother's hand and felt a little pang of sadness that her father was gone and wasn't the one making her mother laugh anymore. But Ed was a lovely man, who obviously cared about her, and cared for Ellie, so if her mother had to move on, she was glad it was Ed who was helping her do it. They were silent for a time, both lost in their own memories. They watched a couple of patients be taken into an examination area and hoped they would be next. Jane was remembering her father, and then her own husband. Both gone too soon and sorely missed. Fae was thinking about the same thing, but also about how her daughter was too young to not try to be happy in a relationship again.

"What about you?" Fae asked.

"What about me?" Jane said, knowing what was coming next. Her head had begun to throb, and she wasn't sure if she was up to the lecture, she felt coming her way.

"You try again too," her mother said, in a tone that Jane recognized from her teenage years. "You're too young to just give up on love, Jane. You're only thirty- three. You are beautiful, talented, strong, any man would be lucky to have you go on a date with him."

"Thanks, Mom, but I'm just not ready." Jane said, trying not to sound like the snotty teenager who once deserved to be lectured. "I have Ellie, I have the café, I have my memories of Tom, that's enough for me."

"Well, if you ever change your mind, that man Anders Brookstone might be a good place to start." Fae tried to slide the idea past her daughter, hoping she wouldn't notice her noticing Jane's growing attraction.

"I wouldn't know," Jane said, not looking at her mother. Inside herself, however, she began to acknowledge that he was a very attractive man, if you liked the tall, dark sort of look, and he was kind, friendly, nice to Ellie. Maybe he wasn't so bad after all. Maybe, just maybe she would consider the foolish idea her mother presented. But only for a moment or two. It was best not to get her hopes up since she never wanted to be left alone again like she had been when Tom died. No, scratch everything she had just thought. Anders Brookstone was of no interest to her. She was fine in her little world all alone. No tall, dark and handsome needed.

12

Back at the Michaels' house, Valentina and Ellie were making dinner. Alec had brought in his tool box and was fixing some odds and ends around the house. Nothing that needed serious fixing, but things that were a pain, like a lose curtain rod, sticky doorknob, and a squeaky closet door. Things that busy women like the Michaels' might not get around to dealing with because they just didn't have the time. Anders had set the table and gone outside to brush as much dust out of his hair as he could. Now he was wandering around the house looking at family photographs. There were probably a hundred snapshots of Ellie growing up scattered on nearly every surface or wall space available. There was also a black and white photograph of Fae and her husband on their wedding day. Mr. Michaels was very handsome, wearing glasses with thick black frames, while Fae's hair was long and looked to be light in colour, though it was difficult to tell in a black and white photograph. Suddenly, it occurred to him that Fae had the same last name as Jane, which wasn't right since Jane had been married.

"Ellie," he called into the kitchen.

"Yeah?" she responded, sounding very much like some teenagers he'd seen hanging out at the mall. She was getting older by the minute and Jane was going to have her hands full with this girl.

"Do your grandma and mom have the same last name?" he asked.

"Yep. Mom never changed hers when she got married," the girl responded. "My name is hyphenated, Michaels-Jenkins. My dad's name was Tom Jenkins."

So, she hadn't changed her name when she'd married. Interesting. He kind of liked that about her, liked that she wanted to keep her own identity. He wondered if Meredith would do the same when he married her. Then he stopped himself and realized they had never even discussed it once, so it wasn't a good idea to go off imagining things like that. Ellie came over from the kitchen and pointed to a picture of her dad, so Anders could see.

"Here's my dad, with his motorcycle. He got into an accident and died. I was just little." She looked at the picture sadly. "I don't really remember him much."

Anders wasn't sure what to say but thought he should offer acknowledgement. "You have his eyes," he said. The girl gazed at the picture for a bit and nodded.

"Thanks," she replied, and went back into the kitchen. Anders followed, his mouthwatering at the delicious smell coming from the pot Valentina was tenderly caring for on the stove.

"Yum." His stomach grumbled. "That smells almost good enough to eat." Ellie sat at the kitchen table and Anders joined her, noticing a large binder labelled *Ellie's Cookie Creations* in the centre of the table.

"My wife sure knows how to cook, don't you babe?" Alec came in and replaced a screwdriver in his toolbox, tucked it by the door, and took a seat at the table on the other side of Ellie.

"Yes, I do," Valentina said smiling. "Ellie, every woman must know how to cook. It is important to keep your husband happy. What is the saying, 'the way to a man's heart is through his stomach?' It is very true."

"I can't cook," Ellie said, her eyes cast downward.

"Sure, you can," Anders said, jumping in. "I had one of your mud puddle cookies and it was delicious. And look here—" he pointed to the binder on the table, "—here is an entire binder of cookie recipes you created."

"I created the recipes, but I didn't bake the cookies," Ellie said, adopting the teenage tone again. "Those are two totally different things."

"Well, I tell you what, I will teach you how to cook so all the boys will fall in love with you," Valentina said. Ellie's eyes lit up but were overshadowed by doubt.

"If you can convince my mom to let me cook, then I would love to take lessons from you," Ellie said, sounding doubtful. "She never lets me do anything on my own."

"We can convince her, I know it," Valentina said and winked.

Anders looked through the binder on the table, amazed at the number of cookie recipes there were inside the covers.

"Where did you come up with all these ideas?" he asked, and his stomach growled again when he landed on a recipe for oatmeal, cinnamon, macadamia cookies.

"I dream most of them," Ellie said. "Or, I sometimes see something on T.V. that gives me an idea, like my carrot-cake-zucchini cookies with cream cheese and pecan frosting. I got the idea from a cooking show where the chef was making ratatouille." Anders noticed how her excitement began to grow as she talked about the recipes. "I have two more binders like that one full of recipes. I just can't seem to stop coming up with ideas."

"Wow, three binders." Anders was impressed. He wondered if there was something other than selling the cookies at the café they could do with the recipes. Maybe, there was a way they could do something to help the Michaelses out of the jam they were in?

"Boy, I hope your mom and grandma get back soon," Alec said. "I'm starved."

"You go ahead," Anders said. "I'll wait to eat with the ladies when they come back. I'd like to hear about how things went at the hospital."

"Are you sure?" Valentina inquired.

"Yes, absolutely," Anders said. "Well, actually, I am sort of hungry. Maybe I'll just have some bread to tide me over."

Everyone sat around the table. Anders with his bread, the others with their pasta. It was a good meal, comfortable in its own way, despite Ellie not really knowing any of them. She really liked Valentina and hoped that one day she'd grow up to be beautiful, friendly, kind, and colourful too. Until then, she would take as many cooking lessons as she could get from her new friend.

After dinner, Anders rounded Ellie up. "Come on, kid, time for bed I think," he said to her. Ellie was tempted to disobey but decided otherwise. The Brookstones were doing her mom a favor. Her mom had a head injury and a flooded café, she really didn't need a bratty daughter too. Anders waited in the hall while Ellie brushed her teeth and got changed into her pajamas. Then he tucked her in, wishing her a sweet sleep.

13

Four hours later, Fae and Jane were home again. It was dark, and they were starving, having only had some snacks from the vending machine to tide them over. The cafeteria in the small country hospital they went to was, of course, closed by the time they made it through triage. Alec and Valentina were nowhere to be found. Fae phoned the house when Jane went for a CAT scan, realizing they probably wouldn't be home any time soon, giving instructions to Valentina on Ellie's bedtime routine and told the gang to go ahead and eat. Fae also remembered to phone Iris, who had had the day off, to fill her in on the disaster at the café.

The Brookstones' truck was nowhere to be seen when Jane and Fae pulled their van into the drive. A dim light glowed in the front window, but otherwise the house was quiet. A fear gripped Jane's heart, beating in time with the throbbing of her head, which had luckily only been a terrible goose egg and headache, according to the doctor. What if the Brookstones had left Ellie all alone? Hurriedly she threw off her seatbelt, grabbed her purse and ran as fast as her sore head would let her, up to the front door. Not wanting to wait for her mother who had the keys, Jane found the plastic rock hide-a-key in the garden, bursting through the front door as the lock gave way to the key's click.

Feeling somewhat frantic, throwing her purse down on the nearest surface, she scanned the room. There, fast asleep on the couch was Anders. Still wearing Tom's T-shirt, he was stretched awkwardly across their chesterfield, a foot resting on the floor, the other hanging over the arm of the couch, his dress slacks riding up slightly, exposing his muscular calf. He looked as peaceful as a child, all the lines of his face at rest, arms wrapped around one of Ellie's stuffed animals, draped in the old pink and yellow afghan Jane kept folded nearby for rainy afternoons when she might get the chance to read a book. Admittedly, that had not happened for months because she was always at the café, or with Ellie. Jane felt her stomach lurch, a mixture of hunger pangs, terror over losing the café, and something familiar she felt at having a man asleep in her house, sent her on a retreat to Ellie's room.

There she found her daughter, curled under her cloud-patterned quilt, the glow in the dark stars on her ceiling shining away, lighting the way for her daughter's dreams. Jane was glad to see Ellie's walker within easy reach for her daughter, in case she needed to get up in the night. Jane bent to kiss her daughter's forehead.

"Mom?" Ellie turned sleepily toward Jane. "Are you O.K.? Do you have a concussion?"

"I'm fine sweetie," Jane said, simultaneously stroking Ellie's hair and lightly rubbing her goose egg. "Just a bang to the head. The doctor says I'm supposed to rest for a couple days and drink plenty of water." Jane was unsure how plenty of water would help, other than washing down the super-strength painkillers he gave her for the headache. "Did you have an alright night with the Brookstones?"

Through a yawn, Ellie responded excitedly, "Yes I did. Valentina showed me how to make garlic bread. It was fun. She let me drizzle the olive oil. And she made really yummy pasta with meat sauce. Alec fixed the squeaky door hinges, and Anders read me a bedtime story, even though I'm too old for that kinda stuff."

Ellie pretended to pout, but Jane could tell that her daughter liked the attention. Her own heart panged painfully at the thought of all the nights Ellie missed since Tom's death that she could have been sharing bedtime stories with her father. Jane shoved the feelings aside, trying to sound much more chipper than she was feeling.

"Where are Valentina and Alec now?" Jane asked, wondering if they had driven all the way back to the city.

"They went back to the café," Ellie said, yawning again. "Alec said they would check out what work needed to be done in the morning and that they would camp out near the river for the night. They always carry a tent and sleeping bags with them wherever they go. Isn't that a good idea?"

Jane's eyebrows rose up a bit, causing a sharp pain in her brain. "It is indeed," she said, but she was more surprised that they went back to the café so late in the evening. They didn't even know her and yet they had sacrificed their entire day to helping her out. "Go back to sleep now, sweetie, you've got school in the morning."

"Goodnight, Mom, I love you," Ellie said through another yawn.

Jane left her daughter with another kiss, pulling the door closed behind her. Back in the kitchen she found her mother, and a note from Alec explaining they had gone back to the café to do some clean up.

Anders stayed to watch Ellie. They were having fun looking through her cookie creation binders. He was waiting for you to return to have dinner, which is in the oven.
Hope your head is feeling better,
A & V

Jane looked up from the note to meet her mother's gaze. Her mother gave her a small shrug. Fae couldn't believe how nice the Brookstones were either. Jane rose from the table, holding her head onto her body, and went to the living room to wake Anders while her mother got out some plates. He was still asleep, his jaw flexing in some dream time movements. She saw some plaster dust still clinging to the edges of his hair and found herself reaching out to brush it away. Her long fingers grazed the side of his face and the hair at his temple. His eyes fluttered open at her touch and for a moment, their eyes locked. Anders felt a momentary confusion as to where he was and why his foot was asleep, but the face before him was one he would know anywhere, even if there was a large purple-black bump currently residing on it.

"Hi," he said.

"Hi," she said back. "You read Ellie a bedtime story?" she asked, taking a step back, even though she already missed the feel of his skin under her fingertips. She held one hand on her head, while the other rested on her hip. Anders wasn't sure if this was a gesture of annoyance at having read to Ellie, or if it was a way to keep herself together because of the pain in her head.

"I did," he said. "We had a fun time. Her recipes are really great," he said, a genuine delight spreading across his face as he sat up. Realizing he was cuddling a pink stuffed lion, he practically threw it down next to him. Jane laughed. That was the first time he'd heard her laugh, and even though it was at his expense, he knew he'd always want to hear her do it again.

"Ellie told me her lion would keep me company until you got back…" He trailed off a bit.

"She must like you," Jane said. "That lion is her favourite." She turned and gestured for him to follow her to the kitchen.

Fae set out plates of pasta with the garlic bread on a platter in the centre of the table. For herself and Anders she poured red wine.

"Can't I have some wine?" Jane complained, "I certainly could use it after the day I had." She grimaced as her mother plonked the jar of pills the doctor gave her and a glass of water down next to her plate.

"No, you may not have some wine. Take your painkillers and eat your dinner. I'm sure those babies will do you in well enough without the help of alcohol." Fae was stern but kind with her words.

"A little wine won't hurt, Mom," Jane said sounding more like a teenager than Ellie did lately. "These pills probably won't do anything."

Anders smirked into his noodles, enjoying the interaction between mother and daughter. Chewing the delicious bite, taking a mental note to tell Valentina that she was an excellent cook the next time he saw her. He asked Jane how she was feeling.

"I've been better, but no concussion," she said, then threw back the pills and took a large gulp of water to get them down.

Anders eyes softened as he reached over to touch her hand. "I'm glad."

Their eyes locked a moment more and Fae turned away pretending to dry a glass to give them some privacy.

They all tucked into their meals, starving from the emotional toll brought on by the day. Jane started to get drowsy by the end of her meal, her painkillers in full effect, resulting in Fae ushering her to the bathroom to brush her teeth and then tucking her in bed. Something she hadn't done since Jane was close to Ellie's age.

"You can sleep on the chesterfield," Fae said to Anders' back as he washed up the dishes. "There is an extra toothbrush for you on the bathroom counter."

Anders dutifully brushed his teeth and returned to the crammed quarters on the couch, cuddling the pink lion again after he was sure Fae was asleep.

14

The next day, Ellie woke up first. She made her way to the bathroom, washed up, got dressed, and went to the kitchen where Fae was warming a semi-stale lemon cranberry muffin she'd fished out of one of the bins they'd rescued from the café. Fae left to dress while Ellie ate. They were both being as quiet as possible, so that Jane would be able to rest and not to wake Anders. They were too late for Anders, who had left before sun up, folding the blanket and stacking the pillow and stuffed lion on top at the end of the couch. He'd left a note next to the lion:

Dear Jane, Fae, and Ellie,
 I hope this note finds you feeling better, Jane. I am off to the café to find Alec and do some more cleaning. I'll be back to visit soon.
Anders.

Shortly after breakfast, Fae trundled Ellie off to the bus stop, dressed in her work clothes, intending to help with as much clean up at the café as she could manage. They left Jane sleeping, covers pulled up to her chin.

When Jane awoke several hours later, she was confused, and her head throbbed as she rolled away from the way too bright sun shining in the window. She squinted one eye open and saw the time on the clock said 12:37 p.m. Leaping out of bed from the sight of that number on the clock, she quickly sat back down as the blood rushed to her head.

"Okay, so, go slowly," she said to herself aloud, placing a hand on the side of her head to stop her brain from moving with the rotation of the earth. When she found her equilibrium again, she saw out of the corner of her eye a note from her daughter.

Dear Mom,
Stay in bed today, doctor's orders.
xo
Ellie

The note was propped up on a tray laden with a bowl full of green grapes, next to a chocolate filled flaky pastry Jane recognized was one rescued from the café yesterday. A mug with pink and red hearts on it sat next to a thermos. Jane opened the lid to find it steaming with the smell of cinnamon tea. Her bottle of painkillers rounded out the little display. Envisioning Ellie preparing the tray with the help of her grandmother made her heart glad. Ellie was such a good daughter. Tom would be so proud of her, she thought to herself, fighting back the need to sob. If she started, she just might never stop. She sat up a little more.

The tea smelled delicious and Jane found she felt hungry. First though, she needed the bathroom. Sleeping for more than twelve hours, her bladder was currently protesting. She stood up gingerly, shuffling her way down the hall. After finding relief, she studied herself in the mirror. Her hair was a mess, and the bruise on her forehead was still protruding out a good two inches from her face. It had changed slightly in colour overnight, darkening to a blackish purple that clashed nicely with her freckles. Jane flipped some hair over the bruise to hide it from herself but winced when it landed on the lump.

"Ouch," she said, turning out the door, shuffling to the kitchen to grab a glass of water and another chocolate pastry, just in case. She peeked into the living room, expecting to see Anders there on the couch, but of course he wasn't there.

He was gone, along with Tom's T-shirt, she assumed. Something inside her lurched and she couldn't tell if it was because of her head or the memory of Tom's T-shirt alive on someone as strapping and fine-looking as Anders. Though Alec had worn one of Tom's T-shirts too, it was the sight of Anders she couldn't get out of her head. He was handsome, very handsome. It was okay she admitted it to herself. She was still a living, breathing woman. Even if she never wanted another relationship again, she could still find a man attractive. Besides, this man, she knew, would destroy her business. After the collapse of her ceiling, she didn't hold up much hope for Cutie Pies any longer. *What am I going to do?* she thought to herself, feeling a list inside herself once more, thinking about Ellie's need for a new wheelchair, losing her business, paying bills—

Her head throbbed as she quickly shuffled back to bed, where she opened the window and tucked herself in. She turned on the radio and found some soothing classical music station that didn't make her head spin. Jane couldn't remember the last time she was home in the middle of the day and despite the pressing circumstances life was handing her now, she hurt too much to worry about anything except lying there, listening to some woodwinds and the birds outside. Jane ate her breakfast, drank her tea, chasing down a couple more of those pain pills in the process, and promptly fell back asleep.

15

At nine that morning, Anders phoned his father to deliver the news about his latest venture. He dreaded the phone call, knowing that his father would say to demolish the building, which is exactly what Blair had done. Anders normally would have just gone along with whatever his father had said, but today, a day in which he started out the morning by hugging a stuffed, pink, toy lion, and eating some still delicious left-over pastries he had argued with his father.

"No, Dad, I think you should come see this place." Anders felt disbelief at his own words, looking at his reflection in the rear-view mirror of his brother's truck which he'd borrowed earlier that morning. "It's different, here. It's not meant for condos." A flash of what could be came into his mind and Anders tried to hold onto the feeling of everything being right in the world, an unfamiliar feeling that scared him a bit, though it was nice for as long as it lasted.

"Son, I read your report that you left on my desk," Anders imagined his father, a granite-like block of man sitting up straight behind his glass and chrome desk, glasses perched on his nose as he flipped through the report. "I see no reason to try to save this place. I can't imagine what you see in this property. But if you insist,

I'll make the trip up in two days. I'll bring your mother as well. She might like the drive. Find us a place to stay and we'll make a weekend of it." Blair barked orders to his son.

"Yes, sir," Anders said, and thought about how he would find them a place to stay, but no matter. He had won a small victory in convincing Blair to come to Millvale at all.

His father abruptly hung up the phone as Anders felt his brow break out in a sweat. "What do I do now?" he said aloud to his reflection. His reflection had no answers for him.

When Anders borrowed the truck from his brother, he had retrieved the keys from Alec and Valentina who were huddled around a small camp fire down by the old mill where they had pitched their tent. When Anders left Jane's house, he walked through town and discovered it was wooing him with its charms. Old Victorian houses with well-kept gardens lined the street, with the sidewalk running close to the front doors of the homes so it would be easy to say hello to your neighbours. It was a warm and inviting place, with much to offer in terms of beauty and scenery, but not much to offer in terms of amenities and entertainment. Though there was an old railway track that had been turned into a conservation and walking trail, aside from the building that housed the café, travel agency, hairdresser, and variety store, there was not much else to see and do, except maybe some fishing in the meandering creek down by the mill at the back of the café property. As Anders walked through the town, he felt more and more at home, his bones settling into the quiet pace of the streets, the sound of the creek rippling through the air soothing him.

Deciding to take a drive to see what lay in the neighbouring town, Anders took the truck, and pulled off the side of the road to phone his father. Now, he continued his journey, past sod and potato farms, horses and cows behind wire fences, on a wide-open road that led straight to the larger town of Bellfield. Here he found a dry cleaner, where he dropped off Jane's husband's T-shirts. Then he found a farm supply store and bought himself some working clothes, so he could pitch in around the café with the cleanup. He found a small bistro where he ordered coffees and breakfast sandwiches to take back with him. The town was quaint, with interesting art shops, some small restaurants, a bowling alley, and a theatre. On his way back to Millvale, he took a different route and discovered there was a ski resort within a short drive, as well as three golf courses in the area.

Anders also spotted a nice-looking bungalow for rent on his drive back. He pulled into the driveway and phoned the Realtor who came to meet him quickly. Anders toured the house, discovering the property was warm and inviting, and was available for rent on a nightly basis as well as for longer term. The place was furnished in warm tones, like his office. He felt at home, and noticed his shoulders relaxed a bit. He would stay here for the next few days, give his parents a place to rest, and maybe even Alec and Valentina too. Then he would show his father around and try to convince the difficult man that an inn was what the area needed.

A plan was developing in his mind when he pulled up in front of the café, to find his brother and his bride, along with Iris, Fae, and an older man working on clearing out the debris from the ceiling collapse. He soon discovered the man was Ed, Ellie's bus driver, and by the looks of things, Fae's boyfriend.

The business owners in the other shops were here too, looking out for their friends and lending a hand. It was clear that the people of Millvale looked out for their own. Anders handed round the goodies, including the now cold coffee he'd brought with him to the crowd of rag tag helpers who had assembled, feeling like one of the crowd, even though he knew that the people who owned businesses here were suspicious of his presence. He couldn't blame them, and he wanted to reassure them that he was there to help, not destroy their lives. But it was too early for him to say anything. So, he got stuck in with the cleaning effort to try to prove through his actions that he wanted to look after the businesses of Millvale. When a quiet moment came, he pulled Alec aside and they put their heads together as to what they would tell Blair when he showed up, and how to break the news to Jane when they saw her again.

16

Later that afternoon, Meredith called. Anders was surprised to see her number light up his phone. Answering on the third ring, a lump of guilt ran down his throat. Anders forgot about Meredith. That can't be right, could it? He wanted to marry her, and he hadn't thought about her at all since he got to Millvale. He was just preoccupied with the café and now with finding a place for his parents to stay, and the plan he was developing to save the space. That's all.

Without warning, the image of Jane smashing her face floated into his mind while Meredith told him about the latest funeral they'd had yesterday. He caught himself drifting into the memory instead of listening to his girlfriend. He'd never minded listening to Meredith's funeral stories before, why did he stop listening to them now? He was just tired from staying in a new place and all the physical labour he'd been doing.

"Honey, I'm really tired," Anders said, feeling slightly panicked. "Do you mind if I phone you again tomorrow?"

"Yes, alright," Meredith said sounding just as she always did. Calm, collected. "Any idea of how long you will be in Millvale?" she asked.

"I'll be here for a few days. My parents are coming to check out the café property," Anders responded, feeling a bit surly at her questioning him. He shook it off. "I've rented a house until Monday next week, so we'd all have a place to stay."

"That's a great idea," Meredith said, and Anders agreed that it was a great idea too. Close to the café, close to his project that he hoped he'd be able to make work, and close to Jane and Ellie. He shook his head again. He really must be tired. Why did he keep thinking about Jane? And now Ellie too?

"Okay, Meredith. I'll talk to you tomorrow." He felt the urgent need to get off the phone and figure out his mind.

"Goodbye, Anders," Meredith said.

"Bye," he said quickly and hung up his phone. Maybe he should have a nap. He could try out one of the beds in the house he'd rented. He'd set up a little work station after the day of clean up finished. Insurance adjusters had come to inspect the property. He, along with the crew they'd assembled, finished clearing away as much debris as they could. Alec and he had climbed on roofs and tarped whatever looked like it might leak. A meeting was made for the next morning that would convene at Anders' house around the large oak dining table that came with the place. He would present his ideas to the group. If they liked them, he would show them to his father the next day.

After he left the clean-up crew, and before he came back to the house, Anders stocked up on some snacks and drinks, and bought an orchid, his mother's favourite, to put in the window. Somehow, he hoped that having her favourite flower would make up for this house that he knew his parents would hate. Anders, on the other hand, really liked it here. There was a large fenced yard in the back, and the property had a long winding driveway, which was always something he'd dreamed of having since he moved into the condo. The idea of walking down a peaceful lane each morning to pick up the paper appealed to him. The yard was flanked by a forest on one side and a corn field on the other. The interior of the house was just what he would like in his dream home. Aside from a few different choices in paint colours, he could see himself in a place like this. Comfortable furniture, fire in the fireplace, happy photos on the mantle, some toys scattered around. In his mind, the place felt like home already.

This wasn't his home. It was a temporary stop, required only to accomplish the job he had been sent to do. He looked at the clock on the kitchen wall that he could see from his work station in the dining area. It was a quarter to five. He was to be at Jane's house at five-thirty, on invitation for dinner from Ellie. Evidently, it was the last day of school for the year and she wanted to have a celebration dinner. How could he resist a celebration during all the upheaval he'd been dealing with the past few days? He'd even bought her a small gift when he was shopping. He decided that instead of a nap, he'd have a shower to soothe the sore muscles and revive some sense of normalcy to his mind.

After his shower, he dressed in some of the new clothes he bought that day. A white golf shirt and jeans he'd picked up at the men's clothing store he'd found in Bellfield. He was surprised at all the interesting and useful stores he'd found. There was also a big box department store, that had groceries and other things one might need like diapers, kid's clothes, and tires. One stop shopping at its finest. Exactly what he needed, where he needed it. He also had time to pick up Tom's T-shirts on his way through town. Imagine, it was cleaned in less than one day. Anders supposed that was one of the perks of small-town living. Not so many other people in the way.

In the yard, he waved to Alec, who was loading a contraption made from PVC pipes in the back of the truck.

"What's that?" he asked as he climbed in next to Valentina who was in the middle of the bench seat.

"You'll see," said Alec, with a half happy, half excited smirk on his face that he tried to hide when he climbed in the driver's seat.

They drove down the winding drive and out onto the road that took them back into town, to Jane's house.

17

Jane sat on the couch, holding a bag of frozen peas to her forehead. She was feeling much better, though her head still throbbed a bit. Two doses of those extra strong painkillers and sleeping all day had done wonders. She had managed to have a shower, being careful to avoid the still darkening lump, and she had gotten dressed in shorts and a T-shirt with her damp hair thrown up in a messy pony tail on top of her head. As she rested from the effort, she listened in to Ellie and her best friend Sally who were sitting at the kitchen table working on her new cookie binder and laughing, happy to be done school for another year.

Jane had felt terrible when Ellie came home singing "No more pencils, no more books—" and celebrating the end of another school year. Jane had completely forgotten that school was ending this week. With the worries of the café, the flood, and thinking about how they would pay for a new wheelchair for Ellie, Jane had just let it slip from her mind.
But Ellie hadn't minded. She had planned a party for herself, asked her grandmother to cook, and now Iris, Ed, Valentina, Alec and Anders Brookstone were all coming over for dinner. A bit of a strange group, but Ellie had taken to Valentina right away. Jane felt pride as she

thought about how confident and capable her daughter was becoming. Since Valentina was a strong and confident seeming woman herself, it was fine by Jane that Ellie have another example of what kind of woman she could be one day. Though the thought of Ellie out there in the world alone frightened her more than she wanted to admit, Tom would be so proud of how she was growing into her own person. She felt a lump rising in her throat just as the doorbell rang.

"I'll get it," she called into the kitchen and quickly let out a breath to erase the sad memory. Today she would have some fun and celebrate with her daughter. Despite everything else that was weighing on her mind. She let the hand holding the peas drop from her face to her side as the door opened.

"Ouch," Iris said, giving a quick hug to Jane in the doorway. Her curls floated around her shoulders, rubbing slightly against the goose egg on Jane's face.

"Yeah," Jane said with a half-hearted chuckle. Behind Iris followed Ed, who was smartly dressed in tan slacks and a crisp blue polo shirt that complimented his greying hair.

"Hi, Jane, these are for you. I hope you're feeling better." Ed handed her a small bunch of deep pink carnations. In his hands he held two more bunches of flowers. One, a nosegay of yellow daisies for Ellie to celebrate the end of school and to thank her for all the cookies she'd made for him over the past school year.

"Thanks, Ed," Jane called over her shoulder after Ed, who was delivering the third bunch of flowers to her mother which was a small bouquet of pink sweetheart roses that were the approximate shade of Ed's cheeks as he gave them to her. This impromptu dinner fell one day before their date, for which both Ed and Fae were obviously excited. Ed offered to help with the dinner preparations. After handing him an apron, Fae had him set to work chopping cucumbers for the salad. Ellie pushed her walker over to the cupboard and pulled out three mason jars for the flowers.

"Let's all have vases of our own," she said, filling them with water and putting her daisies in the centre of the dining table.

"Good idea, sweetie," Jane said. She turned to put her flowers in their jar when she saw the Brookstone truck pulling over to the sidewalk. She waited in the doorway to greet them. Valentina gave her a big hug, and a jar of chamomile paste she whipped up.

"It will soothe your lump," she said with her thick accent, making the thought of smearing weird herb paste on her forehead sound somewhat appealing to Jane.

"Thank you," Jane said, smiling.

"Valentina," Ellie said excitedly from the kitchen. "Come meet my friend Sally."

"Hello lovely Ellie, and Sally, it's nice to meet you." Valentina's voice drifted toward the kitchen, where the girls started laughing over something Jane didn't catch. She felt a sense of warmth spread though her at all the happy noises coming from the small room.

"Hello, Alec, come in," she said to the blonde Brookstone brother. Alec nodded, trying to be polite and obviously not looking at Jane's bruises. Bringing up the rear was Anders, who looked good, very good to Jane's utter amazement. He was a good-looking guy, she had remembered that much, but seeing him now, dressed in jeans with a well-fitting polo shirt loosely tucked, was surprising. He looked normal, like a regular guy who wasn't out to ruin her business. *Careful Jane*, she said to herself. But why would she need to be careful? She was not interested in dating, never mind this guy, of all the men who came into her café. Never this guy.

"I come bearing gifts, of sorts," Anders said, holding out Tom's shirts on wire hangers, covered in a dry-cleaning bag and a new binder for Ellie which he deposited on the kitchen table.

"Awesome," Sally said.

"Thanks," Ellie replied happily.

"Oh," Jane said, surprised to be getting the shirt back so quickly. "Thank you. Let me just put these things down," she said, feeling awkward. Placing the peas back in the freezer and her flowers in their vase.

"I'll carry it," he said, trying to follow her down the hallway to her room.

"Um. No, that's alright," Jane said, taking hold of the opposite side of the hanger. Anders tugged back a bit, his eyes twinkling just a bit too much for her liking.

"I wanted to talk to you, alone, if you don't mind." His confidence waned and returned in a microsecond. Jane noticed, though she didn't think Anders knew it had happened.

"Okay," she said against her better judgement, and nodded for him to follow her down the hall, past the partiers in the kitchen who were all busy laughing and helping to get dinner ready.

When they reached the closed door to her room, Jane turned and said, "I'm sorry but it's kind of a mess. I was not really feeling up to being neat today." She frowned. Anders felt compelled to stroke her face and caress away the painful looking bruise. He resisted.

"It's fine. Really," he said instead. She opened the door. The room was just like he thought it would be. Cozy, like the rest of the house, with light blue walls and a blue quilt embellished with kittens in different fabric patterns chasing after colourful balls of yarn. A large bed, with a silver framed photo of Tom on one bedside table, his side he assumed, along with a reading lamp and some new looking books on her side. Dirty plates and cups sat there from her day in bed, alongside the bottle of painkillers. The windows were covered in yellow drapes, and there was a long, low white dresser on the wall opposite the bed. He liked it.

"Your room is great," he commented with an approving nod.

"Thanks," she replied, doubtfully. She took the shirts from him, discarding the hangers and bag on the end of the bed, pressing the fabric to her face. She was visibly disappointed as she neatly folded the shirt and put it back into a dresser drawer. She didn't mention that she could no longer smell Tom on the shirt, even if that was never possible, since he passed away so long ago. But in her memory, she could still smell him. The memory of that shirt had been altered since she saw Anders wearing it and would never be the same. She shook her head.

"That's a nice photo of your husband." Anders gestured awkwardly to the framed picture.

"Thank you." Jane focused on the frame, crossing the room to caress it.

"Ellie said he died in a motorcycle accident?" Anders let the question drift, hoping Jane would fill in the rest.

"Drunk driver ran a red light," Jane offered up by way of an explanation.

"I'm sorry," Anders said.

"Me too." Jane's face looked hurt. Anders felt the need to take away the pain and crossed the room to stand close to her. He reached out to place a hand on her shoulder.

"What was it that you wanted to talk to me about?" Jane said, dodging his hand then turning away slowing to prevent her head from spinning.

Anders rubbed his hands nervously on his thighs. "I think you should sit down for this."

"Okay," Jane said, feeling butterflies rise in her chest. Anders took a few deep breaths. "You're making me nervous," Jane said. "Out with it."

"Okay, here goes," Anders started. "I think I have a plan to save the café, and I wanted to run it past you first before I told everyone else."

"We need to save the café?" Jane knew in her heart they did but was hoping it wasn't true. Her head throbbed a little.

"Yes, otherwise, my father will just tear the building down and put up condos," Anders said, in the voice of a businessman. Jane felt a cold chill settle on her skin, despite the hot weather outside. "My father is a tough man to please, trust me. I've had years of practice in disappointing him."

"Oh," she said. She was quiet for a moment, thinking if she should kick him out or ask him to continue. She hoped what he would say was going to save her future, but how could she trust this man who was a near stranger? She decided to take a leap of faith. "Go on," Jane said.

"I want to turn the café, and the other businesses, into a beautiful hotel, with a restaurant and spa. I want to expand the café into something more. I think this is the perfect location for it," Anders said all of this in one breath. "What do you think?"

"How?" was all Jane had to say.

"We could use the insurance money you would get, along with the insurance money from the other tenants to make repairs to the building and to expand it to make the hotel, an inn, actually. I am going to meet with my father tomorrow to try to get the rest of the money as an investment from Brookstone Holdings." Anders was quiet while Jane thought.

The insurance money could buy a new wheelchair for Ellie. Maybe it was time Jane and her mother cut their losses and Jane got a regular job in the neighbouring town? She wondered what Fae would say. She would obviously need to talk to her before answering Anders. The insurance money would put them afloat for a few months, maybe even six months or more. Could she risk all of it on a new venture? She didn't know if she had the strength to start over again.

"I don't know," she said, and Anders frowned. "I need to talk to my mom about all of this before I can agree to anything."

"Alright, I understand. I have a presentation I can show you both after dinner." He patted the satchel slung across his body, which held his tablet, she assumed.

"Okay, I think that would help," she said, smiling slightly.

"Great," Anders said. They stood for an awkward moment of silence. Jane broke it by gesturing to the door. "I guess we should head back to the party to see what's happening with dinner. I'm starving." She wasn't sure if she was hungry or if she might throw up, but mostly she wanted to end this conversation because her head was starting to swirl again, and she wanted this man out of her room. Anders began to walk ahead but stopped in the hall to look at her.

"I'm not going to lead you into ruin," he said, looking so sincere that Jane felt the hard part of her heart that had his name on it shift a little. She nodded, staring back at him. He turned and walked to the kitchen, with Jane right on his heels.

18

The laughter in the kitchen was loud and Jane found herself smiling despite the terrifying news Anders had just given her. Should she put the insurance money into this new venture or give it to Ellie and buy her a new chair? This might be the last chair they would need to buy for a while, so that was a consideration. Her heart leapt a little, but she wasn't sure if it was because of this turn of life that was happening to her, or if it was because Anders looked so good in the jeans he was wearing. Okay, fine, she admitted to herself that she was attracted to Anders. But that was it; she was not going to do anything about it. He was effectively forcing her to end her business, and so what if she was going to get the chance to help him build something bigger, and maybe even better. He was forcing her to change her life and she was not happy about it. She liked things to be the same, to be stable. Her safe cocoon of predictability where she kept Ellie and her mom sheltered and where she would never have her heart broken again.

She pulled herself back from her racing thoughts when they turned the corner and she looked in the kitchen. Ellie was standing at the kitchen counter with a small paring knife in her hand. Ellie was helping to make dinner, which was natural enough, but suddenly it dawned on her that Ellie was standing. How was she standing? Jane looked again and saw that her daughter was strapped into a PVC pipe frame that had an angled support pressed against Ellie's back that held her daughter upright. Jane's heart sank.

"What's going on?" she asked with mild panic pushing past Anders who was in the hallway in front of her.

"Mom!" Ellie cried, obviously overjoyed with being able to stand at the counter and help cook. She had a cutting board filled with sliced mushrooms in front of her and a huge grin on her face. Jane walked quickly over to where Ellie stood to look at the contraption that surrounded her daughter. There were wheels at the bottom of the frame, along with a belt that held Ellie against the back support, and two padded supports for her shins to press against and support her legs.

This was attached to a U-shaped frame that travelled around Ellie's backside. There was an open space at the front, so her daughter could press right up to the counter, along with arm rests in case she needed support on the side. She thought it looked safe enough but was unsure.

"Alec built it for her, Jane," Fae spoke quietly from the kitchen table. "I thought it would be alright to let her try it." Her mother was cautious, knowing how protective Jane was of her daughter.

"Yeah, Mom, isn't it great?" Ellie said, smiling wider and wider every time she looked at Jane. Inside Jane screamed to herself that no, it wasn't alright. None of this was alright. Who are these Brookstones anyway? Coming here and changing her life all around.

"You should have asked me first," Jane said to the whole crowd. Alec cleared his throat to draw her attention.

"My apologies if I overstepped, Jane." He looked at her. Jane felt annoyed because he had a sincere face and was obviously trying to help. "When we were here the other day, I saw how much Ellie enjoyed cooking with Valentina and I thought I could help make it easier for her to learn and help you. I promise I made it as safe as possible," Alec said. He looked so earnest that Jane felt another hard piece shift in her heart, only to be replaced with guilt that she, Ellie's own mother, had never thought of getting something like this made for her own child.

Before she could respond, Ellie spoke up.

"Don't be mad, Mom, I like it," Ellie said, looking worried.

"Yeah, it's awesome," Sally said from the kitchen table. Ellie looked at her, and they both beamed at Jane. Jane felt defeated, guilty, tired, and confused. She also felt so proud of her daughter for being brave enough to try something new, and that's more than what she could say for herself lately.

Not sure what to say she ended the conversation with a lame, "Well, just be careful." She went over to the freezer, pulled out her bag of peas, and went out to the couch to sooth herself and her now throbbing head with the frozen vegetables.

The rest of the evening went along without incident. They enjoyed a tasty dinner of mac and cheese with a side of summer vegetable salad, Ellie's mushrooms featured prominently in the bowl. They topped off the meal with slices of one of the rescued strawberry pies from the café. Most things, what would fit anyway, had been packaged and stored away in the freezer. The rest were in the fridge or on the counter, waiting to be eaten in the next day or so.

Ellie and Sally declared the evening's party a success, and went off to figure out how to use Iris' video camera, which she'd brought along to upload the footage of the storm damage of the café to Anders' tablet for it to be sent to the insurance company and for him to have on file for Brookstone Holdings. The adults sat around the kitchen table for a while chatting and enjoying the company. Anders told the others about his plans for converting the café building into an inn. Fae shot Jane covert looks across the table, which promised they would be having a lengthy discussion in the morning. Jane excused herself early and went to hide under the covers, promptly falling asleep after the painkillers kicked in.

Anders cornered Fae while Alec and Valentina tidied up the dishes. He wanted reassurance that Jane was alright. He didn't want to think that he was the source of her need to leave and go to bed early.

"She has worked to make everything stable and the same since the day Tom died," Fae said, looking a little past Anders to a place he couldn't yet understand. "This is hard for her," she said and patted his arm. Anders knew he would have to proceed with caution but had no doubt that he wanted Jane on the hotel project. Not only because she was clearly a fantastic cook and would make the new restaurant a sure-fire success, but also because he genuinely liked her.

Yes, he liked her.

19

In the early morning, Anders met with the other tenants of the building. They liked his plan to expand the building to an inn. The salon decided they would invest their insurance money into adding a spa to the hotel, while the travel agents, who happened to be a married couple, decided they would move their office into their home. They had a daughter in college and wanted to use the insurance money to pay her tuition. He could understand that. The variety store agreed to invest as well, offering to run the gift shop inside the inn. After he finished this meeting, he prepared to meet his father. He felt a bit nervous, but Alec assured him that his plan was solid, and that he wanted to help to make the hotel the best place around.

At midmorning he went home, and laid out his plans again with Alec, making sure they were perfect. Their father was set to descend with his mother sometime in the early afternoon. They had preliminary drawings that Alec laid out, a land survey showing the large property that went all the way down to the creek and the beautiful old mill that was included as part of the property. He laid out how they could refurbish the mill and use it as a backdrop for wedding pictures. They had drawn up some plans for an English country garden with rambling paths and a flurry of colourful flowers. The restaurant would seat one hundred, while the banquet hall could handle two hundred. The spa would have massage rooms, and an aqua bath where people could bathe in the healing waters of the countryside. The spa would also offer a full-service salon. The new hotel would employ one hundred fifty people year-round.

He estimated that the hair salon would receive thirty thousand dollars from their insurance company, the variety store around fifty thousand, while Jane would receive around sixty thousand dollars. Then, with that money in line, he would ask his father for another three million that he believed he would need to complete the rebuild and transformation of the property. He felt a sinking in his stomach when he realized how much money he was about to ask his father to provide to complete this build. If only he knew for sure that Jane was in. Not so much her money, though that was important, but more so her talent. He knew his father loved good food, and Jane was one of the best cooks he had ever met.

"What if Jane doesn't agree to come along on the project?" Anders looked worried as he spoke to his brother, who looked casual as always.

"She will," Alec assured him, as he draped his arm over the back of the wooden kitchen chair he sat upon.

"How can you be so sure?" Anders paced, doubtfully back and forth across the checkerboard floor of the large kitchen.

"If you're not sure, ask her," Valentina said.

Ask her? Anders thought that was sensible and wasn't sure why it hadn't occurred to him earlier. He had asked her the day before, but she seemed to shut down. He didn't want to see her do that again.

"I don't think she likes the idea," Anders said, and paced some more.

"I think she's just nervous," Alec said, looking decidedly not nervous. Anders wanted to punch him for looking so calm.

"What if Father refuses the deal?" Anders said, feeling a worried boring in his stomach, images of Jane and Fae crying on their couch, while Ellie sat crouched in her too small wheelchair. He felt responsible for helping them, for making them happy, for making Jane laugh.

"He won't," said Valentina, reassurance in her voice. "It's a great idea. I would love to stay in a beautiful hotel like the one you have described."

Anders paced some more and decided the only thing he could do was to phone Jane and invite her to come to the meeting with his father. He stepped outside onto the wide-open porch that overlooked the meandering driveway of his rented house and dialed. She picked up after two rings.

"Hello," she answered, sounding better than she had the night before.

"Hi, Jane, it's Anders Brookstone," he said, feeling formal and nervous.

"Hello," she said, sounding detached. Maybe that was just his imagination.

"I was just calling to see if you had a chance to think about our discussion last night?" Anders found a seat on the porch swing. His view now landed on a field of corn that was about ankle high.

"As a matter of fact, I have," Jane said. "I was going to call you actually. I heard from the insurance company earlier this morning. They are giving me $100,000 for the café." Her voice grew colder, and Anders knew he should proceed with caution.

"That's wonderful," he said.

"It is," Jane agreed and sighed. She took a deep breath. "After discussing it with Mom, she's decided to retire, and I will continue on with you at the new hotel. But there is a catch.

"Okay," Anders said. He had unconsciously stood up with excitement when she said she was going to join him at the hotel.

"I won't give you all that money. I can't. You can have $80,000, and I'm keeping the rest, so I can buy a new wheelchair for Ellie and look after my family until the restaurant is up and running at the hotel."

Anders thought to himself about how he liked how practical Jane was, and how fiercely she protected her loved ones.

"I think that's great," he said, noticing the sun suddenly turning the corn into a bright green light shining in the field beyond the window.

"And one more thing," Jane said, her tone growing even more serious, if that was possible.

"Yes," Anders said, and held his breath.

"You better not screw this up," she said. "I'm trusting you." She said, sounding shaky. "I don't trust people, and I'm trusting you. I hope you understand how big this is for me, and for my family."

"I do," Anders said. And he did. He felt a bead of sweat drip along his spine, realizing suddenly how humid the day was becoming. "I won't steer you wrong. I promise," he said, wiping his forehead.

"Alright," Jane said. There was a pause as they considered the conversation.

"Great," Anders said. Jane started to say her goodbyes when he called her back. "Oh, I was actually phoning to ask you something else too. Would you be willing to come over this evening to meet my parents and possibly cook them dinner? I wanted to show off my new restaurant chef to my father, help him see the value of his investment."

"I'd have to bring Ellie along," Jane said sounding concerned. "Mom has her date with Ed tonight. Uh—" she paused. "Is your place accessible?" Anders looked around. There were two steps up to the porch, but other than that the house was all on one level.

"Yes, absolutely," he said, smiling into the phone. "I bet my parents will find Ellie just as charming as I find her." Jane laughed a bit and he could hear her relax.

"Okay, what time would you like us there? And what would your parents like to eat?" she asked.

"How about dinner at six- thirty?" He felt his stomach flip again. "I'll put a key under the mat, and you can let yourself in whenever you like. And make whatever you want. You're a fabulous cook. Whatever you make will be perfect."

"I'm glad you have such confidence in me," she said, sounding somewhat unsure.

"I have a good feeling about you, Jane," Ander said, softening his voice. "I promise you, everything is going to work out," he said this to her but was not so sure himself.

"I hope you're right," she said quietly. "I'm putting all my eggs in this basket you're weaving."

"I know," Anders said. They both paused again, lost in the seriousness of the moment.

"Okay, I better start thinking about tonight," Jane said as the silence stretched out a fraction too long. "See you later."

"See you later," Anders replied, feeling the world spin a little faster. "I'll send you the address in an email. Bye." He heard her disconnect. His heart beat a bit faster. He hoped he was making the right decision. Really, he was basing all of this on a single meal that Jane had cooked. What if that's the only thing she knows how to make? Of course, that was silly. She was running a café. She must know how to make other dishes. He hoped. That worry swirled around his mind for a bit, only to be replaced by a new worry.

What if his parents, his father, didn't like Jane? Would he forbid the project? What would Anders do then? Anders had never met a child with a disability before meeting Ellie. What if his father hadn't either? What if he thinks she's some sort of terrible monster? No. That's crazy. Or was it? Who knew? Anders certainly didn't feel that way about Ellie. She was lovely. Surely, she would charm her way into his father's heart, just like she did to his own.

Maybe all of this was just a terrible idea from the start?

20

As Jane disconnected their call, she felt her stomach churn. It wasn't her head that was causing this reaction any longer since the lump had gone down overnight, leaving only a greenish yellow bruise in the centre of her forehead. It was sore to the touch, but not sore in general anymore. Maybe it was the thought of getting a $100,000 cheque in the mail one of these days that had her feeling unnerved. She'd never had that much money all at once, and to think that she was just going to give the majority away to Anders, a man she'd only met a week ago, in the blind faith that he would improve her life, or at the very least, change it forever. She wasn't sure what to think of herself, or this entire situation. It felt as if she were on a rollercoaster with no end in sight.

She had to admit that she was happy to not be at the café right now. She was tired — so, so tired of working so hard and not getting any farther ahead. And now she would have the money to look after Ellie, which was the biggest relief of all. The thought of Ellie crammed into that wheelchair was breaking her heart. Even though they got a subsidy to purchase a new chair, she still hadn't had the money to make up the difference. Now she did. She had the opportunity to breathe for a minute, something she hadn't been able to do for eleven years.

When Tom died, she steeled herself against life and all the bad things it had to offer. A daughter with special needs, while a blessing filled with love, was also a difficult burden at times. They had made the best of the challenging situation, and Ellie was growing into a strong, fierce young woman. Jane couldn't feel prouder of her daughter, herself, and her mother, as well as everyone else who had touched their lives over the years. But it was hard, to be climbing and climbing a never-ending hill. Now was a chance for a new start, and Jane was afraid to admit to herself that she was excited at the path that lay ahead.

Just then, Fae came out of her bedroom wearing a lovely blouse and skirt combo. The blouse was a light green with darker green leaves patterned all round. The skirt matched the darker green colour. The outfit made her eyes pop.

"What about this one?" she asked, doing a slight twirl.

"That one's nice, Mom," Jane said, stifling a giggle. "It makes your eyes look lovely."

"That's what you said about the last one." Fae sounded annoyed.

"I can't help it if you're an attractive lady, Mom," Jane said, laughing.

"Well, you're no help," Fae pouted in an elegant way. "Do you realise how long it's been since I was on a date? Forty years. That's how long." She flapped her arms around and went back to her bedroom. Jane flopped herself down on the couch and yelled back toward her mother's room.

"Ed already likes you, Mom. You don't need to be so worried about how you look." Jane put her feet up on the coffee table. The day was getting warm and they had a fan oscillating. The breeze felt nice on her bare toes. Moments later, Fae reappeared.

"What about this?" She twirled again, making the skirt of a tight red dress flare out a bit around her knees. The dress was form fitting, showing off Fae's small frame. It had a sweet heart neckline and small flutter cap sleeves. It made Jane's mother look at least ten years younger.

"Wow," Jane said. From the corner where Ellie had been reading a book while listening to her favourite music, she pulled off her earphones and joined in.

"Yeah, wow, Grandma!" Ellie grinned.

"Really?" Fae said, spinning a bit more.

"Yes, really," Jane and Ellie said almost in unison. "Where'd you get that dress?" Jane asked.

"I ordered it online," Fae said, sitting in the overstuffed armchair next to Jane. She closed her eyes in pleasure when the fan came her way. "I thought it was time I got something nice for myself."

"I'm glad you did," Jane replied. "Does Ed take heart

medication? Because if he does, you better give him some head's up about how smoking hot you look." Jane laughed as Fae swatted her arm toward her daughter. "Seriously, Mom, that dress is great. Perfect for celebrating your date with Ed, and your retirement."

"My retirement," Fae repeated, somewhat disbelieving. "Are you sure you're okay with my retiring?"

"Of course, Mom," Jane said without hesitating. "It's time for a change for everyone around here. You've been such a big help to me and Ellie—"
Fae interrupted her.

"I always will be," she said, getting teary eyed.

"Of course, and we always want you to be, don't we, Ellie?" Jane asked her daughter.

"Yeah, Grandma, we do. You're always so helpful. But I'm getting bigger now. I can do more things." Ellie grinned again. "Like I can help with cooking more now that Alec gave me that amazing stand-up frame." Ellie stood up and came across the room with her walker, flopping down on top of her grandmother in a big bear hug. "Don't worry, Grandma, I washed my hands and face after breakfast, I won't get crumbs on your dress."

Fae hugged her granddaughter tightly. Jane leapt up and joined in, squishing Ellie and Fae in a bigger bear hug.
Speaking into Ellie's wavy hair Jane said,

"Guess what, kiddo? I have to help Anders with cooking for his parents tonight. I need to impress them since Anders wants me to be the chef at the new hotel restaurant, I was hoping you might help me make dinner, Ellie, over at the house Anders rented."

The women squealed in happiness. "The restaurant chef at the new hotel!" Ellie was so happy for her mother.

"That's great honey, what a wonderful fit for you," Fae said, her voice sounding muffled. "Okay, enough, I can't breathe under here." The ladies all laughed. Jane got up and helped Ellie right herself.

"Sure, Mom, I'll help you. We should make shepherd's pot pie," Ellie suggested, with final certainty.

"What is shepherd's pot pie?" Jane asked, sounding doubtful.

"It's shepherd's pie, but with crust instead of potatoes," Ellie said, sounding somewhat breathless with excitement. "And the best part is I can help you cut the mushrooms if we bring my cooking frame."

Jane had to admit that the dish sounded good, and just fancy enough to impress Anders father who sounded like a snob from what she could gather. Maybe if she fancied it up with pearl onions and a rich red wine mushroom sauce, and chunks of steak instead of ground meat it would be just the thing, despite the hot weather. She'd serve it with a light fennel salad to freshen up the plate.

"That sounds like a great idea, sweetie," she said to Ellie.

"We should get matching aprons, so we look like professionals," Ellie suggested.

"Another great idea," Jane agreed. "Alright, let's get going, we need to go to the grocery store. Did you brush your teeth?" Ellie rolled her eyes.

"Yes, Mom, of course. I'm going to be twelve soon, I don't need you to remind me." Ellie sounded like a teenager again.

"Of course," Jane said, hiding her delight at her daughter growing up. "Let's go then."

"I'll get the grocery bags." Ellie went into the kitchen and came back with a bunch of reusable cloth bags hooked to her walker. She transferred herself and the bags to her wheelchair.

"Oh yeah," Jane said, winking to her mother behind her daughter's back. "I forgot to tell you, we are going to get you a new wheelchair next week."

"Really!" Ellie turned around to face her mom. "Can I get a red one, with stars?"

"A red one with stars?" Jane said laughing.

"Yeah, I want a red one, so I can look fabulous like Grandma does in her dress, and I really like stars." Ellie's eyes lit up.

"Well, your grandma does look marvelous," Fae said, striking a pose.

"We'll see if they can get you a red one with stars," Jane said, rolling her eyes at the ladies she loved more than anyone in the world. Then she laughed, grabbed her purse and headed out the door with her daughter toward their uncertain future.

21

In the early afternoon, Anders stood in the sun outside the café, sweating from the heat. Or at least he thought it was the heat. His white dress shirt and blue tie were beginning to wilt, and there were creases in his slacks that he hadn't noticed in the morning. Alec, on the other hand, sat with his back against the trunk of a big maple tree with his eyes closed. Valentina looked lovely as usual. Anders couldn't understand how they weren't stressed. Blair Brookstone was due any moment.

Anders paced back and forth, practicing his speech under his breath. He wanted to make his pitch well. He'd never pitched anything to his father before. Normally, his job was to appraise, then recommend a course of action. That course of action was almost always the course of action Anders knew Blair would want, and by almost always, he knew it was, in fact, always what Anders did. His father liked to describe him as "reliable" and "predictable" and "dependable." He'd never once heard his father describe Alec in such boring terms. Instead, Alec was described as, "flighty," "irresponsible" and "a fair-weather son." That is until recently, when Alec returned with a beautiful wife and took his rightful place with the Brookstone family. Still, those descriptions had never bothered Alec in the first place. He didn't care what his parents thought of him. Anders, on the other hand, cared entirely too much.

A black stretch limo came up over the crest of the hill and stopped across the street from the café. Alec stood, brushing the dirt from his shorts. Valentina subtly fixed her hair, and Anders wiped his brow. It was show time.

"Hello, son," Blair said, slapping Alec on the back while he shook his hand. Anders received the same treatment. Valentina got a strangled looking hug.

"Hello, dear," his mother gave him a hug and then turned to hug his brother and Valentina.

Behind them followed Meredith.

"Meredith?" Anders said in surprise, his mouth hanging slightly open. "What are you doing here?"

"I asked your parents if I could come along, since I hadn't seen you in so long, and it seems that Millvale has stolen your heart." She laughed, but looked hurt.

"Well." Anders was somewhat flummoxed, startled by the way she managed to look so chilled in the heat. "I'm happy to see you." He hugged her and gave her a kiss on the cheek. There was an awkward pause as they all stood around. Then Blair broke the tension.

"Alright, down to business," he said, looking slick and put together while he buttoned the top button of his steel gray blazer.

They donned hard hats and toured the café, checking out the water damage, the cracked foundation, and the roof that needed replacing. Among the bad items, Anders made sure to point out the old style of architecture, and all the lovely natural features the property offered as they walked down to the creek to look at the mill. All the while, he answered questions and pitched his idea. Alec was silent, unless there was a construction question to answer. Valentina made a point of highlighting any beautiful features by agreeing or saying "hmm." Anders appreciated their support.

After they had finished, Anders joined his parents and Meredith in the limo, while Alec and Valentina followed behind in the truck as they toured the countryside, checking out the golf courses, skiing areas and neighbouring towns. Anders gave the hard sell that this location would make an excellent setting for an inn. They pulled into the driveway at Anders' rented house around six.

"Oh my, what's that delicious smell?" his mother asked.

"That's whatever our hotel restaurant chef Jane is cooking us for dinner," Anders said, as they walked up the planks Alec had laid down for Ellie over the steps.

"What are these planks doing here?" Blair asked, sounding annoyed. "This is where we are staying tonight?" he asked, sounding even more annoyed.

"Yes, as you have seen, there are no places to stay in the area, so I rented this house for the time we are here," Anders replied. "Yet another reason why I think investing in the hotel would be a wise decision for Brookstone Holdings." He herded everyone into the house, where he found Jane and Ellie cooking in the kitchen, wearing matching bright pink aprons. He assumed Ellie had picked them out. Jane looked calm, and the lump on her head had gone down to just an ugly looking green bruise, that strangely, brought out her freckles. He winked at her across the living room. Meredith saw the way Jane winked back and exhaled, but no one heard her.

"Welcome, Mr. and Mrs. Brookstone," Jane said wiping her hands on a towel before extending the right to greet this important couple. "Jane Michaels, former owner of Cutie Pies Café, and hopefully, the future chef of the restaurant in the hotel." She smiled, trying to look confident.

"Lovely to meet you, dear," said Mrs. Brookstone. "What is that lovely smell! We could smell it all the way out at the car." She looked around, hoping to find the source.

"It's shepherd's pot pie," Ellie yelled from the kitchen. Then she came out in her wheelchair to say hello. Blair sucked in his breath at the surprise of seeing the girl who was just standing at the counter in a wheelchair.

"This is Jane's daughter Ellie," Anders said.

"Hi!" Ellie said, in an excited way that made everyone relax.

"Hello, dear," Mrs. Brookstone said.

"Ellie is my helper tonight. It was her idea to make this dish for you," Jane said, sounding proud.

Anders added,

"Ellie is great with inventing food combinations, especially cookies, right Ellie?" Anders encouraged the girl to join in the conversation.

"Yup, I have binders and binders filled with recipe ideas at home," she said, with a bright grin on her face.

"And her cookies are delicious," Anders said, nodding with authority. At this moment, Meredith spoke, introducing herself.

"Hello, I'm Meredith Quill, I'm Anders' girlfriend," she said, sticking out her hand to Jane, and then Ellie.

"Oh my, yes," Anders said, looking flushed, "I'm sorry. Meredith, Jane and Ellie." Jane looked somewhat surprised but shook the woman's chilly hand. How could her hand be so cold when it was so hot outside?

"Very nice to meet you," she said, while not meeting the woman's eyes. Trying to move past the unexpected awkwardness she encouraged everyone to take a seat in the living room. "Can I get anyone a drink? I have the makings for Old Fashioneds, martinis with vodka or gin, and red or white wine from the local vineyard."

Anders gave her a thumbs up for last choice. She was on the team and he didn't even have to tell her how to play. "We also have sparkling water, or coffee and tea if you prefer."

"I'd like a red wine, please," said Mrs. Brookstone.

"Old Fashioned for me," said Blair.

"Dry gin martini, three olives," said Meredith.

"Dry, yes, of course," Jane said, completely unsurprised by this choice.

"Two more Old Fashioneds please," said Alec and Anders. Valentina went for red wine as well. She came over to help with the drinks and gave Jane a squeeze around the shoulders to let her know she was doing well.

Once everyone had drinks, Ellie brought around a platter of appetizers. She served crisp leaves of endive with an olive tapenade, and shrimp wrapped in bacon with a sweet fig dipping sauce. Everyone was happy with the selections.

The men hovered over the plans Alec had prepared with Anders' input, discussing the details of the ballroom, courtyard, and restaurant. The women were in the living room talking about where Valentina lived in Italy. Jane and Ellie were busy in the kitchen.

There would be fifty rooms at the hotel, all beautifully decorated to match the architecture of the original building. Anders didn't want to see the history of the place erased and he stressed this point to his father. They would offer tours to the local wineries, and shuttle busses to the golf courses. It would be a popular vacation and wedding spot and would possibly bring further development opportunities to the area. Blair liked this idea.

"Okay," said Ellie, from the kitchen. "It's time to eat this yummy food, clear the table." Blair laughed at the excited girl's spirit and helped clear the table of plans. Blair almost never helped with anything. Anders had a good feeling for how the evening was progressing. If only Meredith hadn't shown up unexpectedly. He carefully took a look at her. She seemed, fine. Maybe annoyed? It was sometimes hard to tell. Her lips were pursed. He wasn't certain that he'd seen that look on her face before. He really didn't like it.

22

They sat at the large oak dining table eating mostly in silence. Jane wasn't sure if that was a good thing, but she assumed it was going well when she looked up to see Anders watching her. He gave her a wink. Her heart flipped. She instinctively looked to Meredith to see if she had seen the secret conversation between them. Her head was down, her black bobbed hair swinging along her jaw a little as the small woman scooped another mouthful of food onto her fork.

Jane had to admit the shepherd's pot pie was delicious. The rich beef gravy enrobed the caramelized pearl onions and dark roasted mushrooms. The beef was tender, and the peas she added at the last minute were a bright addition to each mouthful. Ellie had cut the circles of puff pastry with the circle cutter Jane had picked up when they were shopping. It was amazing to have Ellie cooking alongside her at the counter. Her daughter was resourceful, using her less capable hand to steady bowls on the counter as she stirred together the salad dressing. Yes, she needed help with more complicated tasks, but overall, she had done well for herself. Perhaps Jane had overestimated the inabilities of her daughter. She shook her head to herself. No. No, she had been protecting Ellie, was still protecting her. She was a good mother.

She didn't feel so sure of herself.

"This salad is so fresh," Mrs. Brookstone commented, breaking Jane out of her self-doubt.

"Thank you,' Jane said, smiling toward the impeccably dressed woman who wore tailored linen slacks, a cream blouse and colourful silk neckerchief.

Jane was dressed in a pale purple blouse and a soft tan skirt that fell below the knee, with a pair of sensible black flats; she had thought she looked pretty good. When she met Mrs. Brookstone, she immediately felt shabby and like a country simpleton.

"What is in the salad?" Valentina asked, smiling warmly at Jane. Ellie piped up.

"The dressing is honey, white wine vinegar, and olive oil, with some fresh thyme." She sounded proud. "I mixed it."

"Great job." Valentina nodded with approval.

"The salad is green apple, fennel, with dried cranberries," Jane finished reciting the recipe.

"It is just delicious with the pie," Anders said.

There was a chorus of agreement around the table. Even Meredith agreed. Jane was surprised, though she wasn't sure why. Meredith seemed pleasant enough. The group finished their main course. Jane poured more wine and water after clearing the dishes away. She brought out two small cheese platters to the table, one for each end. She had thought that a cheese course in the middle of the meal might be somewhat unorthodox, but she was out to impress. If the Brookstone's were accustomed to fine dining, they would not be strangers to a cheese course at the end of the meal, however, there was still a surprise desert to come.

    Jane busied herself in the kitchen preparing the special cookie recipe she and Ellie had chosen from one of her binders: strawberry shortbread. Soon enough the kitchen was filled with the sweet aroma of summertime berries cooking into a delicious sauce. Ellie stayed in the dining area with the group. One thing about her daughter's physical challenge that was both a positive and negative was that Ellie often became invisible to the people around her. Jane and Ellie realized this would probably happen when Blair Brookstone had attempted to engage Ellie, speaking slowly and way too loudly. This was evidence that he had probably not met many physically-challenged people in his life, or if he had, he hadn't bothered to see them as individual people who have abilities that manifest in different ways.

Jane and Ellie decided to use this to their advantage to find out more about what the land development tycoon thought of Anders' plan, and her cooking. Now, Blair held the attention of the table, discussing the costs of the rebuild, but Jane couldn't really hear what was being said, except for the occasional numbers being thrown about.

Jane whipped the cream by hand to try and limit the noise emanating from the kitchen. She brewed strong coffee and readied a tray with mugs, sugar, and cream. She placed a cookie on each plate, topped it with the warm strawberry sauce, then placed a neat quenelle of strawberry ice cream she had made earlier in the day atop that. Then a cloud of softly whipped Chantilly cream, and another cookie on top. She pulled out every trick she'd learned watching cooking shows, completing the plate with a flourish of icing sugar dusted over a strawberry shaped stencil.

Ferrying the plates to the table, they were met with soft gasps, followed by oohs and awes. She poured the coffee and passed around the cream and sugar. Everyone ate in silence, savouring the sweet plate filled with the best summer had to offer. Anders nodded at her across the table, ending the exchange with a wink. She felt a blush creep up her neck and light a flame in her cheeks. Wishing her hair was down around her neck became her new pastime.

When the meal ended, Jane received many compliments, the nicest of which came from Mrs. Brookstone who said she'd never had such a unique dessert. Jane gave Ellie a hug to show her appreciation in sharing such great culinary ideas. Valentina helped clean up, with Meredith offering to carry all the dishes to the sink. That was nice of her, Jane thought. She tried to force her mouth into a pleasant shape while she faced the small woman, but it didn't come out right, settling into something that looked like gas might be rumbling in her stomach.

After the kitchen was tidied, Jane caught a glimpse of Ellie who had fallen asleep in a chair in the corner of the room. This had been a long day for her, with much more standing than she was used to. Her little girl must be so tired. Jane approached Anders who was chatting with Meredith in the living room.

"Excuse me," Jane interrupted their conversation. From what she overheard they were discussing Anders' apartment. She thought she caught Meredith shoot her the cut eye, but when she blinked and look back, she stood there with a pleasant look on her face. "Sorry to interrupt, I just wanted to say that I'd better head out for the night. Ellie is pretty tired." Jane gestured toward the chair. Anders nodded.

"She was a great assistant today," he said, smiling down at Jane. Jane felt the blush creeping again, so she turned her face away to look at her daughter.

"She is just enchanting," Meredith said, reaching out to shake Jane's hand. "Your food was lovely, thank you for a delicious meal." Jane tried to read something into this exchange but couldn't get a grasp on any ill intent. She cleared her throat.

"Thank you, I enjoyed cooking the meal for all of you." She bared her teeth forcing a broad and overly genuine grin at the woman, feeling a pang of something uncomfortable in her chest. She smoothed her now sweaty palms on her skirt and attempted to end the conversation by saying, "Well—"

"Right," Anders said, thankfully, taking the hint. "I'll help you with your things." They loaded the car with Ellie's kitchen frame, her walker, and her wheelchair, and Jane's case of knives and any other equipment she brought with her. They stopped to watch Alec and Valentina walking hand in hand under the starry sky as they strolled toward the corn field and the large oak tree nearby. Anders' gaze lingered on them as he wondered if he could ever convince Meredith to take a stroll in the dark out toward a corn field that was probably filled with mice and snakes. Though, he wasn't totally sure that she minded mice and snakes, but something told him, she did. They had always frequented dimly lit restaurants, or bars, or stayed in at his apartment if they were on a date. Meredith never seemed to be the type of girl who would enjoy a nighttime stroll in the country. Perhaps he could ask her? He turned and saw Jane's eyes focused on the newlywed couple. She had a wistful look on her face.

"Everything okay?" Anders asked. She turned her face, so it was in profile.

"Yes, I was just remembering…." She trailed off.

"Remembering what?" He couldn't help but pry. He also couldn't help noticing how beautiful she looked with half her face lit up by the porch lamp. He knew he shouldn't be enjoying her face this much, but he just couldn't help himself.

"I was remembering when Tom and I were first married." She sighed a little, smiling in a sad way. "We took a motorcycle trip across country, just us, a change of clothes, a couple bed rolls, and a tarp in case it rained. We camped out in fields along the roadside, at the edges of farms, or streams. Places that looked a lot like where those two are headed." Jane stopped speaking, lost in a memory that Anders could tell hurt her, but also made her happy.

He just stood watching her for a while until they both became aware of the silence. Her trance was broken by the sound of Anders breathing too near to her. She could feel heat coming off his skin. The blush started again, but this time she was bold, looking into his face, and feeling so lonely she felt her heart stop for a second.

He reached his hand out and took her hand, his eyes tracing the curve of her lips, the rise of her cheeks, the sweep of her brows and lashes. Jane knew she shouldn't let him see her, but she didn't try to stop it either.

"You were wonderful tonight," Anders said, desperate to look upon true contentment on her face, instead of the melancholy lingering there in the small creases on her forehead. "You and Ellie, you were both wonderful." At the mention of her daughter, Jane's face relaxed.

"Do you think your father liked the meal?" she asked, looking concerned.

"Absolutely," Anders said, eager to reassure her. "You did a wonderful job. The food was inspired. I'm sure he will see that having you at the helm of the restaurant in the inn would be a boon for his investment. That is, if I can convince him to invest." He saw that she looked concerned. "Don't worry about that though. It's my job to worry," he said, smiling. He pulled her in for a hug, and whispered congratulations in her ear.

She leaned in with more enthusiasm than he expected, molding herself into his body a little. She smelled like strawberries and he realized she had a small dollop of sauce on her neck. He resisted the urge to kiss her to get it off. He cleared his throat and the hug broke. He suddenly felt cold, even though the night was very warm.

"You have sauce, uh—" he paused awkwardly, pointing to her neck.

"Oh no," Jane said, laughing uncomfortably. "Well, that's embarrassing." She scrubbed at herself, making her freckles pop out of red rubbed skin. There was an awkward silence once more until Jane broke it by saying.

"Ellie." They both turned to gather her up. "Oh wait, how will I get her to the car? We packed her chair."

"Not to worry," Anders said, "I'll carry her out."

"Oh, alright." Jane was unsure. They took a few steps together toward the house. Just then they saw Meredith in the window, the light behind her making her small frame look all sharp angles. Anders paused. Jane kept walking; her head held high.

Inside, Anders made a beeline for Ellie, careful to pick her up gently enough not to wake her. He avoided Meredith's eyes as he carried the girl to the car. She was surprisingly light. Having not carried any other children, he wasn't sure why he was surprised. Jane brought up the rear, nodding goodnight to Meredith as she zipped up Ellie's backpack and slung it over her shoulder. The elder Brookstones were nowhere to be found, and she assumed that they had gone to bed.

At the car, Anders slid the girl into her seat and buckled her in as quietly as possible. She didn't even stir. Jane hopped quickly into the front, flinging the backpack onto the floor in the passenger side.

"Goodnight, Anders," she said, with a finality that made his heart sink.

"Goodnight, Jane," he said, swallowing hard. "I'll phone you on Monday and let you know what my father says about the plan. I still have one more day to convince him so try not to worry." She nodded, drilling holes into him with her dark eyes as he shut the sliding door of her van.

As she drove away, Anders saw her lips were drawn into a thin line. He would do almost anything to never see her face like that again. He hoped his father was ready to open his pocketbook and invest in this cockamamie project.

23

Anders placed his hand on the door knob, not wanting to walk inside. Breathing deeply, he stepped through the threshold, keeping his eyes on his shoes.

"Did Jane and Ellie get on their way alright?" Meredith's asked the other side of the room.

"Yes, yup," he responded, still not looking up. He walked quickly to the kitchen and put away a couple of odds and ends left out on the counter. "How did you like dinner?" he asked the back of his girlfriend's head.

"It was delicious." Meredith tilted her head as she spoke. "I can see why you want Jane."

"I don't want her," he blurted, taken aback by Meredith's forward attitude.

"Yes, you do." She stood and turned to face him. "As the chef at the new restaurant." She placed a hand on her hip, her hair swinging against her jaw.

"Oh. Yes, I think she would be a great asset to the project," he said, in earnest. He moved from behind the counter to sit on the chesterfield and gestured to her to join him. She sat down gently on the edge of the cushion next to him.

"I like Ellie. She's sweet." She gazed at him. He reached out and touched her back, she didn't move. That was a good sign.

"I like her, too, she's a good kid." He looked off in the distance, feeling a nervous flutter in his stomach. Now that they were going into this venture together, he felt responsible for Jane, Fae and Ellie, to make sure they were going to survive, and thrive in life. His eyes glassed over as he imagined what it was going to take to ensure theirs, and his survival.

"Hey." Meredith touched his knee, her hand feeling warmer than usual. "Where'd you just go?" Her eyes ran over the lines of his face in a worried way.

"I was just thinking about the risks we are all taking to make this new venture work." He was quiet for a moment. "About how much Jane has on her plate; how much she has gone through."

"Yes," Meredith said. "You are taken with her, I see." She stood and moved across the room, standing in front of the window where she had watched her boyfriend embrace another woman in the driveway. "I think I shouldn't have come here today." She turned to look at him. He stood, wanting to move to her, to make her doubts go away.

"No, I'm glad you're here," he said, earnestly.

"Really?" She turned her back to him again. "I saw you, and Jane, outside before she left."

"You did?" Anders lied, pretending to have not noticed her figure in the window moments earlier, the heat of Jane's body still on his clothes.

"Yes, you know I did." Meredith turned again, dropping her hands to her sides. "Look, just tell me, what are we doing here? I don't want to play games with you." She furrowed her brow, her light eyes looking watery.

"I'm not playing games." Anders felt panic rising in his chest. Maybe he was playing games? He wasn't sure. He didn't know the rules. "I'm happy you're here."

"It doesn't feel like you are." Meredith sighed and sat heavily in an overstuffed chair covered in red and green checked plaid. "It feels like I intruded on something, but to be honest, I don't know what that is, or, at least I don't want to know."

"You didn't intrude." He walked across the room to her, knelt in front of the chair, his hands on her knees. He felt her flinch, but he didn't take them away.

"But you and—" she whispered, gesturing to the last place where Jane had been— "and her. There is something between you. I can see it."

"All that is between us is friendship, and maybe not even that." Anders spoke quickly, wanting to save this situation before Meredith felt any more hurt by what she had seen. "What you saw was a hug between two people who are taking a risk. We are business partners who have been thrown together by circumstances that no one was expecting. We're just trying to make a go of something new. We were celebrating. There is nothing more between us. I swear. Please believe me." He looked away, not sure if he was believing himself. "I'm so happy you're here. In fact." He took a deep breath. "There is something I've been wanting to ask you."

She tilted her head again and he watched her blue-black hair slide along her pale skin. She was beautiful, in a haunting way, and he wanted to be haunted by her forever, he was almost certain. What he didn't want was to see the tears building up in her eyes, ever again. He didn't want to hurt her. He loved her. She was important to him and it was time that she knew that and threw away her doubts. He just hoped that he would be able to do the same once he said what was on the tip of his tongue.

"Meredith, will you marry me?" He shifted his weight to one knee and held her small hand in his.

"What?" She looked at him in surprise, her eyes wide, her mouth held open a little.

"I've been thinking about it, and I want us to be married, Meredith. I know that we would be a great couple." He felt himself have the urge to ramble, to cover up his doubts, but he restrained himself. Meredith was quiet for what felt like forever to him.

"Yes, alright, I'll marry you," she said, and smirked carefully as she watched his face.

"You will?" He was excited, but something inside him deflated.

"I will." She laughed at his disbelief. They stood, embraced, and kissed quickly.

"Wow," he said while he held her to him. His arms longed for the softness of Jane's body. He ignored their desires. "Oh, wait." He stopped, pulled her away from him. "I don't have a ring to give you," he said.

"That's alright, you will," Meredith said. "The important thing is that you asked, and now we can think about our future together. I'm so happy." Despite not having seen her emote very often, right at this moment Anders stood in awe as a flush of colour came over Meredith's face, and her eyes darkened slightly to a storm cloud blue colour, and they twinkled in a way he could never imagined. He supposed she did love him after all, even though she was not the affectionate type in most situations. He felt himself relax a little. He hadn't wanted to make her sad by what she'd witnessed when he and Jane embraced, but he wasn't sure he had wanted to propose either. Though, he had been thinking about it, so he guessed it was all going to work out. He was engaged. He couldn't believe it.

How was he going to tell Jane about this the next time he saw her?

24

Jane parked the van in the driveway outside her house. No lights were on except the small lamp in the living room window. Her mother was still out on her date with Ed. Good. They must be having a great time, she thought to herself. She woke Ellie and they headed into the house. Ellie was still tired and put herself in bed and promptly went back to sleep. Jane stroked the girl's hair. Her daughter was so amazing tonight. Such a hardworking, enthusiastic, loving girl. She was so lucky to have such a wonderful piece of her heart right there in front of her.

Now that she was home, Jane felt the exhaustion in her muscles pulling her down. Deciding to have a shower seemed like a good idea. She stripped out of her fancy work clothes and stepped into the steam. Washing the smell of cookies out of her hair felt good. She was optimistic about the future, however uncertain it might be.

The Brookstones had liked her food. Really liked it, she thought. *I totally know what I'm doing*, Jane said to herself, doing a careful little dance under the hot water. The pie had been an inspired idea on Ellie's part, and the cookies were the perfect finish. Even Meredith, "*Meredith*," Jane said aloud to herself. Well, she seemed nice.

Jane didn't realize Anders had a girlfriend. But, of course he would, because why wouldn't he. He was handsome, kind, successful, smart, the whole package. *Stop it!* Jane turned the hot water down to a cooler temperature to distract herself from any warm thoughts that were developing. Things were going well, despite life throwing unexpected changes her way, yet again. Jane felt proud of herself at the way she was handling things.

That was very unlike her she realized. Her life since Tom died had been about survival — chiefly the survival of her daughter, who suffered many health problems early on, but was thankfully, a healthy and strong individual despite her physical challenges. Then it had been about making the café survive, to pay for their house, to pay for the car, to buy groceries, necessities, and sometimes splurges. The wheelchairs, walkers, and physiotherapy once a month to keep Ellie on track. It was a lot. And now, some of the worries had been eliminated, by the creation of a disaster.

The café building being sold to Brookstone Holdings had been her worst nightmare, before the flood and hitting her head, of course. Now, here she was, making friends with the Brookstones and finding herself liking them. They were not what she expected, except for Blair Brookstone, who was exactly what she expected. Anders, especially, was not what she expected.

She let herself drift into a daydream of remembering Anders today. Flashes of memories, his face, him winking and smiling at her, holding his hand, hugging him. His body so warm and comforting. She hadn't felt warm like that in so long. Alright fine, she thought while forcefully turning off the faucet. She had feelings for Anders. Not that it mattered. Not that she would do anything about it. They were work partners, soon to be business partners. And that was all.

A sharp flash of Meredith's face appeared in her mind. To rid herself of the image, she violently brushed her hair, spraying droplets of water onto the mirror with each stroke. Dressed in one of Tom's T-shirts and soft jersey shorts, Jane padded into the kitchen, where she found her mother drinking a glass of red wine while sitting at the table. She had a dreamy look on her face. Jane poured herself a glass of wine and sat across from a woman who looked years younger than the last time she'd seen her.

"So, how was your date?" she asked in a cheeky tone, not even trying to hide a grin. So obvious was the good time Fae and Ed had had that it was electric in the air.

"Oh, it was lovely," Fae replied, a wistful distance in her eyes.

"What'd you do?" Jane leaned in, taking a long drink from the wine.

"We went to that Italian restaurant in Bellfield. We ate a three-course meal, it was delicious," Fae continued. "I had the pasta carbonara, antipasto and tiramisu. It wasn't as good as yours, but it was still delicious." She reached over and patted Jane's hand.

"Thanks, Mom," Jane said. She appreciated the compliment but was more eager to hear about the rest of the date. "What'd you do after dinner?"

"We took a walk along the river. Did you know they've hung twinkle lights up in the trees along the path?" Jane did not know this, but it sounded lovely. Fae continued, "There was a busker playing an accordion near the bridge, and a little coffee cart with a couple of tables set up nearby. We danced to the music and enjoyed a second dessert and cappuccinos. We looked at the stars, talked, laughed. It felt good to laugh with someone special again." Fae looked a bit bemused.

"That's great, Mom," Jane said. It was great for her mom, and a little for herself since she was beginning to remember what having a crush felt like as well. "So, the most important question." Jane grinned. "Did he kiss you goodnight?"

"Jane!" Fae was incredulous, considering her glass very closely. "He did." The women laughed.

Jane rose from her chair to hug her mother. "Wonderful. Are you going to see him again?"

"We have another date on Tuesday," Fae said, taking a sip of her wine.
Jane clapped her hands. "Wonderful!" Since she was up, Jane made her way to the fridge where she pulled out some cheese, deciding to microwave the last of her croissants that had been saved from the café. They were a bit stale but would be tasty with melted cheddar and butter on top. With her snack made, she returned to the table. Fae stood up and grabbed some raspberry preserves from the fridge to put on the croissant.

"Good idea," Jane said, applying a dollop to the pool of melted white cheddar and popping a bite in her mouth. Fae took a bite as well.

"I don't know why I'm eating this," Fae said, not really caring why she was eating the snack because she was happy and having fun.

"I'm starved," Jane said. "I could barely eat tonight. I was so anxious."

"How did it go?" her mother asked.

"It went well I think, at least Anders said he thought it went well." Jane tried to hide the sigh in her voice when she said his name. She was not successful. "Everyone really enjoyed the food at least, all emptied plates coming back to the kitchen, so that's a good sign. And Ellie was amazing. She worked so hard." That reminded Jane, in the morning she would have to ask Ellie for all the intel she gathered on Blair Brookstone and the conversation that went on about renovating the café.

"So, Anders thought it went well, did he?" Fae asked, her voice in that familiar "I'm going to pry now" tone.

"Yes," Jane said, downing the last of her drink, and pouring a smaller glass to replace it.

"Would you just admit that you like him?" Fae said, her head tilted to the side as she tried to find Jane's eyes that had been conveniently hidden behind her wet hair.

"Okay, fine, yes. I like him." Jane had raised her voice more than necessary. She blushed. "But it doesn't matter. We are going to be business partners. Nothing more. Besides, his girlfriend Meredith made the trip out from the city with his parents."

"He has a girlfriend?" Fae asked, disappointedly.

"Yes," Jane said, popping another sweet and savoury croissant bite into her mouth.

"What's she like?" Fae was unable to hide her intense interest in this girlfriend.

"Small, pretty, black hair." Jane listed off the woman's attributes. "She was perfectly nice. She looks like the total opposite of me, so clearly, I'm not Anders' type anyway. Yet another reason nothing will be happening between us. I'm happy alone. I've grown accustomed to it."

"Uh-huh," Fae said, not believing a word of it, but choosing to let things drop for the time being. She had seen the way Anders took to the family, to Ellie, and the way he looked at Jane. This woman Meredith had serious competition, even if Jane didn't know that she had entered one yet. "When will he tell you about his father's decision?"

"Monday," Jane said, finishing her second glass and the last bite of croissant, then standing to wash the glasses and the plate.

"Monday," Fae repeated, standing to hug her daughter. "I'm sure it will be good news."

"I hope so." She hugged her mother back.

She felt proud of how the night had gone. Except, well, the hug. Oh my, that hug. It had heat to it. And not just body heat, but, emotional heat, if that was even a thing. She wanted to kiss Anders too. But, then with Meredith watching, that was just a terrible idea.

Why did Jane have to come up with such a bad idea. Cooking an amazing meal, great idea. Getting involved with Anders to rebuild her business, also potentially a wonderful idea. But, kissing him, under an oak tree and a starry sky on a warm night. No. Bad idea.

Super, duper, bad, idea, Jane. Do you hear me?

25

Anders stood sweating on the fairway while his father took a shot.

"Nice one, Dad," Anders said, squinting into the distance to follow the ball as it landed on the green, not far from the pin.

"Thank you, son." Blair looked polished as ever, well dressed in his white golf shirt and tailored khaki slacks. "You were right. This is a fine course, a fine course indeed." Blair nodded to himself striding toward the cart.

Yesterday, they had visited the winery on the hill, and toured the ski hill/golf course that was situated nearby. Today, they were visiting the other golf course near to where the inn would be built, for a quick nine holes. Alec plonked himself down on the back of the cart next to the clubs they had rented. Anders sat next to his father who hit the gas pedal just as his bum landed in the seat. The ladies had gone into Bellfield to explore. He hoped they were all getting along.

He swallowed hard as he thought about proposing to Meredith. He supposed he should tell his father and brother that he was now *engaged*. Okay, so maybe he shouldn't have proposed to Meredith without a ring, or, a plan for that matter. He was thrown off with the connection he felt with Jane and then Meredith had been watching from the window. He didn't want her to feel that he didn't love her. He did. She was nice, smart, and calm. Those were good qualities to look for in a partner. And she fit the Brookstone mold. She was presentable, professional, and unremarkable. Unremarkable? No, that wasn't it. She was reliable, and the kind of woman everyone expected him to marry. He needed a woman like Meredith to take to events and to schmooze when he was trying to drum up business. She was inoffensive, detached. No one would complain about having to talk with her. He imagined Jane in a schmoozing scenario. She'd laugh loudly, be overly friendly, maybe even a hot head if she didn't agree with someone's opinion. And she would talk about Ellie, which was fine he supposed, but he didn't want to alienate any clients because of Ellie's special needs. Maybe that was the problem? Maybe he was a problem. Ellie was wonderful, and so was Jane. But he went and proposed to Meredith, and now here he was.

"I have some news." Sweat trickled down the back of his neck. Neither his brother nor father spoke. Alec was quiet because Alec was a quiet sort, but Blair was probably not listening.

"Hey, Dad," Anders said, trying again to get his father's attention.

"Yes, son," Blair responded, turning his face toward him and then away.

"I have some news," Anders repeated.

"Yes, so you said," Blair's profile looked like a block of stone had been carved to make his face. Anders took a deep breath.

"I proposed to Meredith the other night, and she said yes," he blurted out in a rush of air.

"What did Jane say?" Alec said from somewhere behind Anders' head.

"What does Jane have to do with anything?" Anders asked, annoyed.

"That's wonderful news," Blair said, slapping Anders on the back. "We'll have a drink to celebrate when we get back to your place. How lovely that you're marrying that nice girl." Blair parked the cart near his ball and jumped out to finish the hole. As they got out to take their turns, Anders couldn't help but notice Alec shaking his head at him.

"What?" he said, wanting to punch his little brother in the arm so he'd have a charley horse and not be able to get his ball in the cup.

"Nothing," Alec said, "I'm just surprised that you still want to marry Meredith."

"What's wrong with her?" Anders felt the urge to swing rise again.

"Nothing, there's nothing wrong with her," Alec said while jamming a hand into his pocket.

"Your turn, son," Blair said, turning to Anders. He stepped up to his ball, and in the moment of silence before he swung he heard Alec mumble, "But there's nothing right with her, either."

26

When they returned to the house, the women were sitting on the front porch, drinking iced tea. Meredith grinned at them as they walked toward the porch from the car. Anders felt himself relax a little. She had a nice smile.

"Blair, what have you got there?" Mrs. Brookstone called to her husband who carried two bottles of wine with him.

"We stopped at the winery on the way back, so we could celebrate," Blair responded. Anders was surprised by his father's enthusiasm surrounding his engagement.

"What are we celebrating?" Mrs. Brookstone called, laughter in her voice.

"Anders' and Meredith's engagement for one," Blair said.

Mrs. Brookstone leapt up.

"What?" she turned to Meredith who stood, joining hands with Anders.

"I'm sorry," Anders whispered to Meredith who bowed her head slightly, quickly releasing Anders' hand.

She whispered back, "You said we were going to wait and tell them together." Meredith spoke teasingly, but the laughter didn't make it to her eyes.

"I know," Anders said, wrapping an arm around her waist. Meredith twisted a little, so they absolutely weren't touching.

"You're getting married?" Mrs. Brookstone's voice reached a decibel just below a shriek. "That's wonderful!"

Anders watched Meredith's face and saw she was unhappy but was willing to hide it for the time being. They were swept up in hugs from all round.

"I'll get the glasses," Valentina said. When she returned, they poured two bottles of the best wine the vineyard could offer them. Blair cleared his throat.

"I'd like to make a toast," he said, pride beaming from his being, "To Meredith and Anders, following in the Brookstone tradition of marrying lovely women, and creating successful empires." Everyone drank, but Blair continued. "I'd also like to toast Anders new project. After touring the area, examining the building, and eating that delicious meal prepared by that single mother you had here the other day."

"Jane," Anders interjected, feeling anger rise in his chest.

"Jane, yes." Blair cleared his throat, "I would like Brookstone Holdings to take on the restoration and renovation of the inn." He held is glass in the air as everyone clinked.

"Really, Dad?" Anders was thrilled. He hugged Alec and Valentina, forgetting momentarily about Meredith. He wished Jane were there to hear this.

"Yes, son." Blair looked a little self-important, "I believe that this project has potential to expand Brookstone Holding's future. I will give you all the workers and equipment you need, and two million dollars toward the build."

"But we need three million at least to finish the project," Anders interrupted him, feeling his euphoria dwindle, "Not — not, that I'm not grateful. . . ." Anders trailed off, stammering.

"Yes, you do indeed," Blair said, taking a seat on the nearest rocking chair on the porch. "Son, since you will be getting married soon, and you will one day take over the leadership position of Brookstone Holdings, I feel this is a good time to throw you in the deep end to see if you can swim on your own. You will have to come up with the extra costs above two million yourself to complete this build. And, I expect you to handle all the other day-to-day tasks you would normally handle at the office. I really can't spare you being away much longer." Blair finished.

Anders looked to Alec who had turned away. Valentina had taken his arm in an obvious gesture of comfort. Alec deserved to have a piece of Brookstone Holdings too, Anders supposed, though his brother had been away for so long and Anders had taken up the slack, so perhaps he didn't.

"I accept the challenge," Anders said, shaking his father's hand. He had already been adding up how much money he would need if his father hadn't agreed to the project, including the insurance pay outs from the hairdresser, store, and Jane. He was well on his way, he felt confident.

"Alec," Blair said, calling his youngest son to attention, "You'll work with your brother, help him with the flooring."

Alec snorted, and nodded.

"Yep, sure, Dad." His normally placid expression turned overcast. "Flooring is what I'm all about."

"Excellent," Blair said, clapping his hands. "It's settled, that is, once you draw up the paperwork, Anders." Alec turned and went into the house. "Now, let's call the town car and head back to the city. We have work to do," Blair said, downing the last of his glass.

While they busied themselves packing up, Anders had a moment to speak with Meredith.

"I'm sorry I told them before we were all together," he apologized to his soon to be wife.

"That's alright," Meredith said, folding a blouse into her small rolling suitcase. "So, I guess you'll be up here a lot now?" she asked, sounding a little disappointed.

"Yes, I guess I will," he said, sounding not disappointed at all. He liked it here, liked this house. "I'll have to call the owner of the house to see if I can rent this place longer."

"Will you be coming back to the city?" Meredith asked, sounding worried. He put his arms around her, hugging her to him. For once she let him.

"Yes, of course," he said, reassuring her. "I have to head back to the office, and back to my apartment to pack. I'll split my time between here and there I guess." It only made sense to spend time here, considering the logistics that this build would require.

"I don't know if I'll be able to come up here much, depending on how things are going at the funeral home," Meredith said, "You know summer is a busy time of year, all those young people partying too much, getting in boating accidents, and what not…." She trailed off.

"Yes, I know," he said, trying not to picture it. They were silent for a moment or two. "We'll work it out," he said, breaking their hug, helping her pack. He thought it would be great if they would all get going, so he could go by Jane's place and tell her the good news, thank her for her excellent cooking that helped seal the deal. Meredith didn't seem to be aware of his hustling them out.

When the town car arrived, he helped pack the trunk and sent them off with hugs and hearty handshakes. Meredith got a short kiss, which was just the kind she normally enjoyed. Unbeknownst to Anders however, Meredith longed for just a little more. Plus, they never talked about when they would go shopping for her ring.

"I'll see you in a few days," he said to her as he shut the door to the car. She waved through the glass to him as she drove down the drive and onto the road. Anders turned around as soon as the vehicle was out of sight, to change out of his golf clothing, and shower, then head into town to visit Jane.

27

Tucking Ellie in at night was one of Jane's most favourite things in life. It happened less and less now that Ellie was starting in on the teenage years, but tonight her daughter invited her in to her room and now they were cuddled in bed chatting.

"That man Mr. Brookstone was kind of scary," Ellie said with the earnest honesty of childhood.

"Yes, he was a bit," Jane agreed, because it was true.

"Is he going to help us build a new café?" her daughter asked.

"Well, that's what Anders hopes," she said, stroking the girl's strawberry blonde hair that looked so like her mother's own colour, when Fae was young. "I hope so too. I hope he'll help us build a bigger restaurant, with a hotel attached."

"That sounds good," Ellie said, then yawned. She was quiet for a moment, then said, "I like Anders. He's not scary like Mr. Brookstone."

"I like Anders too." Jane sighed a little.

"Is Anders staying here so he can build the new restaurant?" Ellie asked.

"Yes, I think so, at least I think that's the plan." Jane hugged her daughter a bit closer.

"Oh good." Ellie looked up at her mother. "I hope I can make him some more of my cookie recipes."

"I hope so too," Jane said, really meaning it.

"At dinner the other day," Ellie started up, a bit breathless with excitement, "Anders and Mr. Brookstone were talking about how much it would cost for the new restaurant and hotel."

"How much did they say?" Jane's ears perked up significantly at the change in topic.

"Three million dollars," Ellie said, "That's like, a lot of dollars, right mom?"

"Yes, yes, it is," Jane agreed. She felt her heart beat in her chest, a lump rising in her throat. Three million dollars. That was more money than she could possibly imagine. What was this crazy idea Anders got her into?

"Do you think Alec and Valentina will stay too, if Anders is staying?" Ellie said, sounding hopeful.

"Yes, they probably will," Jane said.

"Good." Ellie wriggled down under the summer weight covers a little. "I like them, especially Valentina for showing me how to make yummy tomato sauce, and especially Alec for building the frame so I can stand at the kitchen counter."

"You like them both most especially?" Jane laughed a little when Ellie giggled.

"Yes, I do. And Anders," Ellie said, enthusiastically. "I've never had so many friends. It's nice."

"It is nice." Jane thought about it, about how she had always had lots of people to talk to at the café, but none of them were really her friends. She never had people over, never spent time around their kitchen table, laughing and eating good food. Things the past week had been different, and even though she feared the changes, she also kind of liked the way they made her feel.

Jane and Ellie stayed quiet for a bit. Jane wasn't sure if Ellie had drifted off to sleep, but she wanted to ask her daughter something that had been on her mind.

"Ellie, you still awake?" Jane said quietly next to her daughter's perfectly curved ear.

"Yep," Ellie said, not sounding fully asleep, but not fully awake either.

"Do you like that kitchen frame a lot?" Jane said, feeling bad inside.

"I really do, Mom, it's great," Ellie said, sounding enthusiastic despite her sleepy state.

"I'm sorry I never thought about making one for you," Jane said, guilt choking her up.

"It's okay, Mom, I never thought of it either," Ellie said, nonplused. "Besides, you were too busy at the café and stuff around here. It's okay, Mom. I have one now." She yawned. "I'm going to go to sleep now, okay?' Ellie scrunched down in bed. Jane kissed her head.

"Okay," she said, a lump of guilt burning a hole through her digestive tract. She climbed off the bed, closing the door behind her. She stood in the hallway feeling a little lost. Her mother had gone out again with Ed, because neither of them had been able to wait any longer for another date. Maybe she should make some brownies?

That sounded like the best plan she could come up with, so she went to the kitchen to begin. Wrapping a colourful apron around her waist, she got out a bowl for melting the butter and chocolate over a double boiler. Chopping up the chocolate block and cubing the butter, Jane placed the lot into a metal bowl that sat atop a lightly simmering pot of water. Meanwhile, she whisked together eggs, vanilla, and sugar, tempering the mixture with the chocolate and butter once it was melted, to prevent the eggs from scrambling. Just as she was about to add the remaining chocolate mix there was a knock at the door.

Padding over to answer it, she found Anders on the other side. He was beaming and sweating and looked like a little boy.

"Hi," she said. "I wasn't expecting you."

"No, you weren't." The sun was just finished setting and it lit up his black hair with a wild orange. "Can I come in?" he asked, stepping by her as she made room for him in the doorway. "Wow, it smells good in here." He paused a moment to inhale.

"I'm just making brownies," Jane replied, motioning for him to follow her to the kitchen.

"Wait," he said. She turned. She looked at him, questioningly. She looked just like the day he'd met her, determined, and beautiful. The fading light filtered in through the front window of the house and ignited her hair like autumn leaves. He swallowed hard and took a deep breath. "The project is a go," he said, exposing a mouth full of gleaming white teeth.

"What?" Jane couldn't believe what she was hearing.

"The inn, the restaurant, the renovation, it's a go." He laughed, waiting for her to take it in.

"Really!" She clapped her hands and whooped. Then clapped her hand over her mouth. "Ellie's sleeping."

They laughed.

"And there's more." He took a couple steps toward her, taking her arms in his hands. "I was thinking about it on the way over and I want you to use my house as a test kitchen, to develop the menu for the restaurant. I don't want you to worry about money. I'll pay you, and I'll pay for the ingredients. It's the least I can do for your help with this project." He watched her face, hoping to see something there, but he wasn't sure what it was exactly.

Jane looked at him, stunned, "I can't accept that," she said.

"Yes, you can," he argued.

"But I'm going to be an investor in the business, and it's already costing three million dollars. Where are you getting the money for that, never mind for allowing me to experiment in the kitchen." She broke away from him, starting to pace nervously.

"Where did you find out how much it is going to cost?" he asked, a bit stung that the information was so easily gained.

"Oh, from Ellie," she said, wiping her hands on her apron. "Everyone forgets she's in the room." She raised her eyebrows in a way that suggested he was one of those people.
He thought back to the dinner party, the last time he'd seen her, and Ellie. He'd known Ellie was there, but Jane was right. He paused a moment, then went on awkwardly,

"Right." He cleared his throat. "Look." He took hold of her again, stopping her pacing. "Don't worry about the money. You can invest your portion in the business, my father has agreed to invest two million, and I will worry about the rest. That's my job. You have enough to worry about without worrying about that. I want you to have creative freedom to build the menu however you want. You need more space than this kitchen can give you to do that."

Jane looked around her kitchen. He was right, her house was squidgy, and her appliances were old. She would need more room to try new dishes, write a menu. With the café under construction, his place was the perfect spot. But it wasn't really his place, it was just a rental.

"But that house you're in, it isn't yours," she said, sounding doubtful.

"It is, I've rented it for the foreseeable future," he said, brightly.

"Really?" Jane said, with too much enthusiasm. The idea that Anders might leave had been weighing on her, she realized just then. But he was staying, and he was helping her, which she had to admit was a huge change, for what appeared to be the better. He was helping her by letting her do what she wanted, which was amazing. She hugged him when a thrilling rush of adrenalin flew through her veins. As she pulled away, she went to kiss his cheek, but her lips landed on his mouth. It was warm, and soft, and they both lingered a little too long. She liked the feeling of his hands on her back, the smell of him mingling with the chocolate in the kitchen, and the way his strong body felt against hers. She leaned in a little, Tom suddenly becoming a distant memory. When they pulled away, they gazed at each other, stunned.

"The brownies," she blurted.

"I'm engaged," he said, simultaneously.

28

"You're engaged?" she demanded.

"Let's make those brownies," he said at the same time, taking a couple large strides toward the kitchen.

"You're engaged," Jane said again. This time, as a statement, not a question.

"I asked Meredith to marry me the other night, after you left." His back was still to her.

She watched his shoulders slump a little. To her surprise, Jane found she couldn't breathe. The wind whooshed from her lungs as she grabbed for the nearest chair.

"Why?" she asked. "Never mind, you love her, obviously." Jane landed on the arm of the easy chair. As she spoke, she slid over the arm, so her feet dangled in the air. They were both quiet for a bit. Anders, taking a seat at the kitchen table, watched her feet through the doorway. He couldn't see her face and he supposed that was better.

"Why did you kiss me?" she asked, the question coming out flat and hurt.

"Well." He paused considering. "Actually, you kissed me."

"What?" She sat up. "I did not, you kissed me." She stood up in anger to face him.

"Look, I don't want to argue," he said holding up his hands, palms out to her. "But you did kiss me. You hugged me, and then you kissed me."

She huffed and turned away.

"You didn't exactly protest," she said, venomous.

"No, I didn't," he said. He stood and walked to her.

"Stay over there." She pointed to the chesterfield. She felt her heart racing and breaking at the same time.

"Look, I'm sorry," he said, looking like a sad dog. "I do love Meredith. We have been together for a bit and it was time we became engaged."

"I see," Jane said, sitting down in the armchair again.

"You are beautiful, Jane." He searched for her eyes until she looked at him.

"Well, beauty isn't everything," Jane said, hurt that it was all just physical. "So, what do we do now?"

"Right." He thought quietly, feeling hurt that she was somehow rejecting him, even though he was the one who was engaged. "We'll keep it professional. We'll be friends."

"Professional," she tried the words on. "Friends."

"Yes," he said, trying to sound final. "Everything I said stands. I want you to create the new menu, and to use my kitchen. You can bring Ellie over whenever you want. You are both welcome."

She stood then walked across the room and stuck her hand out to shake on the deal they were making.

"Professional. Friends," she said, avoiding his eyes. They shook when he took her hand. The electricity was still there, but she shivered it from her spine as she walked to the door. "I'll be there tomorrow morning at ten," she said, opening it in a gesture that he should go.

"I actually have to head back to the city for a few days," he said as he stood. "I'll leave you a key under the mat. It's your key, you can keep it. Just come and go as you like." He felt himself trying to smooth things over. Jane felt her heart tumble to her feet when she heard he was leaving, even if only temporarily.

"Fine," she said, gesturing, again, for him to go.

"Good." He stopped, looking at her. She lowered her eyes. He left quietly. She shut the door behind him.

Jane walked to the easy chair, slumping down on the comfortable cushions. Then she remembered the brownies. Finding the bowl on the counter, she found her chocolate had hardened and the eggs had congealed in the bowl.

"Guess I'll start over," she said, dumping the lot in the trash.

29

"So, he's engaged," Iris said, just before she took a big gulp of tea from the steaming mug. Jane caught her friend and former employee up on the story of Anders Brookstone's love life. "But he kissed you anyway?"

"Yes," Jane said, grabbing a brownie off the platter sitting between them. This batch was pretty good, probably way better than the last batch she started.

"Man," Iris said, shaking her head. "But I thought you didn't like him."

"I didn't," Jane said. "But now, I do." She hated to admit that Anders was a nice guy, who had a brother who was a nice guy, and a sister-in-law who was a nice lady. Aside from his parents, who seemed a bit out-to-lunch, the Brookstones all seemed lovely, helpful, and genuine people. "Things changed."

"Evidently," Iris said, her eyebrows shooting up into her curls.

"Hey, I'm entitled to like someone," Jane said, chomping into the brownie with some force.

"Yes, absolutely," Iris said. "I encourage it. You deserve happiness, you deserve love." She reached her hand out and put it on top of Jane's

"I'm happy," Jane said, almost believing herself. "Or at least, I was so busy that I didn't really notice I wasn't happy. Then the Brookstones come along and do nice things for me and promise me my own fancy restaurant in a fancy hotel and kiss me." She huffed.

"And you realized that you weren't as happy as you thought you were," Iris finished, taking another brownie for herself.

"I wasn't unhappy," Jane said, considering. "I was lonely. I thought that maybe I might not be lonely any more. Since Tom died, I thought I'd just be alone, be a mom, you know." Iris nodded. "But then I started to see that Ellie was going to be okay, that I didn't need to be so worried all the time, maybe." Jane sighed.

"You can still feel that way," Iris said, standing to put her empty mug in the kitchen sink. "You just don't get to feel that way about Anders Brookstone."

"I guess," Jane said, finishing the last of her tea.

"What are you going to do about the café?" Iris asked out of interest for her friend's life, but also her own, since she was working at a restaurant out of town for the time being.

"I guess I'm just going to proceed as if I hadn't kissed Anders, and as if it wasn't a really great kiss," Jane said, seriously.

"A really great kiss." Iris shook her head. "I don't know if I could do it." Iris took another brownie, then went to put the kettle back on to boil. Clearly, they needed more tea.

"I can do it," Jane said to herself, and Iris, and the wallpaper. Really to anyone or anything that would listen. She needed to do it. "I have no choice. I have a little girl who needs me to be stable and secure, so she can grow."

"What's the plan?" Iris passed the platter to Jane, who hesitated, but took another brownie anyway.

"The plan is to invest in the new restaurant, and to go to Anders' place to practice the menu, and for me to keep at arms' length from him. It's just business. I'm going to be part owner and he is going to be part owner, and we are going to be equals, and friends." Jane nodded in agreement with herself. Iris looked doubtful, but Jane decided to ignore this, changing the topic. "How's your new job?"

"It's not too bad," she said. "Not as much fun as working in the café, but it pays the bills." Iris poured some hot water from the kettle into the pot over English breakfast tea bags. The smell wafted up a comforting scent. "I wish it was closer, but the drive is fine while the weather is nice. Plus, there's this cute waiter."

"Oh, a cute waiter?" Jane laughed in excitement for her friend. "Do tell!"

"Well, he's tall, with tanned skin, and dark brown hair. His name is José," Iris grinned.

Jane felt a pang of jealousy, imagining Anders' face and dark hair while she spoke. But this wasn't about her, it was about Iris. "He's from Guatemala, and he has the nicest accent." Iris crinkled up her nose in delight. Jane couldn't help but grin at her friend.

"Has he asked you out yet?" Jane poured the tea into their mugs after retrieving Iris' from the sink.

"Not yet," Iris said. "But maybe soon." Her nose crinkled again.

"Well, I hope he does," Jane said. "And if he doesn't, you ask him out. We are modern women, after all. We don't have to leave everything up to the men."

"No, we certainly don't," Iris said, and they clinked their mugs together in a toast to sisterhood and independence.

"So, do you think you'll have some free time to help me design the menu for the restaurant?" Jane asked her friend.

"Really?" Iris said, hopefully.

"Absolutely!" Jane was enthusiastic, "I'm not going to open a new restaurant without my right-hand woman beside me."

"Oh good," Iris was relieved. "I was afraid you'd let me rot at my new job."

"Let you rot?" Jane laughed. "Of course not. I thought you said you liked it there."

"I do." Iris drank from her cup. "I just miss working with you."

"I miss working with you too," Jane said, and stood up to give Iris a hug. Iris hugged her back and they swayed back and forth until they burst out laughing.

"Hey, listen." Iris pulled out of their hug. "How much are you investing in the new place?" Jane was somewhat surprised but decided to answer the question honestly.

"Eighty thousand, why?"

"I was thinking, I'd like to invest," Iris said, looking a little embarrassed. "It's time I stop working for everyone else. I want to be a part of the bigger picture."

Jane considered what her friend said.

"That's a great idea," Jane said. The thought of Iris getting involved made her feel somewhat less scared at the prospects of all the new things to come. "We can get into the unknown together." "Yes, we can." Iris laughed. "I have ten thousand saved up. Do you think that would be enough to get my feet wet and be part of things?" she asked, sounding unsure.

"I think so," Jane said. "But you should talk to Anders. I'll give you his email address."

Just then, Fae came in the front door, practically floating.

"Hi, Mom," Jane said. "Did you have a good night?"

"Yes," Fae said, rushing past them.

"Wait," Iris called after her. "What was that I saw on your neck?"

"Nothing," Fae said, closing her bedroom door behind her.

"It was definitely a hickey," Iris said, shooting a look at Jane.

"A hickey, Mom," Jane yelled after her mother. "Don't think we aren't going to discuss this in the morning."

"It's not a hickey," Fae yelled from behind the door. "I got bitten by a mosquito."

"So, Ed's a mosquito now, is he?" Iris said, and the women practically fell from their chairs with laughter.

They passed the rest of the night speculating on Fae's "mosquito bite," chatting, gossiping, and generally catching up. Jane hadn't realized she needed this. Needed the time and friendship of another woman. With everything that had been going on lately, she hadn't realized how much she missed talking to Iris every day at work. They agreed that they would come up with menu ideas and meet on Wednesday morning, Iris' day off, at Anders' place. The new restaurant would be family friendly, but upscale. It would serve breakfast, lunch, and dinner, and have an amazing dessert menu. It might even offer snacks too.

After Iris left, Jane got herself ready for bed. Tomorrow she'd drop Ellie off at Sally's place. They were going to make a video with the camera Ellie had borrowed from Iris. Jane would go to Anders' house, and pretend she didn't care. It was just business, research for business. She would consider his house her test kitchen. Nothing more.

As she tucked herself under the covers and closed her eyes, she could still feel his lips pressed to hers.
Yep, just friends. No problem.

30

Back in his office in the city, Anders tugged at his tie. In just a few days, he had become accustomed to loose-fitting collars. Another thing about being in the office that he found off putting was the strength of the air conditioning that was currently blowing down on his shoulders. He missed the fresh, naturally temperate, air in Millvale.

On his desk was a stack of property acquisitions. They were mostly in the city, but some were, of course, way out of the way. His father was not one to stick to the downtown area. If a property looked like a good opportunity, he would snap it up, seemingly no matter how far it was located from their city headquarters. He decided to pay a visit to his father to see if some of this work could be passed on to a junior employee, so he could have some free time to work on the inn. As it was, this was at least three weeks of work alone, not to mention having to get the other project rolling.

Anders walked down the hall toward Blair's icebox he called an office.

"Hi, Amy, is he in?" he asked the receptionist. She nodded and buzzed his father.

"Anders is here to see you, sir," she spoke into the telephone receiver. A moment's pause. "He'll see you now," she said, gesturing to the large wooden door, the gate keeping the lion inside.

"Thanks." He moved past Amy feeling an immense amount of gratitude for her. She must be a saint to put up with his father's demands.

"Hello, son," his father said without looking up from the cup of coffee he poured himself. There was a large insulated carafe on the corner of his desk. "Have a seat." He gestured to the chrome and leather chairs. "What can I do for you?"

"I wanted to discuss the case load you've given me," Anders said, trying to look respectable and dignified while sitting in the world's most humiliating chair.

"What about it?" Blair took a long drink from the steaming mug.

"I was hoping you'd allow me to give some of the items to a junior employee, so I can place most of my focus on the Millvale project." He got straight to the point. His father did not tolerate dilly dallying.

"No," Blair said flatly. "Anything else?" Anders adjusted his tie, suddenly feeling smothered.

"Dad, look, I know I agreed to maintain my usual level of work, but I just don't think it's possible," he said, trying to look tall and important. "I'll have to be spending at least half the week in Millvale to oversee the project."

"And you'll be planning your wedding I suppose," Blair added. Anders tilted his head back in surprise.

"Yes, I suppose so," Anders said, unsure of where this was headed.

"But I want you to supervise whomever you pass work along to, alright. Just because you're busy elsewhere doesn't mean these acquisitions aren't still your responsibility." Blair took a long drink from his mug, finishing its contents. He stood to pour another cup. He looked at his son over the rim of the freshly filled mug as he took another long drink. Man, oh man did his dad drink a lot of coffee. No wonder he was so intense.

"Have you bought her a ring yet, son?" Blair resumed his seat at his desk. He looked superior and important, just like his portrait that hung behind him.

"Not yet," Anders admitted. "My proposal was sort of unexpected."

"I see." Blair considered his son. "The same happened with your mother. I just looked at her one day, and I couldn't help myself. I blurted it out, right there at the bus stop."

Anders laughed, surprised he'd never heard this story before.

"Wait, you and mom took the bus?" He could hardly believe what he was hearing.

"Oh yes." Blair nodded as he remembered.

This was going to be a strange day, Anders thought to himself. He'd never really seen his dad smile before. Frown, yes, lots of times, but he didn't know that his mouth could turn the other direction.

"Your mother and I were poor when we met. I worked at a dry cleaner's; she was a deli girl in the local grocer. We were so in love. I just couldn't wait to make her my wife."

Anders had never known any of this. He didn't know his mom had ever worked, never mind his dad having not been the boss of his own company. The whole thing was unsettling. He was happy to know his parents were in love. That was nice, since he never really noticed that sort of thing between them. He assumed it was an upper-class thing, to hide your emotions. It went to show how you just never know what's happening behind closed doors.

"How did you know she was the one for you?" Anders asked, feeling doubt about his own decision-making skills.

"I couldn't stop thinking about her." Blair's eyes sparkled, and Anders was taken aback by suddenly seeing his dad like this. Weekend mornings, when his mother would make pancakes, his father would sometimes grab her around the waist and twirl her, making her laugh. Since he hadn't been living at home for a while, he'd forgotten. "She was so beautiful, so funny, so frustrating." Blair laughed, and Anders joined in.

Suddenly, an image of Jane's face floated into his mind. Was Jane the one who made him laugh, made him frustrated? He wasn't sure. He tried to replace the image with Meredith's face. She made him comfortable. But was that what he wanted?

"Go to Tiffany's, son, get her a nice ring, she'll be happy," Blair said, drinking more from his cup.

"It's not her I'm worried about," Anders said, to his own surprise. Blair's interest was piqued.

"Who then?" he said.

"Myself, I suppose," Anders said. He couldn't ever remember a time when he'd had this much of a conversation with his father.

"Cold feet, that's all," Blair said, looking important and presidential again, his image in tandem with that of the portrait. "I didn't have them, but lots of men do. It's nothing to worry about. Go home tonight, give that little Meredith a kiss. You'll see."

"What will I see?" Anders sounded doubtful.

"That she's the one. You'll know." Blair said, self-assuredly.

The phone rang, and Anders took that as a cue to leave. He set out down the hall to grab the files he planned to delegate. First thing was first, he was getting rid of any file that required him to leave the city. After distributing the tasks, of which he kept five for himself, five close-to-the-office-or-home tasks, he made some phone calls and finished his day. On the way to his condo he wondered about knowing if marrying someone was the right decision. Could it be as easy as knowing from a kiss? He wasn't sure. When he kissed Jane yesterday, he knew something was different about her. Though, he had known that since the moment they'd met. But the kiss. Oh boy, the kiss. He would remember it for the rest of his life, that's for sure. He couldn't say that any of the kisses he'd shared with Meredith had been so… he searched for the right term. All encompassing? Yes, that was it. They were always nice, always enjoyable, but he'd always craved more than just a nice, enjoyable kiss.

Maybe Meredith's kisses were like packaged chocolate chip cookies, and Janes were like homemade. He just had to figure out which ones he liked better, he supposed. He wasn't sure if that was going to be easy, since he made the proclamation to Jane that they would just be friends.

"Bonehead," he said to himself. Then "no, nice guy," and it was true. He was a nice guy, who wanted everyone to be happy, all the time. And now, here he was, engaged to a woman whom he cared for and had been with for a long time, but he also had doubts. Big doubts. Like if the choice to marry Meredith was ever going to make him happy. And if anyone really cared if he was happy, if they were happy.

"Chocolate chip cookies, indeed," Anders said to himself as he walked to his car. Delicious baking was what got him in this mess in the first place.

31

On Monday and Tuesday, Jane ferried supplies back and forth to Anders' place. There had been a note left for her from Valentina next to the stove.

Hello Jane,
Make yourself at home. Alec and I are at the building site getting ready to start. I hope you make lots of delicious recipes! If you need anything don't hesitate to contact us.
Valentina.

Jane decided she would leave all the dishes she'd created for the Brookstones to try and critique. She'd purchased two small notebooks, one for recipes and reviews, and one to track the money Anders had given her to try out the new recipes. He'd left her a cheque for ten thousand dollars, which she deposited in a new account at the bank. This was business after all. She wasn't going to go monkeying around with money that didn't belong to her.
She kept her notebooks, a few pens, a stapler, and calculator in a small purple box Ellie had decorated that was lying around the house, which she now left on top of the refrigerator. In her finances book she stapled every receipt for all

the items she purchased, keeping a running tally in the back to track her expenses.

Every recipe would be made as a double batch. One, she would test with her family, or Iris if she was there, and one she would leave for the Brookstones with instructions for reheating. Once she had everything she needed, she put it away in the kitchen. There were essentials left here by the landlord. One pot, one pan, four soupspoons, four forks, four knives. One very dull chef's knife, one ugly looking cutting board, four large plates, four small, four bowls, two mixing bowls, along with assorted mugs, glasses and plastic cups. Jane loaded the cupboards with an arsenal of restaurant style cooking equipment, putting a sticky note label on every drawer and cupboard so it would be easy to find everything until she became familiar with the layout.

She filled the pantry and fridge with the ingredients she would need over the coming days, also labelling those items to keep them separate from those of the tenants of the house. Her mixer, a heavy-duty beast, took pride of place in the centre of the counter top. Now she was ready.

On Wednesday Iris arrived armed with pages of ideas for dishes, menus and recipes. They got to work on some lunch dishes. A mixed-bean soup with rapini and spicy sausage, a peach chutney-smothered chicken sandwich served on thick slices of freshly baked pecan bread, spread with a tangy blue cheese and toasted in a press. The side salad featured arugula, raspberries and thin slivers of pear. Pumpkin seed crackers with warm brie, caramelized onions and a sweet-and-sour tomato jam. A warm square of black olive and roasted pepper frittata served alongside German potato salad featuring smoked pig cheeks instead of bacon.

    Iris also brought a notebook with recipes for exotic drinks. Preserved hibiscus flowers in a tart syrup, topped with sparking water and a sweet lime reduction created a beautiful pink drink the women placed in a large glass pitcher. Blueberry puree with ginger ale and peach nectar and a ginger beer with muddled mint and a club soda press filled glass mason jars.
"These drinks will be perfect for brunch," Jane said to Iris who was kneading dough. Flour was spread across the mid-section of her apron. She looked happy.

    "You think?" Iris said, smiling. She swayed to the music they had on in the background.

    "I do." Jane took a drink of the hibiscus mix and felt a tingly tangy thrill run through her. "These are great," Jane did a little dip and twirl to the music. They laughed.

    "This is fun," Iris said.

    "It is," Jane said, despite herself. She had missed the kitchen, she realized now. She hadn't been away from cooking for such a long time, ever, since she started the café. It was so great to stretch her creative culinary muscles, even if she was nervous of where all of this would take her.

"So, José asked me out yesterday," Iris said, interrupting Jane's mulling.

"He did?" Jane nearly squealed. She felt giddy. Friendship, food, fun. Today was a good day. "Did you say yes?" Jane said teasingly.

"Yes, of course," Iris said as she split the dough, she'd been working on into two loaf pans, covering it with a damp tea towel to let it rise. "We are going to go for a walk near the river and get ice cream."

Jane watched her friend's eyes light up, feeling happy for her, but sadness for herself.

"That's great," she said, feeling sincere, but not sure if she sounded so. Iris stood pouting, staring at the loaves she'd just prepared.

"I think this need basil," she said. "What do you think?"

"Sure." Jane quickly chopped up some fresh leaves. Iris dumped one loaf out and folded in the herbs, then put it back in the pan.

Jane busied herself writing out instructions for each dish. It was time consuming, but they got a lot accomplished that day. Plus, everything was delicious. Though she'd been away from the kitchen, she was happy to see she hadn't lost her touch.

"This is a great start," Jane said to Iris. They high fived.

"I'll just write out a copy of preparation instructions for the Brookstones, and we can clean up." Jane tore a page out of her notebook.

"You're getting them to try everything?" Iris said, sounding skeptical.

"Yes, of course," Jane said, not looking up from her work. "Anders is funding this, and I want him to see the work I've done. Plus, we need taste testers." She continued to scribble.

"Not hoping the old saying is true?" Iris smirked.

"What old saying?" Jane stopped writing to look at her.

"The way to a man's heart is through his stomach." Iris laughed.

"Hey," Jane said. "It's just business. Totally professional." Jane sounded like she was firm in her stance, but Iris saw the blush creeping up her neck.

"Okay, sure, I believe you." Iris wiped the counter down, depositing the flour residue into the trash.

There was a knock at the door just as they finished putting away all their equipment. Iris went to the door and found Ellie, Sally and a woman who looked like Sally's mom at the door.

"Hello," Ellie said. Iris moved aside to let the girl through. She called to Jane to come to the door. Jane arrived, wiping her hands on her apron.

"Hi, honey." She hugged her daughter, realizing she had missed her lovely face today. "How was your day?"

"We made a movie." Sally excitedly animated the process as she told Jane about it.

"They had a good time," Sally's mom Anne, said.

"She wasn't any trouble?" Jane asked.

"Never." Anne kidded.

"The movie is online, Mom. We can watch it tonight," Ellie said.

"Sure," Jane said.

"We'll see you soon," Sally said. Anne waved, and they left.

"What kind of movie did you make?" Iris wanted to know what her camera was used to create.

"We made a cooking video," Ellie said. "I was the star."

"You were?" Jane laughed in happy disbelief of her wonderful daughter.

"Yup, I used the support that Alec built me, and Sally's mom helped, and Sally stirred things. We made cookies from my recipe book. We called the video *Ellie and Sally Bake*.

"That sounds like fun," Jane said, feeling a lump in her throat. Her daughter was so imaginative. "I can't wait to watch it."

"Sweet," Ellie said, sounding again like a teenager. "Mom, it's so hot in here. Do you have anything to drink?"

"Do we!" Iris ran to the fridge to get one of the fancy drinks for her. She returned with a big glass of the pink hibiscus drink. Ellie's eyes widened. "That looks tasty," she said, then she took a sip. "Mm, delicious. This should go on the menu for sure." She took another big gulp, then let out a belch.

Jane laughed and yelled, "Excuse you," over her shoulder as she turned on the air conditioning, so the house wouldn't be too warm for the Brookstones that evening. She wanted to leave everything in her test kitchen just right.

32

Driving out of the city on Thursday morning, Anders felt the stress of the crowded and noise-filled city sliding from his vertebrae, only to be replaced by a new stress, one that resided in his chest. This stress was the one that told him he was crazy for taking on the project of building an inn, of going in a different direction to the family business plans. A project that looked like a broken-down historical building with two women breathing down his neck.

He rolled his shoulders and focused ahead at the empty road stretching out over rolling hills. Fields of wheat and knee-high corn undulated along the roadsides. Wild flowers filled his vision, while the blue, cloudless sky, reinforced the prospect of heat that would come later in the day.

He loved this drive. Loved the idea of the inn, despite the ulcer he was probably going to give himself. To save a building, to turn it into something better, was something Anders never knew he held a passion for but was quickly learning about himself.

The money was a worry. Raising one million dollars was doable, he hoped. The running tally in his head didn't really help too much. So far, he knew they had secured over one hundred and fifty thousand, including Jane's money, along with the salon's money, and the small investment from Iris. He thought about where else they could find the capital but hadn't come up with any ideas yet.

Pulling into the job site, he saw Alec hunched over some blueprints with their architect Gretta Butler. Anders always liked working with Gretta, one of the many architects on the Brookstone's roster.

"Hey." Anders shook the woman's hand firmly. "Nice to see you Gretta. How are things looking?" He wanted to get right down to business. He only had a few days each week in Millvale, so there was no time to waste.

"As I was telling Alec," Gretta gestured to his brother, her yellow hard hat struggling to stay put atop her head of fluffy salt and pepper curls, "we are in good shape to really get rolling. We will save the façade, just like you wanted." She looked at him with approval of his choice to save the history of the site. Her brown eyes crinkled in a way he always liked when he worked with her. "Then, we will build on to the back, leaving the restaurant at the front with big picture windows so people will be able to look in on the action in the kitchen and dining area. The reception will be in the other parts of the building that is currently on site, and we will add on to the back to include the rooms and ball room area. There will be a courtyard with an archway over the path to the gardens and old mill by the river. I thought that perhaps you might like to place one or two exclusive cabins for honeymooners and such down here for those guests that might like extra privacy."

Anders was impressed by the drawings and Gretta's delivery. He looked to Alec who nodded his approval.

"Looks great," he said, shaking her hand again. "I'll review the drawings and let you know if I think we need any changes." Gretta nodded and headed out with a wave to the men who stood by Alec's truck.

"What do you think?" Anders needed to settle the doubts in his stomach.

"It's great," Alec said. Always one to get to the point, he didn't mince words elaborating. Anders noticed that Alec wasn't meeting his eye.

"What's wrong?" Anders ducked his head, trying to catch Alec's eye.

"Nothing. I just—" He stopped himself.

"What?" Anders insisted. "Come on, don't wimp out. Just tell me," Anders almost whined.

"I wanted to ask you if you would let me take over site coordination and the role of foreman on this project," Alec huffed the request out, looking nervous. Something Anders was not used to seeing on his normally confident brother's face.

"But you do flooring, stone, marble, not general contracting," Anders said.

"I know, but I want to expand, learn, apply my skills." Alec looked away; frustration evident on his face.

"Well, I don't know. What did Dad say when you asked him?"

"I didn't, I'm asking you, you are overseeing this project," Alec said, his face growing red around his hairline.

"I think we should ask Dad," Anders said.

"Of course, you would think that," Alec said, turning and stomping away toward the guys who were redoing the roof.

"Hey." Anders chased after him, grabbing the yellow hard hat Gretta left behind. Shingles and nails flew past their heads as Anders caught up to Alec near the dump bin next to the building. "It's just that…" He addressed his brother's back, a flush of anger visible on the skin of his neck. Anders looked for the right thing to say. "You're not always so reliable. I mean, you run off to Europe, come back married, don't tell anyone. I just don't know if this kind of spontaneous behavior is what I want in someone running my job site."

"I'm not reliable?" Alec's voice rose. Anders noticed the roofers slowed down their pace to stop and stare at them. "Well if I'm not reliable, you're too reliable." He spat the word reliable in Anders face. Anders recoiled as the hot air from his brother's lungs brushed across his chin.

"How can a person be too reliable?" Anders demanded.

"Well, let me think." Alec listed things off on his fingers. "You're boring, you're predictable, you let Dad walk all over you, and you're engaged to Meredith. At least I have some adventure in my life, take some risks, try something new now and then. You're just under our father's thumb."

"Leave Meredith out of this," Anders growled, his fists balling up at his sides.

"Why?" Alec roared. "Do you even love her?"

"Yes, of course I do." Anders lifted his chin.

"What about Jane?"

"I barely know Jane."

"That doesn't matter." Alec stepped closer to Anders, their noses practically touching. He lowered his voice. "I saw the way you look at her. The way she looks at you. The way you looked like you wanted to run away when you announced your engagement. What are you doing?"

"Meredith is the right choice, what Mom and Dad and Brookstone Holdings expect, need." Anders listed reasons on his hand, mirroring Alec's movements from moments before. "If I'm going to take over the business, then Meredith is the right choice."

Alec turned on his heel, his face stormy. "That's another thing," he yelled over his shoulder. The roofers had completely stopped their work now, openly gawking at the argument as it unfolded below them. Alec bellowed at them, "Get back to work or get off the roof!" He turned to Anders. "Why is Dad giving you the business? We should each get half."

"Get half?" Anders huffed. "You haven't been here. You haven't had to deal with Dad every day. You haven't put the time in. You don't know anything about how the business works. Why would you get half?"

Alec stared at his brother. It amazed him that they could look so much alike and have turned out to be two such different people. "You're right, I've done nothing but disappoint everyone. I decided to live my life like it belongs to me. How silly. I should have been more like you. The family lap dog."

Wounded, Anders turned without a further word and walked to his car. He threw his hat on the passenger seat, peeling out onto the town street leaving his brother in a cloud of dust.

33

Anders drove up the drive of his rented house to find Jane's car parked out front. He was feeling a bit happier than he had moments before, but it was quickly replaced by a feeling of awkward apprehension. He hadn't seen her since they kissed, a kiss that was causing him a lot of trouble.

What did Alec know anyway? You couldn't tell anything about anyone just by a look. It took time, patience, to know what and how you felt about someone. Take Meredith for instance. He had known he found her attractive, wanted to get to know her better. So, they started dating, then when an appropriate amount of time passed, he brought her to a family dinner. Now they were engaged. That was the proper order for a relationship to grow toward a future. Not the way Alec seemed to think it should go, rushing off toward marriage without a thought or care, swept up in passion and lust. That was just not the way to do things. That just went to prove his point of why Alec didn't deserve to be one of the heads of Brookstone Holdings. The company didn't need someone in charge who let his heart make all the decisions. They needed a sensible, calm, thoughtful leader. Anders was this leader, he knew. He had spent a lifetime being reliable, dependable, straight and true as an arrow. He deserved the recognition he was finally getting.

In the rear-view mirror, he looked himself over, checked his teeth, smoothed down his hair that was wild from wearing a hard hat. Climbing out of the Jeep, he grabbed his duffle bag with his clothes for the weekend, and headed inside, swallowing once to quash the anxiety he felt rising in his throat.

We're just friends, he told himself as he placed a hand on the doorknob.

"Hello," he called as he walked through the door, trying not to startle Jane, in case she was presently wielding a sharp blade, or hot pan or something. The smell of tomato sauce rose to greet him. His stomach growled. Some of the annoyance he felt for his little brother was replaced by a desire to eat a huge bowl of spaghetti topped with whatever sauce was filling the house with this delicious aroma.

"Hi," Valentina called. She came to the door. "You are here early," she said to him, taking his bag from his hand.

"Uh, yes," Anders said, avoided her gaze. "Things are well in hand at the site." He hugged his sister-in-law hello and tried not to notice any reasons why Alec could have fallen in love with her instantly.

"Come in. Jane is just helping me with my application for landed immigrant status, and she's cooking us our dinner." Valentina went down the hall and placed his bag in the room where his parents had stayed when they were visiting. Anders noticed Ellie's backpack but didn't see the girl anywhere around. Jane stood next to the oak dining table, looking flushed and awkward.

"Hello," she said, keeping her gaze lowered.

"Hi," he responded, keeping his distance. Her hair was pulled back like the first day he met her. Her apron tied tightly around her waist, showing off her curves. Oh no. What was he going to do?

"Come sit," Valentina called to him, a smirk on her lips and trouble dancing in her eyes.

"Yes, uh, let me just wash my hands first and grab a drink." He wandered into the kitchen, over to the sink. He passed the pot where the sauce blipped and bopped in simmering. "What's this cooking on the stove?" He hovered over the pot, letting the steam cling to his skin.

"It's the sauce for the vegan dish I was trying out today," Jane called. She walked from the table, then closer to him. "Wanna taste?" He turned to her and nodded. She grabbed a small bowl, filled it with a mixture of rice and quinoa, sliced and roasted green, red, yellow, and orange bell peppers. She topped the lot with a gracefully scooped spoonful of sauce. Then she sprinkled chopped parsley, cracked pepper, and finished the dish with toasted pine nuts and a drizzle of olive oil. He took the bowl from her hands as she nodded to him. A truce perhaps?

"Thanks," he said, nodding back.

"You're welcome," she said, not breaking her gaze. He turned away first and went to the table. He heard Jane sigh and then open the fridge. She followed him with a tray of glasses and the day's drink creation. Mandarin and peach juice mixed with elderflower tea.

"You stay away from my papers." Valentina joshed them as she scooped up the books and scattered sheets of paper from the table, stowing them carefully in the buffet behind them. Anders took a bite from the bowl in front of him while Jane filled the glasses. He heard Ellie coming in the front door.

The dish was delicious, of course, but also unexpected. The sauce was deep and rich, with mushrooms and slivered olives in black and green, exploding on his tongue. The black pepper and olive oil made the dish spicy, while the bell peppers were sweet. It was the best vegan dish he'd ever tried.

"This is great. You should put it on the menu for sure," he said, waving his utensil enthusiastically at her.

"Thanks," Jane replied, chuckling.

"So, did you see the plans for the inn today?" Valentina asked, breaking some sort of trance that had fallen between Anders and Jane.

"Yes, I did." Anders nodded, trying his best to stay positive and not fall into the anger he had felt when he was talking to Alec. This was his wife after all. If he had a problem with his brother, it was between them. Valentina had nothing to do with it.

"What did they look like?" Ellie asked as she joined them at the table. Jane poured her a glass of some of the drink then looked at her.

"What is all over you?" She rushed to the kitchen to grab some damp paper towel. Ellie's arms were covered in a yellow dust.

"Dandelions." Ellie laughed. "I was seeing if I was made of butter."

"What is this 'made of butter?'" Valentina asked.

"If you take a dandelion and hold it up to your skin, and you can see a yellow reflection, it means you are made of butter."

"The key word being reflection." Jane tutted as she scrubbed at the girl's arm. "You're not supposed to rub it all over yourself."

"I was just making sure, relax, Mom." Ellie rolled her eyes and Anders tried to stifle a laugh "Tell us more about the plans, Anders." Ellie turned her intensity on him.

"Please," Jane corrected. Ellie whipped her head toward her mother, rolled her eyes harder than before, then whipped her head back to look upon Anders once more.

"Pleeaassee!" She huffed.

"Well," he chuckled, "the restaurant is going to have big glass windows so that the guests can see into the kitchen and the dining room. It's going to be built in the already existing part of the building. The front desk and reception areas will also be in the old part of the building. Then the new areas will hold the ballroom, and guest rooms. There will be a courtyard and a garden, and a path that leads down to the creek and old mill where we are going to put a couple of private cabins."

"That sounds great," Valentina said.

"Yeah," Ellie echoed. "Mom did you hear that? Big windows? Your new restaurant is going to be awesome."

"Yes, it sounds like it will be," Jane laughed.

"Anders, can you build some place for me too?" Ellie asked, sounding hopeful.

"A place for you?" Jane frowned. "Why would you need a place?"

"I don't know," Ellie said, her eyes looking big and sad. "To hang out with you and stuff, like I used to at the café."

"Well, that's kind of a lot to ask Anders," Jane said kindly, trying to let her daughter down gently.

"Now, I don't know," Anders said, the seed of an idea forming in his head. "I can't promise anything to you, Ellie, but I might be able to come up with something. But if I do, it will be a surprise." His voice was tender and kind and filled with so much caring that Jane felt more hard pieces of her heart softening.

"I love surprises!" Ellie said, happily. "Hey, Anders, do you want to see something terrific?"

"Always." He looked at Jane trying to diffuse any uncomfortable feelings in the air.

"May I use your tablet, Valentina?"

"Of course." Valentina passed it to her. Ellie busied herself typing something, and then proudly propped up the screen against Anders' empty bowl so everyone could see. On the screen was a video. The sounds of giggling girls came through the speakers.

"This is *Ellie and Sally Bake*," they announced in excited voices.

"Oh, this is the video you made?" Jane asked, giving her daughter a squeeze on her shoulders.

"Yes, shh." Ellie shushed her mother and Anders chuckled at the girl's seriousness. He realized in a few moments he shouldn't have been so judgmental, as the video played, he saw two friends having fun, making some of Ellie's crazy cookie recipes. They looked delicious, and Ellie proved herself to be a very capable baker. With Sally to help her with anything she needed an extra hand to get done, and a woman, Sally's mother he assumed, to deal with the oven, they created a fun and entertaining video.

"That was great," he said with genuine enthusiasm.

"Really?" Ellie beamed, obviously proud.

"Really," Valentina and Jane spoke almost simultaneously.

"Nice!" Ellie said. "It was really fun. We are planning to make another one this week."

"I can't wait to see it," Anders said, truly meaning it. The seed in his mind started to sprout. Though he wasn't going to mention it to anyone yet, he was formulating a plan for something great he suspected that Ellie would love. Just then, he heard the door open and Alec came in.

"Darling," Valentina cooed.

Anders turned, nodded to acknowledge his brother's arrival, then stood to place his dishes in the sink. Jane watched the scene, noticing the tension between the two, and wondered what was going on there.

Maybe they were fighting about Valentina? Jane couldn't imagine that. Maybe the dinner from the other night? That made Jane have a sinking feeling in her stomach. Surely, one of them would have said something to her if she had done something wrong. No, it mustn't be that. What else could it be? The inn? Now, that was a possibility. She hoped there wasn't trouble brewing surrounding the inn. She didn't have time for more trouble. Not now, not ever.

34

Early Friday morning, a week later, Jane padded out to the kitchen in her bare feet. She put on the kettle and filled the French press coffee maker with beans she'd ground the night before. Breathing in the fresh scent of coffee made her feel happy. This morning, she felt especially happy. They were going to the children's rehab hospital in the city so Ellie could get fitted for her new chair. Though the series of events that led to this moment had been stressful and uncertain, right at this moment, Jane counted her blessings that she was able to get the new chair. This chair would last Ellie through high school, she hoped. She'd noticed that lately her daughter was using her walker more and more. She had to admit to herself that Ellie was becoming more independent, that cooking video proved the point nicely. But, this was the way of life, even for special-needs children. She wasn't going to be a little girl much longer and Jane knew that she would have to practice letting go, practice not feeling her heart fly up into her throat every time Ellie tried to do something on her own.

Alec making that support frame was a huge step in this direction. She still kicked herself for never thinking of it, for not letting Ellie into the kitchen to help with more than just writing recipes. There were probably lots of ways she could have accommodated her daughter's needs better than she had done in the past, but if she were honest with herself, she didn't want to let her daughter do things for fear she would hurt herself, or worse, injure herself beyond repair. Jane knew this was improbable, and perhaps even irrational, but there you had it. The truth was, most often, ugly. And this was an ugly side of herself. She coddled her daughter, spoiled her too, even. Besides her mother, Ellie was all Jane had left.

When Tom died, she had been devastated. A widow at twenty-six, her friends, most of whom hadn't even been in long-term or serious relationships, didn't know how to help her. Left with a little girl who had challenges, alone in a city far from home, she was lost, confused, and deep in depression. Her mother had come to see her and demanded she move home with her immediately. They got a little bungalow together, and her mother had quit her job as a secretary to work with Jane and open the café. Together they spoiled Ellie, looked after her, and doted on her. While those things didn't need to stop, Jane was starting to see that her daughter needed to spread her wings, to try things, and fail or succeed. Ellie needed to learn about life a little bit more.

When the kettle boiled, she poured the water over the grounds, then got two mugs, put a splash of cream in each and set them on the table. She'd heard Fae moving around down the hall and figured she'd appear soon. Then she got out the carton of eggs and whipped up a big omelet to share with her mother and daughter. Laughter drifted down the hallway and she knew Ellie had gotten up and was chatting with her grandma.

Ellie had been so excited the night before, knowing she was getting a new chair today. It was all she could do to get her daughter to go to sleep. Ideas of how she wanted her chair to look had morphed since she'd learned that she'd be getting a new one and now she was leaning toward a purple chair with glitter. Jane didn't know if such an item would be a wise idea, considering they hoped the chair would last many years. Ellie would most likely tire of that combination, but maybe Jane would just let her daughter be happy here and now and hope for the best in the future.

Soon granddaughter and grandmother arrived, all dressed and ready for the day. They ate and chatted, Ellie still going on about her ideas of what her new chair should look like. At eight o'clock, Jane dashed off to get dressed, and then load up the car.

"Mom, would you take a picture of my kitchen support, so I can show Mike at the hospital? I think he'd like to see it."

Mike was the technician that helped to fit chairs to patients, or build prosthetics, braces, etc. He was great with kids and Ellie always liked to see him, even when he had fitted her with a brace on her good hand when she was little, to make her weak hand stronger. Unfortunately, it hadn't helped much, but Mike had made the negative experience more fun than it otherwise would have been. Jane grabbed her phone and took a few quick pictures, then snagged the bag of snacks for the trip she'd packed the night before, and they were off. Except, when they got to the van, they noticed the light was on inside.

"Oh no," Jane said, and hopped in the car. The battery was dead. "Oh, no." She cursed under her breath. "I left the light on yesterday when I dropped my debit card under the seat at the bank." That's what she got for using the drive through instead of going inside the bank to get some money out. "Shoot."
She tried to think quickly. This was their only vehicle. How would they get to the city?

"Mom, do you think Ed would let us borrow his car?" Jane tried to keep the panic out of her voice. They had waited so long for this appointment; she really didn't want to reschedule.

"I'll call him." Fae pulled out her cell and dialed Ed. They spoke quickly, and Jane could already tell the answer was no. "He has a dentist appointment in Bellfield today, he needs his car, sorry."

"Okay." Jane thought some more. *I guess we could reschedule.* Unbeknownst to her, Ellie had grabbed her mother's phone from her purse and was dialing.

"Hi, Anders," she spoke cheerfully into the phone.

"Ellie!" Jane balked, horrified.

"Anders, our van is broken down and I have to go get my new wheelchair today, can you come help us?"

"Ellie, hang up that phone now!" Jane started to blush. Fae was laughing. The girl hung up moments later and turned to her mother with a triumphant look.

"He's coming right over." Ellie grinned.

"You shouldn't just take my phone like that, and you shouldn't be bothering Mr. Brookstone." Jane blushed harder.

"It's fine, Mom, he's our friend, right? He wants to help us." Ellie rolled her chair around the driveway, oblivious to the trouble she was causing. Since there wasn't much Jane could do now, she phoned the hospital and told them that they might be late for their appointment. Minutes later, Anders pulled up in his Jeep.

"Good morning, Anders," Ellie yelled, rolling her eyes at her mom, as he got out and walked up from the curb.

"Good morning." He greeted her warmly, then nodded to Fae. To Jane he said,

"What's the problem with the van?"

"I accidentally left the cabin light on all night and half the day yesterday," Jane said feeling ashamed.

"I see." He popped the hood and went back to his car. Out the window he called to Ellie and Fae to move to one side, so he could pull up. He was going to try and boost the van. He rolled up the sleeves of his nicely pressed light blue button-down shirt and got to work connecting wires to batteries. Jane secretly admired the look of concentration on his face, and the way the front lock of his hair fell in front of his eyes as he bent forward. She resisted the urge to brush it away. He turned on his car and then Jane hopped in and turned hers on. Nothing but a click-click noise from the key.

"Try again," he called, and she did. Still dead. "Looks like you need a new battery." Anders wiped his hands on a rag he had hidden in a bag in the trunk.

"A new battery." Jane's mind whirred while she tried to figure out how she'd be able to get a new battery and still make their appointment.

"Okay," Anders said cheerfully, evidently not put out at coming to her rescue one bit. "You better hop in. We don't want Ellie to miss her appointment. But Fae, I'm sorry, you will have to stay behind. I'll have to fold one side of the back down to make room for Ellie's chair."

Jane thought he seemed genuinely sorry that he wouldn't be able to fit everyone in his vehicle.

"Not a problem." Fae's eyes twinkled a bit. "I'll stay here and call the tow truck. You go on." She made a shooing gesture to the girls.

"Oh, no, we can't ask you to drive us," Jane said. Meanwhile Ellie had already parked her chair next to the car door.

"Come on, Mom, we have to go," Ellie pleaded with her.

"It's really no trouble." Anders spoke softly, trying to reassure her. Jane stared him down, attempting to read his face. She saw nothing but kindness there.

"Well, okay," she said reluctantly.

"Great," he said, going to work on folding down the seat. Ellie climbed in the back as Jane put the chair in and secured it with some bungie cords she found in the trunk. Anders phoned Alec and had a clipped conversation about how he wouldn't be back today. The exchange sounded strained, but he turned on a sunshine-y voice when he spoke to them again.

"Everyone buckled in?" he asked.

"Yes," Jane and Ellie replied.

"Super. Then, we are off." He backed out of the driveway while Fae waved. Jane couldn't help but notice the large grin spread across her mother's small face.

35

At the hospital they managed to park and make it just in time for the appointment. Anders stayed in the waiting area while Jane and Ellie went inside. He read some of the posters on the wall that talked about the work the hospital did, how they made the braces and prosthetics, and looked at the smiling faces of the children who had been helped. This place was impressive, he thought to himself. He lived not too far away and had passed the grounds but had never gone inside, because he never needed to. It was nice to see that a hospital like this was available to those who did need it, though.

He wandered around a bit while he waited, looking at everything there was to see. There were bright colours everywhere, artwork on the walls with kooky animals and exciting scenes. There were large windows overlooking a big pool. He watched some of the kids work with physiotherapists in the water. It seemed like fun, but also hard work. Some were practicing walking up a ramp that was submerged underwater. I supposed that made things easier on their joints. A couple kids were doing arm exercises using special floating devices that provided resistance. He wondered if Ellie had ever tried any of these types of exercises when she was younger.

In the cafeteria he ordered a coffee for himself and tea for Jane, as well as picking up an apple juice for Ellie. He looked out the windows onto a beautiful garden with wide pavement paths winding through different vignettes of flowers and shrubs, or tall trees with wooden figurines painted by children. There was an overriding theme here, that of happiness, or at least cheeriness. He knew some children were here for serious illnesses. He'd seen one or two being wheeled past on gurneys. He imagined what it must have been like to find out that Ellie would have physical challenges. His heart ached for families who had more seriously challenged children.

Lately, Anders had been thinking about Ellie, her budding skills, and her blossoming confidence. An idea had come to him after he saw her baking video, and she'd asked for her own space. He would build her a baking studio, with a small shop attached. It would be offset from the restaurant, with space to film the videos if Ellie and Sally wanted to work there, and a place for Ellie's Creations to be sold. The guests would love it, and he thought Ellie would love it too. He assumed there would be several kitchen staff, so when Ellie was at school or living her life, there would be someone to take over. He couldn't wait to build it for her.

Outside of the excitement and anticipation he felt for working on the inn project, he felt a passion for creating a space for

Ellie, something he'd never felt before in his adult life. Sure, he'd loved Hot Wheels, and baseball, but this was something entirely different. He could help her, make the space accessible, and give her a place to succeed at her dreams.

He'd been researching accessible kitchen equipment, and there was a fair amount available. He'd stock the shelves with bowls that stuck to the counter and install accessible pull-down shelves to make it easier for Ellie to reach things above if she was in her chair. He'd also invest in ovens where the doors tucked in, so there would be no unnecessary obstacles in her way. The plan was to keep it a total surprise, right down to the paint colour. Now, he'd just have to let Alec, and Gretchen the architect, know of his plans.

Returning to the waiting area where the ladies left him, he found Ellie in her new chair looking out the window that overlooked the parking lot. Jane was at the counter.

"We're donating the old chair for someone else who might need it," she said to the woman behind the counter.

"Wonderful," the plump and smiling woman answered. "I'll get you a tax receipt and you can be on your way."

A man in a white lab coat walked briskly out to the desk and had a quick discussion with Jane. She turned and looked at Anders, then Ellie, and turned back. Jane waved Anders over.

"What's up?" he asked as he handed her the cup of tea.

"Oh, thanks," she said, surprised. "Mike wanted to know if he could contact your brother about the frame he made for Ellie." Jane asked. "Do you have a business card, or, his cell number or something?"

"It was a very impressive item that your brother created." Mike shook Anders' hand. Somewhat startled, Anders handed the juice and coffee to Jane. She took them awkwardly trying to balance one cup on top of the other.

"Here you go." Anders handed over a business card upon which he'd written Alec's number. "I'll let him know you liked it." That was, if, and when they were on speaking terms.

"Great, thanks." Mike shook his hand again, "I'll be in touch. Lovely to meet your husband, Jane. Ellie, I'll see you around," he called across the room to the girl who waved in return.

"He's not my hus—" Jane stopped as Mike disappeared around the corner. She was blushing again, the red creeping up the back of her neck and onto her ears.

"Here's your receipt, Ms. Michaels." The woman at the desk handed it to her. Jane piled the cups in Anders' hands again.

"Thank you." She placed the receipt carefully in her purse. Then she turned to Anders, taking the apple juice, removing the top. They walked over to Ellie.

"I see you settled on iridescent blue." Anders nodded in approval at the stylish new chair. She had done nothing but talk about what her new chair would be like for the entire drive into the city.

"I did. I thought this way it would get to look like it is a bunch of colours all at once." She grinned.

"Good thinking."

"It's efficient too, it has a longer battery life, and look at this!" Ellie flipped a small table up from the outside of the arm where the controllers sat. It was big enough to hold a drink, or a small notebook, maybe even a tablet, and then could be returned to the side out of the way when not in use. "Isn't this great? It's going to be so handy."

"Leave it up," Jane said, handing Ellie the bottle of juice.

"I love apple juice." Ellie took a big gulp. "Thanks."

"You're welcome." Anders handed Jane her tea. "Black tea with milk, I hope that's okay." He looked uncertainly at her.

"Perfect." How did he know what kind of tea she liked, she wondered?

They made their way down the elevators and out to the parking lot. Ellie's new chair fit nicely in the Jeep. Once they were loaded in, Anders remembered he'd forgotten to pack a fan and wanted one for his bedroom in Millvale.

"Would you mind if we swung by my apartment? It's nearby and I wanted to get something," he asked the ladies.

"Wonderful! I've never seen an apartment before." Ellie was very excited about this suggestion.

"Absolutely," Jane replied, sounding tired, or maybe it was just relief at getting the new chair situation settled. "You're the driver."

"I'll be quick," Anders promised.

"It's no trouble," Jane said to him.

"You sure? You seem tired or something." Anders frowned at her, concerned.

"I'm just…." Jane looked for the right word. "Feeling overwhelmed and grateful. I'll be fine in a bit." A mix of emotions ran across her eyes.

"As long as you're sure." He searched her face.

"She's sure! Come on, Anders," Ellie insisted, loudly, for that matter.

He paused a moment longer to look Jane over, his heart aching to connect with her.

"Alright, we're off." He turned away from her, suddenly feeling in danger of losing something he desperately wanted to hold on to. He turned on the car. They were on the road to his place in a matter of moments.

36

Parking in the underground garage was a thrill for Ellie, who had never seen one before. The spot was emblazoned with the name "Mr. Brookstone" written on the pavement done with a white painted stencil. Ellie thought this was fascinating too.

They took the elevator up to the fourteenth floor, travelling down the hallway to the left once they reached their stop. The whole time Ellie talked non-stop. It had already been an exciting day, and she was getting a serious thrill riding in a shiny elevator that announced the floors as it passed them, and then the fancy carpeting in the hallway, and how each door to each condo had its own personal porch lamp. It was all new and fascinating to her. Jane mouthed *thank you* over Ellie's head, happy her daughter was enjoying this adventure.

Anders was enjoying the quiet between them, though he was still worried that there was something wrong with Jane. He'd never seen her silent for so long before. Normally she would be pushing forward, taking names, getting things done. But today, aside from the stress she was obviously under from the possibility of being late to their appointment, she was contemplative and keeping to herself.

"Here we are," Anders announced when they reached his door, 1408 was written in brass letters fastened to the door.

"Neat," Ellie chimed in once more. Anders turned to look at Jane, who was smiling down at Ellie. He suddenly felt nervous. Had he put away all his underwear before he left for Millvale the last time?

"Welcome," he said, sweeping his arm across the threshold as he swung the door inward. Ellie burst through. "Make yourselves at home."

"Whoa," she exclaimed upon seeing the view.

"It's lovely," Jane said.

"Thanks," Anders replied, throwing his keys in the bowl by the door. He felt relieved that she liked it.

"It looks just like I imagined it would look," she said, a pleased look on her face. His heart beat a little faster. He wondered what she meant by that.

"Oh, really?" He tried to ask in a nonchalant way. Why should he care what she thought anyway?

"Yes," she said. "It's calm, and comfortable in here."

Anders looked around at the place. A worn brown leather couch and chair faced one another, with the couch facing the window. He had a television, but preferred to read most evenings, or listen to the radio, so a side table with a reading lamp and small AM/FM radio had pride of place. The T.V. was on top of a rolling cabinet so it could be put away when not in use. He had a plant, a rubber plant to be exact, in the window. It was a gift from his mother, and he had been careful to look after it. There was also a large bookcase, made of wood that matched the leather furniture, filled with many books and some knickknacks like his grandfather's old fishing rod, a trophy from when he played baseball a hundred years ago, and a mini Leaning Tower of Pisa Alec had brought back from Italy. The walls of the whole place were a light blueish grey. He liked that it reminded him of being at the lake.

"Thanks, it's my home, so I wanted it to feel that way I guess," he replied, his insides feeling warmer than a moment earlier. They were quiet for a moment. He admired the shape of her face, and he couldn't be sure, but he thought that maybe she was tracing the shape of his lips with her eyes. He felt his heart rate pick up again and resisted the urge to hold her.

"Neat bedroom." Ellie came whizzing back into the room. The battery in her new chair was making it move at super speed, compared to the old one.

"Thanks," he replied.

"Not to rush you," Jane said. "But I think we should probably get going otherwise we'll be caught up in rush-hour traffic for the drive home."

"Right, of course." He started down the hall to the storage closet. "Let me just fish out the fan and we'll be off again."

"He's got a cozy plaid blanket on the bed," Ellie was telling her mother.

He could hear them talking while he moved a couple boxes out of the way and pulled out the fan that had been stored in the back. He removed the plastic shopping bag that he'd placed over the blades to keep the dust off. Then he thought he heard the door to the apartment opening.

"Oh, hello," Meredith's voice was surprised.

"Hi," Jane said, sounding equally surprised.

"What are you...?"

"We were just...," Jane and Ellie spoke simultaneously.

"We just stopped by to pick up a fan." Anders scooted into the room, holding up the fan as evidence.

"I see." Meredith looked cautiously around.

"Anders drove us to my appointment to get my new wheelchair. Our car broke down," Ellie filled in the rest of the story for Anders' confused-looking fiancée.

"Ah." Meredith crossed the room and kissed Anders, who tried to feel natural kissing her back.

"What are you doing here? I thought you were coming up to Millvale after you finished work?" Anders tried not to sound accusatory in his questioning.

"I forgot my allergy medicine here the last time," Meredith said carefully, tilting her head toward Ellie. Jane turned around and walked toward the door where she stood in front of the bookshelf.

"Ellie, come check out these interesting books Anders has." She called her daughter over to try and give them some privacy, though if she were a German Shephard, she'd have turned her ears toward them to listen in.

"So, what's going on?" Meredith whispered, not very quietly.

"Jane's car broke down this morning and since I was in town, I stopped by to see if I could help. The battery is dead, so I gave them a ride because they needed to come into the city for an appointment." He told the story all in one breath.

"There wasn't anyone else who could help?" Meredith sounded annoyed.

"I guess not," Anders said, not having thought about it previously.

"I thought you said you weren't spending too much time with her." Meredith spoke through clenched teeth.

"I'm not, I swear. I haven't seen her in weeks," Anders said, sounding somehow guilty, though Jane knew that she hadn't seen him in a long time, except that one time when she was helping Valentina. Perhaps Meredith wasn't totally oblivious to the attraction between them,

Jane thought to herself. She couldn't blame the woman. Her fiancé was disappearing to a different town for days at a time, and she hadn't really been able to join him much.

"It was just a trip into the city to go to the appointment, then zip back to Millvale," Anders said, his voice growing louder than a whisper with each syllable.

"And the fan?" Meredith was not ready to let go of her accusatory tone.

"I just remembered I wanted it," he spoke to her in a familiar way. "You know it's warm at the house at night."

"True," Meredith said with knowing in her voice. Jane wanted to hurl.

"I'm just going to drop the ladies off, and then I'll meet you at the house for dinner, alright?" Anders sounded as if he wanted to defuse the argument, Jane could tell.

"Mom left you some yummy dishes to try in the fridge," Ellie replied, way louder than necessary.

"Ellie," Jane scolded her.

"What?" Ellie said, confused.

"I'm sure she did." Meredith spoke through tight lips.

"Right," Anders agreed. They all paused.

"Maybe we should get going?" Jane said, clearing her throat awkwardly.

"Right." Anders said again, fan in hand, making his way to the door, turning back a moment to kiss Meredith lightly on her hair. "I'll see you later, don't be late." He laughed nervously.

"I won't," Meredith said, doubt dripping from her words as she watched the trio leave.

37

Ellie lay on her side in bed, the breeze from the ceiling fan fluttering and tickling her hair. She was so happy lately, like super-duper happy. She had been mostly happy before, but lately she had been especially happy. She liked having her mom around more, and she liked being on summer vacation, though she always liked school too. But this summer was great because she got to see her mom whenever she wanted, and she didn't have to go to camp. Not that she really minded camp, but it was nice to have a summer to do whatever she wanted. And what she wanted to do was hang out with Sally and make baking videos. The videos were getting popular, over one thousand views each. Though, most of those were probably her mom, or grandma, or Iris, but still, that was a really big number.

Sometimes they took videos of Mom trying out new recipes. People on the internet were getting excited about the new inn. She didn't think her mother knew about that, but Ellie thought it was neat to see people so interested. And, since they got the insurance money, her mom had bought Ellie her own tablet to make videos, which was way easier to use than Iris' camera.

Ellie could see her mom was happier too. She seemed stressed out still, but not like before. Somehow having the Brookstones around had made her seem calmer, though her mother would never admit it. She had also overheard her mom and grandma talking about how relieved they were that her new chair was here, that they were able to get it just in time. Ellie knew she had been growing too fast for the last one, but she couldn't help it. She did like the Brookstones though. Anders was funny and nice, and Alec was quiet and kind, and Valentina was so pretty and so different from her mom. Her mom was always serious and focused, but Valentina laughed and sang a lot, and ran around in the garden, which she'd never seen her mother do.

Lately her mom had been spending time at the inn, picking out everything to finish the kitchen. Ellie wasn't allowed on the construction site, but her mom brought home tile samples and pictures of stoves and sinks, and different plates, and glasses, and cutlery. It seemed there was something new to pick out each day. Ellie got to pick out some of the new stuff with her mom and Iris, which was lots of fun. The kitchen was going to have butter yellow walls and white tiles, with a pale green floor. The plates would be white and oval shaped, and the glasses were tall and clear.

Then, one day, Anders stopped by and asked Ellie for her favourite colours but wouldn't tell her or her mom why. Anders was always doing stuff like that. He also stopped by and asked her what her favourite flowers were, and her favourite tree. Who would have a favourite tree? Ellie thought that was a crazy question.

Sometimes Meredith was around when Anders was around. She knew that they were getting married, but she just couldn't see it. They never laughed, or fought, or seemed that excited to be around one another. Alec and Valentina were always hugging and kissing and laughing or arguing and then kissing. Even Ed and her grandmother were like that. Holding hands or looking at each other softly when they thought no one was looking, but Ellie always saw them.

Ellie watched Anders and Meredith carefully. Meredith was nice, quiet, polite, but kinda boring. Like, she was also kinda weird. Working with dead people? Ellie and Sally had laughed and laughed when they found that out. Weird. Really weird. Ellie couldn't imagine it. All those zombies and ghosts, at work every day. No. Thank. You.

Ellie really didn't understand why Anders liked Meredith. There wasn't anything wrong with her, per se, but, when Anders and her mom were together, his eyes looked sparkly, and Mom laughed more and looked rosy like she'd been out in the snow, even though it was summertime. Ellie secretly thought Anders should marry her mom, but she'd never say that to anyone. It would be perfect if the Brookstones could be around more. She had started to imagine stuff. It was kind of embarrassing though, because the stuff she imagined was about Anders becoming her dad. She loved her real dad, but she didn't really remember him and all the fun stuff they must have done together when she was little. Ellie liked that Anders was fun to be with and that he made her mom smile. Plus, if Anders and her mom got married, that would mean Alec would be her uncle. Maybe he would show her how to use tools. And, Valentina would be her aunt. Valentina could teach her Italian and all about Europe. They could plan a trip to go there together one day when Ellie was older.

    Nope, she'd just keep making her videos for a couple more weeks, then she'd be back in school and would just forget all about that silly idea.

38

Several weeks had passed since Anders and Jane kissed, and Anders was feeling good about how things were going. Now, he was strolling hand in hand, a miracle in itself, with Meredith along a quaint street in the centre of Bellfield, enjoying the end of summer breeze with its refreshing brush against their skin. He hadn't thought of the kiss much at all lately, things were too busy with the build and his time spent in the city, though he had to admit to himself he was finding reasons to be in Millvale. Meredith joined him most weekends, where they would spend time exploring the area or quietly reading on the front porch. Meredith commented often on how delicious Jane's cooking was, and this pleased Anders to no end, though he would never admit it.

Today was a big day, however. Today was the day that Anders was taking Meredith to pick out her engagement ring. On one of their trips to town, they had walked past a picturesque jewelry store. The front awning was done in a sage green and in the windows were displays filled with sparkling rings atop plump velvet pillows done in a colour to match the awning. On the window was written The Silver Lining in pink script with grey outline. Out front, the shopkeepers had done nice window boxes, bursting with fresh flowers. Meredith had commented on how attractive and inviting the store was, but they hadn't gone in because Anders needed to get back to the inn to approve something that was being delivered. But today they would go in, Meredith would choose her ring, and their engagement would be officially official. Finally.

 His parents had been on him lately as to why Meredith didn't yet have a ring. His father kept insisting Tiffany's was the right way to go. Anders didn't agree, so now he would do things his way, with Meredith.

 Since the day she walked in on Jane and Ellie at his apartment Meredith had been somewhat distant. While she was not one to be overly affectionate normally, she had pulled away even farther. Today it seemed as if he was forgiven, though he had done nothing wrong. He was helping a friend, just as Meredith would want him to do if someone was in need, right?

 Since that day, Anders had thought a lot about how to incorporate more accessible spaces into the inn. Ellie wasn't the only person who needed such spaces, but to be honest, he had never thought about anyone who might need to access a space because they moved through the world in a different way than he did. Now it was something he couldn't shake, and he wanted to use his project to do something about it. He'd decided to call in an expert because he would be making three of the new rooms at the inn accessible, as well as the dining area, banquet hall, public washrooms, and garden, so that Ellie, and people like her would be included. He hadn't told anyone about his ideas yet, but he would soon enough. He suspected that the changes he wanted to make to their plans for the renovation might cost some more money, but he was sure he could swing it. Maybe. He hadn't had much luck in the fund-raising department, and he needed to figure that out soon.

They arrived in front of the shop.

"We're here," Anders said happily to Meredith.

"Oh, we're going in?" Meredith sounded excited. She rarely sounded excited. "Did I ever tell you I love antique jewelry?"

"No, you haven't." Anders liked to see this look of enthusiasm on her face.

"I do." Meredith face shone. She looked like a young girl, if young girls could have such unsettling eyes. "I have some of my grandmother's, but I never really wear it as it isn't appropriate for work."

Anders knew that she tried to wear muted outfits to work so that she wouldn't interfere with the grief and mourning of the funeral clients. It was important to be invisible, and available, when you worked at a funeral home. Perhaps that explained the dichotomy of Meredith's personality. She was stark, but friendly, bland and reliable. Perhaps forgettable, yet he found himself initially charmed by her.

She fit into the scenery nicely, and there was something to be said for that.

"Well, let's see what they have inside shall we?" Anders buzzed at the door and they were let inside the first door, then through the interior safety door once the outside door closed. Inside the shop, there were long display cases lining the sides of the space, with a runway down the middle, which held smaller square display cases. Everything was shiny glass and chrome, lined with green velvet display pads and boxes. The walls were a similar pink to that on the sign out front.

"Hello." A polished, friendly looking woman with dark skin stood behind the furthest counter from the door.

"Hi," Meredith said in response, smiling in the woman's direction.

"May I help you find something?" the woman queried. Her wavy black hair was swept up on her head in a fancy twist. She wore a red sundress and a lacy short-sleeved cardigan. Her smile was welcoming and warm.

"We'd like to see your engagement rings, please." Anders felt his brow begin to sweat a little, but mostly he felt calm. "And if you have any vintage or antique rings, we'd be particularly interested in those." He squeezed Meredith's hand as he spoke. She squeezed back, which surprised him. Maybe this was all going to work out all right in the end?

"Certainly." The woman gestured with a graceful arm. Anders detected a slight West Indian accent to her voice. She looked to be in her mid-fifties. "In this case here, we have some lovely antique and vintage jewelry. Each one has an exciting story behind it. Gerald," she called toward the back.

"Yes, Love," a kind voice called back.

"Would you grab the book with the details about the antique rings please," she replied. Meredith was busy surveying her choices. Anders noticed that her name tag said *Love*. That must really be her name.

"You have a unique name, if you don't mind me saying," he ventured.

"She gets it all the time," said a tanned-looking man in his fifties came from the back, dressed in a sharply pressed teal button-down shirt, with an ivory vest on top. Together they made a colourful couple. "My wife is a special woman." He grasped her hand and brought it to his lips, so he could kiss the back.

"Oh, stop it." Love blushed a little, batting her eyes at her husband. The saleswoman returned her attention to Meredith. "Have you found anything that catches your eye, sweetie?"

Anders thought the lilt of her voice was soothing, which was good. He could use a bit of soothing right at the moment.

Meredith had her eyes trained on one ring.

"May I?" she asked, and Love removed the velvet tray and placed it on the glass counter.

"Help yourself, dear." Love gestured. Meredith cautiously reached out for an Art Deco ring, in a platinum setting. She slid the ring on her finger. It was a perfect fit.

"In the centre is a bezel set, cushion cut diamond," Love explained. "The asymmetrical stones on either side are old rose cut diamonds, and the strings connecting them are made of platinum."

Meredith held her hand aloft to catch the light on the ring. It sparkled. Anders swallowed hard at the sight of how perfectly that ring suited Meredith's hand. Also, at how expensive it was bound to be.

"The tale of this ring," Gerald reported dramatically, after he flipped through their book of stories, "is that it was designed by a Russian artist. He gave it to his sweetheart just before World War II broke out. She wore it every day, even when she was forced to escape and travelled to North America. Her love went missing in action, but she kept that ring on her finger until her dying day in the hope that he would someday return."

Imagine, Anders thought to himself. Waiting until you were old and grey for your love to return. Could he see himself doing that if Meredith were to disappear? Would she wait for him? He wasn't sure the answer was yes to either question. But, could anyone ever be certain of such a thing? His mind travelled to Jane, wondering if she would have waited her lifetime for her husband Tom. *Would she wait for me?* The thought slipped into his mind. He erased it immediately.

They were all silently lost in the spell of the story for a moment. Then Meredith faced Anders.

"What do you think?" She looked up at him hopefully.

"I think it's beautiful." He swallowed hard again, the reality of the situation hitting him once more. "And, if that's the one you want, then I think we should get it."

"Really?" Meredith clapped.

"Yes," Anders said. The enthusiasm he felt when they arrived at the shop started to wane.

"Good choice, sir." Love shook his hand, and then Gerald shook it too.

"I'll ring you up." Gerald ushered Anders to the cash register while Love placed the box for the ring in a bag. Meredith kept the ring on.

Anders swiped his credit card and thought about the pros and cons of soft and chewy chocolate chip cookies versus crisp chocolate chip cookies. Crisp chocolate chip cookies were good for dipping and good for saving in case of emergencies. Soft cookies were warm, comforting, and the kind of cookie he wanted to come home to, though he supposed he would get used to the crisp cookies, eventually.

39

A few days later, Jane was summoned to the work site for a meeting with Anders.

"It's a surprise." Was all she could get out of him when she'd asked what it was about.

"Do I need to bring anything?" She enquired, hoping for more information.

"Just yourself," he said, sounding cheerful.

So, she'd grabbed her purse, and left Ellie with Valentina who had come over to teach her how to make her delicious tomato sauce recipe. Her mom was out on a lunch date with Ed, which, if she were being truthful, was pretty much a continuation of every date they ever went on. They were practically inseparable, and it was so nice to see her mom happy after seeing her lonely and sad since her father had passed. Jane wouldn't have been surprised if there would be a wedding in the future between those two. Both Jane and Ellie loved Ed, so it would be a good thing for everyone.

Jane pulled her van up in front of the dusty construction site. She saw Anders, Alec, Gretta the architect and a man she'd never met around a table under a pop-up shelter. Anders stood upon her exiting her vehicle, coming over to greet her. She felt a sad pang pass through her, but it was gone as quickly as it came.

"So glad you could make it." He beamed at her and shook her hand.

"Me too," she replied cautiously. "I hope, anyway. What's this meeting about?"

"You'll see." Anders chuckled gleefully to himself.

Alec nodded to her and had a look on his face that said he didn't have time for this out-of-the-blue meeting. It also said that he had no idea what it was about either.

"Hi, Gretta, nice to see you." Jane shook the woman's hand. Jane noticed there were a bunch of blueprints spread across the table, with rocks on the corners to keep them down in the breeze that blew the dry air in their direction.

"This is Simon Chan, a specialist architect dealing with accessible building projects," Anders said as he made the introduction.

"Hello, nice to meet you." Jane's slender hand was held aloft across the table a moment while Simon stood. He had a small struggle as he placed a crutch on his left forearm to do so. The man was just slightly taller than Jane, with a round face and bronzed complexion. His short greying black hair poked up in places where the wind caught it. His shining dark eyes disappeared in happy creases when he smiled.

"It's nice to meet you too." His hand was warm in hers. "I'm looking forward to consulting with you on these changes Anders has proposed."

"What changes?" Alec sounded exasperated.

"Yes, please, fill us in," Jane said, taking a seat.

"Well, after I took you and Ellie to her appointment at the hospital, I was inspired," Anders said, while excitedly pacing around the table. "I want to transform some of the spaces in the inn to make them extra special and, most importantly, accessible, for guests with physical challenges."

"We already have made plans to meet with the accessible requirements laid out by the building code, and changing things now is going to cost us time and money," Alec growled, voicing a protest.

For a moment, Anders was taken aback. Alec was to be working on floors, but clearly, he had been taking an interest in other areas of the build if he had this information at his fingertips. He made a mental note to talk to his brother about this later.

"I know but hear me out." Anders waved his hands to dismiss his brother's negativity. "I've consulted with Gretta and Simon and we've come up with a few minor adjustments to surpass the code and make the accessible spaces truly special for our guests. Jane, I'd like you to look at the plans and let me know what you think." He moved his hand in an all-encompassing motion over the blueprints.

"Well, if you insist, but I'm not sure I'm really the right person to ask." She hesitated a moment but moved around the table next to Simon when she saw him smiling at her. The plans were, elaborate, to say the least. Three of the guest rooms were to be upgraded with more accessible features. Rather than having just one accessible room as was required by code; they would surpass the code by adding many more useful accoutrements for those who require an extra hand. This room must have a low shower with a seat, and a sink where a wheelchair can fit underneath, and a taller toilet and special platform for the bed to make transfers easier; these rooms were to include high tech. Each room would have a transfer sling, and an accessible tub with a door. The beds would be on hydraulic lifts to make them adjustable to various heights.

She saw in the margins, a note made that there would be a Personal Support Worker on call should a guest need one. The blinds would be remote controlled, or voice controlled, and there would be Braille guidebooks of the area available in all the guest rooms.
She moved on to the plans for the garden and saw that there were changes noted for the materials used to build the pathways. Instead of gravel, which was the original material chosen, it was changed to be a special crushed stone suspended in resin, that would provide a smoother surface, one less prone to becoming

uneven. The paths were also to be wider and winding down the slope to the river to make the climb easier.

Then she saw a small blueprint for something called "Ellie's Kitchen."

"What's this?" she asked. She was feeling overwhelmed by all of this. It slowly dawning on her that Anders had been moved to make sure her daughter would be included, forever, at the inn was more than she had been prepared to take. She was sure when Ellie had requested what Anders had been calling "Ellie's Surprise" that the girl just wanted a safe place to hang out with her mother after school. Not a whole kitchen.

"It's a space just for Ellie, made for her, so she can bake her cookies and film her videos with Sally," Anders said. Jane noticed he became bashful when he spoke about this space. "It's a place where she will fit. Where she can bake and be safe. And we'll sell the baking, and maybe even make a cookbook out of her recipes, if Ellie thinks that sounds okay. The money can go toward saving up for her schooling, or, whatever she might need."

Anders managed to look up into Jane's eyes. He could see she was a mix of emotions. A careful look of delight was on her lips with something else he couldn't quite read in her eyes. He suddenly became very nervous and found himself rambling. "Her videos, they are becoming really popular, and, I just thought that, well, she would maybe like to interact with the guests, and, she could be with you more, and —" He paused awkwardly. "You hate it." His shoulders slumped.

"No. No." A tear escaped and ran down her cheek. "I love it. This is amazing. Not just for me, or Ellie, but for everyone who will be able to enjoy this place when the changes are made." Jane rushed around the table and grabbed Anders in a hug. "It's wonderful," she whispered in his ear. Her hot breath passed across his neck and a shiver ran down his spine, despite the heat of the day. He closed his eyes for a moment, only to open them and find Alec staring him down with a very unimpressed look.

Before the meeting could go any longer, the group turned when they heard a loud horn blasting. They found it to be Ed, driving his school bus, roaring in the driveway, with colourful beach towels flapping in the wind out of a window on either side. When it came to a stop, Valentina hopped out and shouted.

"Come on! We're going to the beach!"

40

When Jane spotted the bus, she turned her face, so Ellie wouldn't see her crying. She didn't want her daughter to know about the plans yet.

"Anders," she hissed to him. "Can we keep these plans just between us for now? I don't want to tell Ellie quite yet." Anders looked hurt and confused. "It's wonderful, truly. I just want to have some time to digest the information first." She placed a hand on his trying to hold in the tears. His face softened.

"Alright," he said.

"Hey, everybody," Valentina said, striding quickly across the parking area. "Don't you want to go to the beach? Ellie said you promised her you'd go before school starts and that is next week."

"You're right." Jane admitted. "I did promise. Alright, let's go."

"And you too," Valentina playfully scolded her husband and brother-in-law. "Let the workers go early. It will boost morale."

"Great idea," Anders said, riding high from the big reveal. Alec noisily cleared his throat in protest but was tut-tutted by his wife who kissed him sweetly on the side of the face and whispered something that was for only their ears.

"Alright, I'll tell the crew. Anders and I will meet you back at the house. Gotta grab our stuff." He strode off to tell the crew, who let out a collective yell of happiness in getting the afternoon off.

Jane collected her things and started toward her van. Gretta was on the phone headed off to another meeting. Simon followed behind, rolling up the plans. He called after Jane.

"Jane?" His voice was kind and inquisitive.

"Yes," she responded, her chestnut hair blowing across her face. She curled it behind her ear looking up at Simon.

"I was just wondering about the beach. Is it an accessible beach?" he asked, smiling, while packing the blueprints into a cylindrical case.

"Yes, it is. It's neat. They have a boardwalk down to the beach, and cement ramps out into the water so you can take a wheelchair right in, or you can rent a wheelchair that has special tires that will roll easily on the sand." She looked at him quizzically, waiting to see if he had any further questions.

"Wow," Simon said, excitedly. His eyes disappeared into the happy creases once again. "Would you mind if I tagged along? I'd love to see that, to check out the design and to maybe get to know Ellie a bit so I can learn about her before we start on the kitchen project."

"Oh," Jane said in surprise. "Yes, of course." She hesitated a bit.

"Don't worry, I won't mention the kitchen to her." Simon's face was sweet.

"Huh, you overheard," Jane said, narrowing her eyes a little at him.

"I did." He held up his hands. "I couldn't help but overhear."

"I see." Jane was embarrassed. "You understand, I mean. It's just so much."

"It's overwhelming, yes." Simon agreed.

Jane felt somehow reassured her hesitation was okay. That things would be fine. She considered him for a moment. He seemed like a caring and considerate man, and it would be good for Ellie to meet an adult who was successful while dealing with a physical challenge. She didn't have much opportunity for that around here.

"Well, why not join the caravan? We're headed back to Anders' house and then you can join us on the bus." She motioned for him to tag along, this time in a friendly way instead of just to be polite.

"Wonderful," Simon said and walked next to her toward the parking area.

* * * *

In Alec's truck, things were less friendly. They drove behind the bus and could see Ellie's enthusiastic hand waving around in the window of the bus. Anders' chuckled as he watched her.

"What the hell is going on?" Alec shot at Anders when they were about half way to the house.

"What?" Anders feigned innocence.

"Changing the plans, now? Are you insane?" he fumed at his brother; his voice much louder than usual.

"What?" Anders repeated. "You're one to talk. You're supposed to be looking after the floors. Clearly, you've been pushing yourself into other jobs on site since you know so much about what's happening."

"Well, since you wouldn't ask Dad if I could be the lead on the inn, I asked him myself," the blonde Brookstone brother shouted.

"So, what did Dad say?" Anders demanded. Alec was silent for a moment, clearly annoyed by having to reveal the conversation with his father.

"He said I wasn't qualified to be in charge," he admitted.

"I told you," Anders gloated.

"Yes, you were right." Alec stuck out his tongue.

"Mature." Anders balked.

"But Dad did say I could work on learning more things, so that is what I've been doing."

"Oh," countered, Anders sounding a bit calmer. "Well, I guess that is a pretty good idea."

They were silent for a few moments, then Anders jumped back into discussing the changes to the building plans he'd made. "I'm not insane, I'm brilliant. This is going to be a great business move."

"Or is it a great move to get Jane's attention?" Alec shot back.

"That has nothing to do with it," Anders said, incredulous.

"That has everything to do it." Alec laughed cruelly.

"Hey," Anders said, insulted. "It's not funny, or a ridiculous idea. Quit it."

"And even if it isn't to get Jane's attention," Alec continued.

"Which it isn't." Anders interjected.

"Where are we going to get the money to pay for it?" Alec continued ignoring Anders' protests. "We're already almost a million dollars short. These plans are going to add on at least another half million."

"Firstly," Anders began, then paused at the breadth of Alec's knowledge. "I've done some research. There are not many accessible places in the area, or even in the surrounding region for people with physical challenges to stay, never mind a nice place in which to holiday like the inn will be when it's finished. I checked out local attractions like the ski hill and the golf course. Did you know that the ski hill has four tracker and three tracker skiing?"

"What's that?" Alec asked, becoming curious with the speech Alec was delivering. Maybe this wasn't such a terrible idea?

"It's sit-skiing. They also do skiing using outriggers. They have a special program, equipment, and lessons available for physically challenged skiers. And, the golf course has disc golf, which is golf played with frisbees that can be played by anyone. So there. Also, Ellie's videos are super popular. The last time I checked she had almost five thousand subscribers online. Just think, the inn could sell her books, teach cooking classes. It would be great."

"Okay, but still, how are we going to pay for it?" Alec repeated sounding a more intrigued than before. Perhaps warming to the idea.

"I'm going to sell my condo," Anders said.

"You are?" Alec said, shaking his head. "Have you told Meredith you're going to sell your condo?"

"No, not yet," Anders said.

"Well, I'd think she might like to know. Where are you going to live when you get married?" Alec asked.

"I thought I'd stay here, in Millvale, stay at the house."

"Of course," Alec said. "So, you can be near Jane."

"No, not because of Jane, but because I like it here. It's a beautiful place."

"And Jane lives here," Alec said.

"Be quiet, will you? That's not why." Anders was exasperated.

"Well, what about Meredith's job? She's not just going to want to leave." Alec tried to reason with his brother. "There are a lot of funeral homes in the city where she can find a job, but here, not so much. There isn't even a funeral home in Millvale is there?"

"Well, no," Anders said. "But there's one in Bellfield, I think."   "You think," Alec scoffed. "You better find out before you ask her to uproot her career to come up here with you. Also, I have one more question. Even with selling your condo, we are still short. What are your plans to come up with the rest of the money? Because Valentina and I were talking and —"
Anders cut him off.

"I'm going to go to Dad, explain why we need these changes. I'm sure he will see how it's a good business decision." Anders nodded to himself.

"You're going to go to Dad, you haven't talked to Meredith, you're in denial about Jane," Alec listed his brother's faults. "You're an idiot."

"I'm making my own way, is what I'm doing." Anders shot at his brother. "Just like you did."

"If you think that's what I've been doing all these years, you're dreaming," Alec laughed bitterly.

They turned off the road into the driveway behind the bus. Tired of talking to one another. Alec parked the truck while Anders hopped out practically before it was fully stopped. There was Meredith's car in the driveway. Anders sighed when he saw it. Of course, she would be here today, a day earlier than he expected her.

"Look, don't say anything to Meredith," Anders whispered loudly through his teeth to Alec.

"I won't," he responded, not turning while mumbling "idiot," under his breath.

In the house the men packed up their swim suits and towels while they got Meredith to tag along. Jane and Simon joined the gang on the bus, Ellie and Fae having packed everything Jane needed before they left the house. Valentina had her suit on under her shorts and T-shirt. The odd group was ready for some fun in the sun.

41

The bus ride to the beach took about forty-five minutes. Jane looked out the window as trees and fields passed by. She swelled with an excited anticipation that she always felt when she went to the lake. Ever since she was little, she had loved the water. Today, even though she was feeling so mixed up inside with the news Anders had dropped on her about Ellie's kitchen, she still felt the call of the waves inside her heart. There was something about the water, something special.

Smiling to herself, Jane recalled one fun summer when her parents had rented a cabin on the water. They strapped on their life jackets the first night there and pushed the long red canoe away from the beach. Young Jane sat in the centre of the boat; the wooden strips pressed against the curve of her crossed legs. Her parents sat surrounding her, her father seated behind and mother in front. It turned out that neither one knew how to steer a canoe, which became a somewhat serious problem when they failed to navigate around a large rock in the rough water. The canoe tipped and they all spilled out in a pile of wet laughter. They swam back to shore with the canoe turned over above their heads.

"Hey, Mom." Jane tapped her mom on the shoulder. Fae turned around from the seat in front to face her daughter. "Remember that time with Dad when we were in the canoe?"

Fae laughed fondly, remembering.

"I had water in my ears for three days after that." She chuckled softly, the laughter sparkling in her green eyes. "Your father said his brain must have been the cleanest ever with the amount of water that went up his nose."

Ed laughed along with Fae and Jane from the driver's seat in front of her mother. Jane liked that he could appreciate a memory that didn't involve him and didn't ask her mother to erase a life she had before him.

Jane turned her face toward the window again, watching the deciduous trees slowly shift to conifers planted in straight lines along the road by loggers years ago. They were getting close to the beach. She smirked to herself remembering the second time she was in a canoe, this time, with Tom, when he took her camping. He knew how to steer the boat, from the rear. He taught her the "J" stroke and how to get back in if the canoe tipped. They paddled to an island off the shore and camped under the stars. Her heart hurt at the happy memory and how long ago that was. It seemed that she hadn't been to the lake since that day, which wasn't true, but she was having trouble remembering when that was. She looked at her watch pulling herself out of nostalgia. They'd be there in about twenty minutes.

Standing, Jane shifted herself to the seat nearest Ellie.

"Time for sunscreen," she said to her daughter who was busy playing a game of tic-tac-toe with Anders.

"Mom!" Ellie was unimpressed with her mother ruining her playing a game with an adult.

"Sorry," Jane said as she pulled the bottle from Ellie's beach bag. "It's gotta have time to soak in, you know that."

"Well, I can do it," Ellie insisted.

"Fine, fine," Jane said squirting a generous glob into Ellie's good hand. "I'll just make sure you get it all rubbed in." Jane proceeded to give herself a generous amount of lotion and began rubbing it on her legs, face, and arms.

"Hey, Mom." Ellie's face was white around the gills where she'd missed rubbing in the sunscreen.

"Yes." Jane absent mindedly rubbed it in for her daughter while Ellie attempted to squirm away.

"Who's the guy with the crutch?" she nodded toward Simon.

"Oh, that's Mr. Chan," Jane said, choosing not to reprimand her for her choice of identifier. She wouldn't have liked to be the "wheelchair girl" but she was a girl in a wheelchair, just as he was a guy with a crutch, so it wasn't technically wrong, but maybe not so polite. Something for them to discuss at a later point she supposed. "He's an architect working with Anders on the inn. He wanted to come check out the beach with us. He's interested in how to make places accessible."

"Oh." Ellie waved. "Hi, Mr. Chan," she yelled. He turned and waved back.

"Hello." Simon waved. "You must be Ellie, it's nice to meet you. And, you can call me Simon if your mom says it's okay."

"Nice to meet you too," she said. Then to her mother, "Well, can I?" Jane grinned at her daughter and her enthusiasm and lack of shyness.

"Yes, that's fine." Jane nodded to Simon. He raised one eyebrow, a gesture she took to mean their secret was safe.

* * * *

They arrived at the beach and unloaded from the bus. Ellie chose to use her walker as they were close to the walkway down to the water and she could take it right into the lake without fear of it being wet. She was in the lead of the group while everyone else grabbed bags and coolers, umbrellas and towels. They found a spot at the base of a dune, so the sun cast a bit of a shadow and they could keep from burning.

Jane popped into a changing area to put on her suit. Her tall figure emerged, wrapped in an emerald green one piece that brought out her eyes and figure. Her long legs were freckled and lovely, her chestnut hair hanging free around her shoulders. On top of her head was a wide-brimmed hat.

She noticed Anders staring as she approached. Meredith noticed too. She saw the scowl on her face. Meredith followed the gaze of her fiancé's eyes, landing on her. Then her small mouth pursed in an ugly way. Meredith's pale body was swathed in a flowing linen cover-up and she also wore a large-brimmed hat. Jane noted, too, that Simon was watching her walk across the sand. He waved to her. Jane waved back, pointedly avoiding Anders' gaze.

"Jane," Meredith said, her mouth drawing into a lizard-like pose as she spoke. Her bony pale hand rested on Anders who tore his eyes reluctantly away from Jane's frame. "We've been meaning to ask you something important, haven't we dear?" She squeezed Anders' thigh.

"We have?" he asked, confused.

"Of course." Meredith's lips pulled tighter. "About the menu."

"The menu," Anders said, still confused.

"For our wedding, silly," Meredith said, squeezing his leg harder. "He's such a scatterbrain." She laughed.

"Of course," he replied, looking down, shamefacedly.

"The menu?" Jane was somewhat unsure what was happening.

"Right, yes," Meredith continued, "We want you to do the food for our wedding."

"Oh." Jane was surprised.

"The food you made at Anders' was delicious," Meredith complimented Jane. It actually seemed genuine. "And we both wanted to have you cater our wedding. We think you'd be great."

Jane looked from Meredith to Anders who was looking down toward the sand.

"Of course, I'd be happy to cater your wedding," Jane said.

"Wonderful." Meredith beamed. "Isn't it wonderful?" She embraced Anders' leg again.

"Yes." He looked up from the sand.

"We can make an appointment to discuss details sometime next week," Jane said. Wanting to get away from this conversation, she looked around to see where she could go to escape. She saw Simon standing in the shade of the dune at the edge of the action.

"Sounds great," Meredith said.

"Good," Jane replied. "If you'd excuse me," said, nodding to them both, even though she wanted to kick sand at them. Catering Anders wedding to Meredith was the last thing she wanted to do. It would be good experience however, and he was helping her get going at the inn. She would consider it payback. Yeah, that would make it easier.

"Hey," she said to Simon. "You okay over here?" She walked across the sand to stand in the shade.

"Yes, sure," he said, his grin hiding his eyes. He had rolled up the sleeves of his dress shirt, but he still wore long pants.

"You're sweating," she noted, while looking out toward the water, watching Ellie play catch with Alec, Valentina, and Ed. Ed was currently retrieving a ball Ellie failed to catch.

"I am." Simon laughed.

"There are some shops along the boardwalk, if you want, I can show you. They probably have some swim shorts," Jane said, lifting her hand to block the sun from her eyes a bit.

"Okay, that sounds like a good idea actually," Simon said, and turning to go to the path she raised her brows as she saw his shirt was plastered to his slim body, showing the muscles in his back.

They walked through the parking lot to the path on the other side. It led away from the beach to a colourful strip filled with shops where teenage boys played arcade games and teenage girls hung around sipping icy drinks in their bikinis. Large inflatable whales, swans, alligators, and bananas hung from strings dangling from striped awnings. The smell of fries wafted toward them.

"Yum," Jane said.

"Yes, I was just thinking the same thing," Simon said. "Come on, my treat." He motioned toward the chip truck parked under a tree. Her stomach growled. She laughed.

"Okay, yes," she said. They went to the truck. She ordered large fries, dousing the food with salt and vinegar when the sizzling fries in a cardboard box were placed in front of her. She put a puddle of ketchup in one corner and grabbed a wooden two-pronged fork. She took a bite.

"Mm, delicious." She closed her eyes to savour the hot potato. Simon watched her, even though she didn't realize. He liked how unhindered she was in her enjoyment.
Simon had ordered half fries, half onion rings. "Oh, onion rings," Jane said, "I'm jealous."

"Have one." Simon gestured as they sat at a picnic table in the sun.

"I couldn't," she said, looking like she just could.

"Sure, you can," he replied, encouraging her.

"Well, okay." She took one, taking a bite of the crisp batter. The onion inside slid out and slapped her in the chin. Simon laughed. "Delicious," she declared laughing. She wiped her chin. What was coming over her? It must have been the lake breeze. She Suddenly felt free and fun, despite everything that should be on her mind, including the now impending wedding menu. They ate for a bit in silence, watching kids on skateboards and scooters zooming past.

"So, the plans for the inn are coming along it seems?" Simon ventured, breaking the quiet.

"Yes, they are," Jane said, stabbing a couple crisp fries with her fork and depositing them into her mouth. She was feeling somewhat giddy at sitting in the sun, enjoying this treat, while someone else watched her daughter. Maybe that was it? Maybe she was just enjoying a blissful, guilt free, non-mom moment. "It's starting to seem really real; you know." She poked another fry and dunked it in the ketchup puddle. "When the café closed, I really didn't know what was going to happen, but I think the inn is going to work. I really do. I'm excited. And nervous."

"I hear you are a great cook." Simon popped an onion ring into his mouth and chewed, waiting for her response.

"You know what, I am. I am a good cook." Jane had a sudden flood of pride. It must be the water. She was feeling like the best version of herself in that moment.

"I look forward to eating at your new restaurant and seeing just how talented you are," Simon commented, sounding very friendly. Very friendly indeed.

"Oh, I'd like that." Jane replied as she felt the blush creeping up her neck, which was more exposed than usual because of her bathing suit.

She blushed even deeper because she had nothing to hide behind.

They finished their fries and continued down the boardwalk, stopping at a shop advertising swimwear. Simon tried on a pair of funky swim trunks in a deep blue with a pineapple pattern. He came out of the change room wearing them to model them for her. She saw that the reason he had a crutch and a limp was because he had a prosthesis on his right leg. But she also saw he was in good shape, sporting a toned stomach and shaped arms. He had a tattoo adorning his left bicep. "All That You Can Be" was written in black script. It complimented his muscles.

He bought the suit and a large red beach towel and some sandals. He placed his work clothes in the shopping bag. They walked back to the beach.

"I hope you don't mind my asking," Jane ventured. "Do you find it difficult to navigate work sites with your leg?" She felt her heart flutter as she asked this personal question.

"Yes and no." He answered, clearly not minding her wanting to know. "It depends on the location now. I can mostly get along anywhere but obviously if there is debris around it is more difficult. When I first was learning to use the prosthesis however, it was hard." He smiled at her; a smile that was becoming familiar. Warm and inviting. "Jane." He stopped walking. She stopped too and faced him. "I was wondering if I could take you out to dinner next week, maybe Wednesday evening?"

She flushed at the surprise invitation. "Oh, well," she responded, flustered. For a moment her heart turning to Anders. Anders, whose wedding she would be catering in mere months. Anders, tall and handsome, kind and caring, the man who created a kitchen space just for her daughter. Anders who kissed her when he was already engaged. "Yes, that sounds lovely." She was done wasting time with Anders. She deserved to find happiness and Simon seemed like a nice man. Why not start her search here?

They returned to the beach and the group having made plans for the following week. He would pick her up at six thirty, they'd go for dinner, and see where the evening took them. Ellie was in the water with Fae and Ed, splashing around.

"Do you mind if I join you?" Simon called out to the people in the lake.

"Not at all," Fae called back.

Simon laid out his towel, then removed his prosthesis, placing it carefully on top to keep it out of the sand. Navigating the beach with his leg and crutch, he headed into the water. Jane noticed Ellie watched the process intently. Presently her daughter sat on the seat of her walker, colourful water wings bobbing up and down with the movements of the gentle waves.

Simon dove in, holding onto his crutch. When he surfaced he floated on his back. "Hi," he said to Ellie, and nodding to the rest of the group.

"Awesome, you can swim holding onto your crutch." Ellie was impressed.

"Yep," Simon said.

"Why do you only have one and a half legs?" Ellie said expressing interest in Simon's leg that was amputated below the knee.

"I had cancer and the doctors thought it would be best if they removed the bottom part of my leg," he said, in a matter of fact tone, undisturbed by Jane's daughter asking such a direct question.

"You're helping build the inn?" Ellie questioned him more, splashing a bit in a wave with a small white cap.

"I am," Simon responded. "I'm an architect. I design spaces so they are easier to use for people like you and me."

"Neat." Ellie was impressed. She looked him over a bit, considering her next question carefully. Simon waited patiently knowing the line of questioning wasn't finished. "Do you have cancer anymore?" She wanted to know, suddenly shy.

"No, I'm healthy now," he said.

"That's good." There was a short lull as some larger waves rocked them back and forth. Then, "Do you want to hear a joke?"

From the shade of the sand dune, Jane watched Simon and Ellie interact. Then there was uproarious laughter floating along the breeze toward her. Seemed like it was going well.

42

Outside, a late summer storm rumbled through Millvale. The night sky lit up with sheet lightning and rain poured heavily on the roof of Jane's house.

"Yikes," Iris said when a large boom of thunder rattled the windows of the house. "Isn't Ellie going to wake up?" She plonked a plate of cheddar and thyme shortbread cookies down on the table, a new recipe they were trying out for the restaurant, something savoury to have with soup or as an afternoon snack offering.

They had nearly used up all the money Anders had provided for test recipes. It was down to the nitty gritty of decision-making time. They had developed an arsenal of dishes and tasty treats to draw from and the women were getting excited about getting to try them out with customers. Next, she poured two large glasses of white wine, something oaky to compliment the cheddar.

"No, she's sleeping like a rock, especially after her day at the beach yesterday."

"Did you have fun?" Iris chomped into a biscuit. "Mm." And then, "you look ridiculous." she said, spraying a few crumbs across the table.

"Nice," Jane said, raising an eyebrow.

"Sorry." Iris hopped up again grabbing a serviette. "Your hair looks wild."

"So, does yours," Jane replied. They decided to switch hairstyles for the night. They straightened Iris' normally bouncy curls and presently Jane's straight hair was piled on top of her head with curlers clinging on for dear life. "How much longer do I have to keep these things in?" Jane carefully stuck a long finger between curlers and scratched.

"I have no idea." Iris laughed. Of course, she didn't, she never used curlers. Jane snagged a cookie from the plate.

"Mm," she echoed Iris. Then with a sip of wine. "Mm. Mm. Maybe we should serve these at Anders and Meredith's wedding?" She finished, a rueful look her face. She rolled her eyes.

"What?" Iris stopped with a cookie midway to her mouth.

"Oh yeah, we're catering their wedding. Meredith asked me yesterday."

"What did Anders say?"

"Not much."

"Figures." Iris drank a gulp of wine.

"We are meeting with them this week, I'll let you know when." She chomped down on another cookie. Iris nodded. "So, I have a date on Wednesday."

Iris choked on her wine. "You do? Who with?"

"I met someone. His name is Simon. He asked me when we were at the beach yesterday." Jane grinned.

"So, you did have a good time," Iris pestered.

"I did." Jane laughed.

"But what about Anders?" Iris ate her third cookie, then rising she went to the counter and sliced up some figs returning with a plate.

"Yes." Jane grabbed a slice of fig placing it atop the cookie. She took a bite and declared it delicious. "These cookies with a bacon fig jam, what do you think?"

"I'm writing it down." Iris grabbed a piece of paper to make note of the recipe alteration.

"What about Anders? He's getting married, we're catering the wedding. It's over." Jane took another bite, closed her eyes, savoured, then a sip of wine before she continued. "But I didn't tell you, he's building a kitchen for Ellie."

"He's what?" Iris stopped chewing.

"He's building her an accessible kitchen, so she can bake her cookies, make those videos with Sally. He thinks we should sell her cookies at the restaurant and even sell her recipes in cookbooks."

"That's actually a great idea," Iris said.

"I know, I can't believe he's doing this for her." Jane sipped from her glass again.

"He's doing this for you, you mean." Iris wiggled her eyebrows at Jane. "No, no he's doing it for Ellie. He was inspired by our trip to the hospital, or so he says," Jane waved her hands around, starting to loosen a little from the alcohol. "He's even having some of the guest rooms converted to make them the ultimate accessible getaway. That's where Simon comes in." Jane took a bigger sip from her glass.

"Simon." Iris popped a slice of fig in her mouth.

"The architect, he specializes in accessible building, and is my date for Wednesday night,"

"Oh." Iris wiggled her eyebrows again. The ladies laughed. "I'm serious though, Jane, Anders, he's making this kitchen for Ellie, sure, but also for you. He wants you to notice. He wants to be with you."

"Well I noticed him, and now I'll notice him as he walks down the aisle. I'm done, we're done. Work friends, colleagues. That's it, that's all." Jane swayed a little as she finished her glass. "This was a large glass of wine, I'm getting drunk."

"And so, you should, you're celebrating." Iris drained her glass. "And I'm complaining, because José and I broke up."

"Oh no." Jane swayed herself off her chair toward the counter where she grabbed the bottle of wine to refill their glasses. "What happened?" She gave her friend a hug around the shoulders while she poured with the other hand.

"It just didn't work. He wasn't funny, or really that nice even." Iris crunched a cookie sadly.

"I'm sorry." Jane hugged her friend with both arms after she put the bottle down.

"There's someone out there for you, don't lose hope."

"I won't." Iris feigned enthusiasm. "Hey, to totally change the subject, do you think we should ask Valentina to work with us at the restaurant when it opens?"

"Yes," Jane said, excited about the idea. "She's a great cook, plus, I like her."

"Me too, even though she's Anders' sister-in-law." Iris ribbed Jane.

"But that's not her fault." Jane finished her second glass of wine.

"How about you slow down a little." Iris' eyes widened as she watched her friend get increasingly tipsy.

"Okay." Jane smiled a wobbly smile that slid off her face a little.

"Yikes, alright," Iris said, jumping up, only a bit tipsy herself. "I'm going to take those curlers out now."

"Yippee." Jane laughed.

"Okay," Iris replied, focusing. She carefully unwound each one. Jane sighed as her scalp felt the freedom of release. "Oh boy,"

"What?" Jane picked up the hand mirror that sat on the table. She looked at herself.

"Uh, oh no." She commented, somewhat

in despair. The end result was less ringlets or sexy beach hair and more poodle.

"Maybe if we comb it out a bit?" Iris offered, running her fingers through her friend's hair. "Nope." All that did was make it puffy.

"Well, I won't be doing my hair like this for my date with Simon." Jane started giggling and couldn't stop.

"No, I should hope not." Iris laughed too. Then she ate another cookie.

43

On Monday morning Anders went to his desk. There was a stack of new acquisitions to sort through. Next, he checked his email. The first one in his inbox was a message from Simon.

I'll be in Millvale on Wednesday to take Jane to dinner if you want to discuss any plans on the inn. Let me know.
Simon
Simon is taking Jane on a date.

His heart sank. He couldn't take her out on a date. No. It wasn't possible. Jane wouldn't be interested in him, couldn't be. Of course not. Why would she be interested in a handsome successful guy like Simon?

Jane was interested in him, Anders. He was convinced. That kiss they shared. He thought about that kiss all the time. Surely Jane wouldn't have forgotten that kiss? Well, even if she did, it didn't matter. He was marrying Meredith. They'd picked out her ring, they were talking about having the wedding at the inn once it was ready. And now Jane would be catering the event, so at least the food would be great. And she would be there, so he could see her one last time. Or maybe he'd see her a lot, since they were technically business partners until he could recoup his investment. And he and Meredith were going to live in Millvale. If he ever worked up the nerve to tell her he was selling his place in the city. No. Jane Michaels no longer mattered to his world. His world was Meredith and Brookstone Holdings. He was a Brookstone and was going to start acting like one.

He set off to work clearing the files from his desk by distributing them among the junior clerks in the office. Next, he crunched the numbers for the rest of the renovation on the inn. Even with the money from his father and the sale of his condo, the build was majorly in the hole. That was even before he decided to make the changes and hire Simon. He supposed he could get a loan, but he wasn't sure that was the right way to proceed.

He held his head trying to think of how to fix this problem. Alec had said he was doing all of this for Jane. So, what if he was? She was a nice lady, with a nice kid. Didn't they deserve someone to help them out? Besides, the changes were a good idea. He knew it. He had the data to back himself up.

He was struck by an idea. He quickly typed up a new report with all the data he'd collected to support his desire to make changes to the project. He called down to his father's office. His secretary said Mr. Brookstone was free right now. Anders put on his blazer, straightened his tie, and marched himself down the hallway, determined to make a presentation to him to get more capital to finish the build. That, as well as he was determined not to sit in one of those damned low chairs.

He knocked. "Hi, Dad, do you have a moment?" He tried to sound confident as he cautiously poked his head through the doorway.

"Hello, son." His father waved him in and then toward the chairs.

"I think I'll stand if that's alright." Anders side stepped around the chairs.

"Suit yourself." Blair poured himself a steaming cup of coffee from the always filled carafe on his desk. "How's my daughter-in-law to be?" he inquired, bringing the scalding hot liquid to his lips and taking a sip. That move alone was enough to make Anders want to run away back to the safety of his warm, non-chrome, office.

"She's great," Anders replied, physically feeling the hot liquid burning his esophagus as he watched his father drink.

"Wonderful." Blair's grin widened. He seemed genuinely happy for them. Perhaps that boded well for this impending conversation. Feeling somewhat buoyed, Anders pressed on.

"Dad, I actually came here to discuss something else with you." Anders tried to stand tall under his father's stony gaze.

"Alright, what is it?" Blair gulped again from the steaming cup.

"Here." He passed him the report. As his father took several moments to read it Anders willed himself to stand still, stand tall, and not to sweat through his jacket.

"No." Blair passed the report back.

"But, just hear me out," Anders begged.

"I already gave you two million dollars, my building crew, and Alec. If you chose to waste those resources, I'm sorry, but there is nothing more I, nor Brookstone Holdings can do for you." Blair poured another coffee.

"Dad, could you stop drinking coffee for a second and listen." Anders started pacing behind the chrome chairs.

"No, it's a waste of money, Anders. It doesn't make sense to pour more resources in for only a few customers." Another scalding gulp slid down into the man's gullet.

"It doesn't make sense to offer comfort and luxury to the people who might need it the most?" Anders paced faster. "You're unbelievable, you know that? You have everything, and you can't see how some people could use more?"

His granite-jawed father considered him for a moment, took another drink and then spoke.

"What's this really about, Anders?" He stared him down with steely eyes.

"It's about providing resources for people who need them, it's about creating something beautiful and useful, and it's about creative freedom." He blew the last part out of his system, sounding about five years old.

"No, it's about that good-looking cook woman and her wheelchair-bound daughter, isn't that right?" Blair folded his hands on his desk. Anders was deflated. He flopped into the closest chair, feeling his knees up by his eyes. He deserved this. Still, he tried to fight.

"Jane and Ellie have nothing to do with this," he protested.

"They have everything to do with it. Since the moment you met them, I've seen you drifting out of your office, out of this business, and northward to that God-forsaken small nothing town of Millvale." Blair stood and came around his desk, perching himself on the edge. He crossed his long legs at the ankle, his stone-grey slacks falling perfectly with nary a crease. "I've seen the way you look at her, the way she looks at you. And the little girl, she adores you, and you clearly adore her back. Look, son, you might be right, this report has some interesting data, and perhaps Brookstone Holdings can look for another project in the future where we can build a special space for those who need it. However, the inn in Millvale is not that space. It's not the time. I gave you the freedom to work on this project because I thought you'd proved yourself, like Alec has."

Anders held his head, disbelief running through his veins. "Like Alec has, really?" He shook his head trying to get his bearings. "You and Mom have been beside yourselves every time he takes off, leaving me to pick up the pieces. I'm the reliable one, the son you depend on. Not Alec," he scoffed.

"You are the reliable one, Anders, but you also don't show any initiative. Alec has always been one to forge his own way in the world and I admire that. Look how he went out into the world and found that lovely wife of his. Valentina is a delight. She's smart, charming, funny, talented, beautiful. And Alec has been taking the time to learn more while on the construction site. He has the drive to change, grow, to be more than he was yesterday. When you approached me with the idea to save this property, I thought I saw a glimmer of promise in you. But now I see you are just the same." Anders moaned and held his head. "Now mind you, if you don't get your act together on this project and bring it in on budget, then I'm sorry, but I just can't see that you belong here at Brookstone Holdings anymore."

"You would fire your own son?" Anders' moan turned into a groan.

"I would." Blair patted his son on the head, the ultimate condescending blow. "It would be for your own good."

Anders rose, his feet leaden as he reached the door.

"Son," Blair called him back. Anders turned with a sigh. "About that cook woman and her daughter...."

"What about them?" Anders rolled his eyes like a teen who had just been grounded for staying out too late.

"If you're in love with her, in love with her daughter, then you should end it with Meredith." Blair pointed a serious nod at his son.

"But I thought you wanted me to have a wife like Meredith?" Anders questioned.

"I want you to be happy, Anders." He nodded again, agreeing with his own ideas. "Successful too, but mostly happy." The man laughed. "You can go now." He dismissed his son, who walked like a robot back to his own office.

Anders sat at his desk in disbelief. His father had said no, had told him he was with the wrong woman, and told him he would be fired if he didn't get his act together. He didn't know what he was going to do to fix all the problems he currently found himself smothering under. To top it all off, Jane had a date with Simon this week. What if he was too late to fix things with her? No, he'd chosen Meredith, made a promise to her. He was going to follow through, his heart be damned.

Now, what to do about the inn? Since Alec was such a wunderkind, perhaps he would know what to do?

44

On Wednesday the Michael's household was filled with excitement. Jane was in the bathroom doing her hair while Ellie rummaged through her mother's closet. Fae sat in the living room flipping through a magazine trying to stay calm.

"You should wear this dress," Ellie said pulling down a floaty mauve number. Jane popped her head out the bathroom door to see which one her daughter had chosen.

"Don't you think it's too fancy?" Jane worried at her hair, trying to place a barrette above her right ear.

"It's perfect," Ellie said as she swooshed it back and forth through the air in front of her.

"Take a sweater," Fae called from the couch.

"Which earrings do you think, sweetie?" Jane applied some shimmery gold eye shadow, then some dark brown mascara and a neutral but glistening lipstick.

"I don't know why I'm fussing so much. He asked me out when I wasn't wearing any makeup at all, and I was in my bathing suit," she whispered to herself while attempting to keep her lipstick holding hand steady.

"These ones." Ellie held a pair of dangling silver earrings that held a delicate clear crystal at the end. "And this bracelet," she paired it with a silver bangle with an Irish saying on it: *May joy and peace surround you, contentment latch your door, and happiness be with you now and bless you evermore!*

"Why not?" She could use as much good luck as possible tonight.

"It's supposed to be chilly, take a sweater," Fae offered again from the living room. Jane hopped across the hall in her slip. "Oh, yes, I like these earrings. Good choice." She gave Ellie an embrace.

"Do you think you're going to marry Simon, Mom?" Ellie asked, running the smooth fabric of the dress through her fingers. "Oh goodness, I don't know sweetie." Jane felt flushed.

"I like him," Ellie said.

"I like him too. That's why I agreed to go on a date and see if we still like each other when we get the chance to talk more." She slid the earrings into her lobes and the dress over her head. Ellie zipped up the back.

"Plus, his prosthetic leg is really fascinating." Ellie held the bracelet in her hand. Jane slid it on.

"It is," Jane agreed.

"He's here!" Fae announced.

"Oh boy." Jane looked at herself in the mirror. "What do you think?"

"You look really pretty, Mom," Ellie said.

"Thanks for your help." Jane cuddled her daughter again, this time tighter than before, hoping to transfer some of that nervous energy somewhere out of her body.

"You need shoes, Mom," Ellie said, squirming out of the hug.

"Oh, which ones?" Jane felt rushed.

"Don't forget your sweater," Fae yelled once more.

"Okay, Mom," Jane said, exasperated. One thing at a time.

"Wear the flat ones. You might go for a walk," Ellie suggested.

"Good point." Jane slid some white ballet flats on her feet, then grabbed her white cardigan.

"Got my sweater." She waved it at her mother as she entered the living room.

"Oh, honey, you look so lovely." Fae folded her hands in front of her. The ladies all stood awkwardly, not sure what they should be doing when Simon reached the door.

"Alright." Jane let out a long held in breath. "You don't stay up too late; you have school in the morning. And get your grandmother to fill out any papers you brought home today, okay?"

It was only the second day back to school. Jane must have been out of her mind to agree to a date this week. Plus, she had the menu tasting with Anders and Meredith looming. It might turn out to be too much.

"Okay, Mom, don't worry. Just have fun." Ellie shooed her mother away.

"Yes, don't worry about anything here," Fae reassured her. The doorbell rang. They jumped. Jane smoothed her hair and dress and answered the door.

"Hi." She blushed. Simon held some sunflowers.

"These are for you," he said as he handed over the bouquet.

"Oh, thank you, sunflowers are one of my favourites." She passed the bouquet to her mother who took them to the kitchen to place them in water.

"And, I have a little something for Ellie and your mother as well." Jane gestured for him to come in. "Hi, Ellie, Fae." He nodded to each of them.

"Hi." Ellie grinned. Fae waved from the kitchen.

"I brought you this box of chocolates to share with your grandma." Simon handed the box to Ellie. Her eyes lit up.

"Oh, thanks," she said excitedly.

"Thank you," Fae said as she trimmed the stems on the flowers.

"Don't eat too many of those," Jane scolded.

"I won't," Ellie said as she put one in her mouth, closing her eyes to savour it.

"Alright, don't worry about a thing." Fae shooed them out the door. "Have fun now," she said shutting the door behind them.

* * * *

They walked out to Simon's car, a sensible sedan in a dark red colour. Comfortable seats for driving around to job sites, Jane assumed.

"Thank you," Jane said, trying not to feel awkward as Simon held the door for her. Once they were settled, he turned to her with a considering glance.

"You look lovely," he commented, his eyes were warm on her.

"Thank you, so do you," she replied. He was dressed in a pale straw linen jacket, grey slacks and a blue and white checked shirt.

"I hope you like Italian food. I made a reservation at a restaurant in Bellfield called L'Oviva Salata."

"Oh, they have delicious food," Jane enthused. "Great." Simon backed out of the driveway and off they went.

"There wasn't much selection in Millvale. In fact, I couldn't find any place to eat at all." He kept his eyes on the road.

"My café, Cutie Pies, was pretty much the only place to eat in town. After it closed to build the inn, the only other places to eat are in Bellfield." Jane gazed at his profile as she spoke.

He had a nice smooth jawline, with a little bit of black stubble shading in the curves.

"How long did you run the café?" He made a left onto a country road with a large bend that took them around a big pond. Some swans swam in the centre, the adults and babies nearly the same size now.

"Eight years. I opened it after my husband passed." She admired the ring of bulrushes around the pond, counted a few butterflies and redwing blackbirds punctuating the brown and green haze with colour. "I needed help with Ellie when she was little, so I moved back home. Mom and I ran the café until the flood. I thought I'd be totally out of a job but then Anders proposed renovating the old building to build the inn, and I ended up with my own restaurant."

"Funny how things work out," Simon offered. "I'm sorry to hear about your husband."

"Thank you," Jane said sadly. "Tom was wonderful. I loved him very much."

"I can tell." Simon turned again, and they entered the town of Bellfield. They rode the rest of the way in silence. Jane was lost in her memories of life just after Tom passed. Simon left her to it.

He parked out front of the restaurant and then opened Jane's door. He ushered her through the doors where they told the hostess of their reservation. Seated at a table in the window they people watched for a few moments. A young couple walked a fluffy white dog to the corner, crossing the street and then turning behind the bank where Jane knew there was a nice walking path through the park.

"Would you like a glass of wine?" Simon suggested.

"Yes, please, maybe something red."

"That sounds good to me too." Simon ordered them each a glass of merlot, something mellow that the waitress promised they would both enjoy. When their glasses arrived, they clinked a toast. "To trying something new," Simon said.

"Yes," Jane agreed. She took a sip. It was delicious wine that filled her mouth with full flavour of ripe red fruits. "So, can you tell it's been awhile since I've been on a date?" She felt herself begin to blush again.

"Not at all," he said kindly, making her relax a little. "I just thought that you seemed like the kind of woman who put her family first, and Ellie is so great, why wouldn't you?"

"Thank you for saying that." Jane grabbed a piece of a warm loaf of bread the waitress had just deposited on the table. She absentmindedly ripped off a piece and buttered it. She placed it on her tongue, realizing she was famished.

"Well, it's true. Your daughter is friendly, funny, inquisitive, and obviously very happy. You're doing a great job." Simon mirrored Jane's actions with his own piece of bread. "Yum, this bread is delicious."

"Thank you." Jane took another bite of bread. "It has been challenging but wonderful too."

"I bet," Simon said warmly.

The waitress returned and took their order. Ossobuco for Simon, lemon risotto with scallops and shrimp for Jane. She switched to white wine and Simon switched to water since he was driving.

"Tell me more about you," Jane said between delicious bites of scallops.

"Well, I was in the army until I was diagnosed with cancer." He chewed a morsel of veal, clearly enjoying the savoury flavour. Jane liked how much he liked food. "Then my career was cut short, literally." He laughed as he gestured to his leg.

Dark sense of humour, Jane thought. But if he could make light of such a serious turn in his life, why not? Jane chuckled at his joke.

"I went to school to become an architect and have been lucky. I've been able to use my experiences to make other people's lives better."

"And the cancer?" Jane asked then quickly covering her mouth. "I'm sorry. That was too forward." She lowered her eyes.

"Not at all," Simon replied. "I've been in remission for ten years."

"That's wonderful," Jane responded, feeling somewhat relieved. The thought of falling for someone who might die soon was way more than she was prepared to take on. They toasted to his remission.

The dinner went on pleasantly. Jane found she began to have warm feelings about Simon, which could partly be attributed to the wine, but also to the company. He was kind, funny, smart, handsome. Everything she could want in a date or possible partner. She wasn't thinking about Anders at all.

"I was over at the inn today," Simon said as they finished a shared plate of tiramisu with a side of cannoli. "It's coming along nicely. Won't be long until you'll be up and running."

"Yes, looks like just a couple months now." Jane took a large sip from her wine glass, polishing it off. "Woo, it's starting to make me nervous."

"You'll be great, I'm sure." Simon reached across the table to take her hand. She let him. "And Ellie's kitchen is going to be just fine too."

"Do you think so?" Jane wondered aloud. "I hope so."

"Is something bothering you about the kitchen?" Simon's brow furrowed.

"It's just—" Jane took a deep breath tears filling her eyes.

"Oh, hey." Simon stood coming to sit next to her on the bench seat of the booth. He put his arm around her and pulled her into a hug. "What's wrong?"

"It's all so generous, you know? I mean, the Brookstones are all so lovely and they have helped Ellie and me out so much, it's overwhelming, to suddenly have help when I've been pretty much on my own. And I'm afraid of what giving a gift like that will do to Ellie. I don't want to force her to become a cook if that's not what she wants. She's too young to be pigeonholed, when she is already pigeonholed so much already in her life." She took a deep breath, tears falling down her face. "Oh, my makeup." She felt suddenly worried her mascara would run since she wasn't used to wearing it in the first place.

"You look beautiful." Simon stroked a tear from her cheek.

"I look tired," Jane said through tears.

"You look like a woman who loves her daughter and has worked hard to defend her in this tough life." Simon held her cheek.

"Thank you," Jane said, laughing a little.

"The kitchen for Ellie, is not a reason to pigeonhole her, so don't worry. I think she's going to love it, and if she grows out of it, you can still use it for prep space or to teach classes. It's multipurpose. Until then, let your creative and brave daughter express herself and maybe make some money on the side. Anders was telling me all about how delicious her cookie concoctions are and that you might sell her recipes as a cookbook and sell her cookies at the restaurant."

"Yes, that's the plan," Jane said, looking worried.

"It's a great plan." Simon wiped away another tear. "And after meeting your daughter, I can't imagine her being anything but enthusiastic to get to have a space to do as much as she can with her creative ideas."

Jane offered, feeling comforted and much less like a terrible mother.

"Thank you," she whispered, looking up at him, his arm nice around her shoulders.

"You're welcome." He gazed into her eyes. Leaned in, planted a soft kiss on her mouth.

She kissed him back, mostly because she was out of practice.

"Simon," she said from pink lips when she pulled away.

"There's someone else, isn't there?" he said with a strong amount of certainty that surprised her.

"Yes, but—" She was confused as to how he could know.

"Anders talked a lot about you when I was drawing up the plans for the changes. It was sort of obvious," he said carefully to her. "It's okay."

"Thank you for the lovely dinner and date anyway." Jane gave him a disappointed look. "I really wanted to like you more than him, please believe me." She gazed down at her empty dessert plate.

"I do." He hugged her again. "Sometimes we can't help who we fall for." He gave her a knowing look.

"Oh, how I wish we could." Jane laughed bitterly.

"Friends?" Simon offered his hand.

"Friends." Jane and he shook on it.

* * * *

Simon returned her home as the late summer sun set. They hugged under the porch light and said goodnight. Jane had had a lovely time. This was a good start for getting back into the dating scene.

"How was it?" Fae asked. She was sitting in an easy chair reading a book.

"It was nice, but not going anywhere." Jane flopped down on the couch kicking off her shoes.

"Oh, I'm sorry it didn't work out." Fae patted her daughter's hand.

"I'm not. At least I got out there," Jane said proudly.

"Absolutely," Fae enthused. "You deserve to be happy, dear. You just have to let it happen."

"Yes," Jane agreed. "I do deserve to be happy and I will find love. I just have to wait for all this Anders business to pass and maybe it'll be easier." She exhaled.

"Yes, maybe?" Fae said in sympathy.

"And, I have a new friend in Simon." Jane punched her fist in the air to celebrate friendship.

"Good," Fae said, then followed suit.

The women stayed in the quiet for a while until Fae got up to make tea sometime later. Jane changed out of her fancy clothes and turned on a funny movie to cheer herself up.

Unbeknownst to either of them, Anders had been sitting in his car, with the lights off and a pair of binoculars, parked down the street. He wanted to–needed to—see Jane with Simon. He watched them hug under the porch light, shake hands and part ways. No kiss. That was good news. Maybe they wouldn't have a second date? Not that he cared because he had Meredith and they were engaged to be married. His life was all planned out. Just the way he wanted it to be.

45

"Anders," Meredith called him to the front porch of the house in Millvale. She poured him a glass of iced tea. "Your drink is out here." She took a long sip from her glass, leaving his on the table. It was hot for a September day, the sun just starting to sink in the sky with the afternoon.

"Thank you." He planted a small kiss on her head as he went past to sit in the rocker next to hers. This is what they would look like when they were older. Somewhat more wrinkled, and grayer mind you, but just the same. Comfortable.

"What do you think about daisies for the centerpieces?" She held a bridal magazine in her lap, condensation dripping a little on the page. She smoothed it out with the hem of her shirt.

"Daisies are fine with me," he said, though he was more partial to lilies.

"White daisies and pink roses." She swooned.

"Sounds lovely." He took a gulp from the cold glass.

"And maybe purple dresses for the bridesmaids and of course purple tuxes for the groomsmen?" She cast a sideways glance to see if he was listening.

"Perfect." He took another gulp and threw his head back against the chair. His rocking pattern increased.

"Anders, really, you want the guys to wear purple tuxes?" Meredith whooshed an exasperated breath from her lungs. "You're not listening." She closed her magazine. "Is something the matter?"

"Oh, I was just thinking about where we would live once we are married," he said with effort. "Sorry, you're right, I wasn't listening."

"Yes, I suppose that is a big decision." Meredith went back to her magazine. "I figured your place, it's bigger than mine. And since you're almost done with the inn project, I thought I would move in once you come back to the city."

Anders was quiet for a long time, not wanting to broach the subject of where they would live any more but knowing he must. He cleared his throat and spoke quietly. "Actually—" he began, cleared his throat and started again. "Actually, I'm selling my condo. I thought we could live here." He couldn't look at her.

"You are, we could?" She was surprised. She closed the magazine in her lap.

"Yes, I'm putting the money into the inn." He didn't look up.

"You are." Her tone suggested she wasn't surprised.

"Yes." He built up the courage to look at her. Her eyes looked like lasers.

"You're planning on putting all that money into that place when we are trying to start our lives together?" She stood up, angry. "What were you thinking? And what about me, what about my career?" She stopped in front of him, then took a long drink from her glass.

"I was thinking I wanted to impress my father by making this place a success." Anders stood too because he was angry with himself. "And that your career would just sort of work itself out."

She snorted, hurt at his lack of consideration. "Well I guess never mind my career, or the fact there are barely any funeral homes here in the middle of nowhere." She stomped her small foot. "I assume you weren't only trying to impress your father, but also Jane Michaels and her daughter Ellie," Meredith shot at him, upset. He began to speak but she cut him off. "Your brother told me about the building plans you changed when we were at the beach. That it was going to increase your budget by at least a half million dollars. You so desperately want to impress that woman that you are willing to give up everything you've worked for, your life in the city, just to dazzle her."

Anders looked at her, sadness washing over him. He was failing at yet another thing he had set out to do to make the Brookstone name a proud one.

"Whether or not I have feelings for Jane is irrelevant," Anders offered. "We are just friends, business associates, nothing more."

"Do you have feelings for her?" Meredith pressed. "Just tell me." Her fingers played with her engagement ring.

"Yes," he had finally admitted it. Guilt ran over him, then relief. He couldn't believe what he was saying. He had feelings for Jane. *Well, that's obvious*, he told himself. *Of course, you do, you kissed her and you can't stop thinking about it. And what you're doing to Meredith isn't right.* "I'm sorry Meredith. I thought you were the perfect woman for me. You are the perfect woman, on paper, but I can't help the way I feel. I've tried."

She sat, deflated, on the porch rail. Then stood once more almost as quickly as her behind hit the wood.

"I should go," she said, not looking at him.

"Go?" Anders was confused.

"I don't belong here." She spoke over her shoulder as she went into the house. She pulled out her suit case from the closet, started to pack the few items she had left here over the past few months.

"Of course, you do." Anders was beginning to panic. His heart was racing. Why did he admit his feelings for Jane?" *Stupid!*

"I don't know, Anders," Meredith said sadly. "I think that maybe we both need to work out what we're doing here. Work it out separately, that is. I mean, I need time to think." She threw items into the case, not folding anything, which was very much unlike her. She was flustered. *He has feelings for her. He has feelings for her. I knew it!* Repeated over and over in her brain. She just wanted to get out of there. Away from this idyllic setting, this pretend life Anders was building for himself, which, evidently, didn't include her. "I'm going back to the city. Don't call me for a while. I need space."

"Meredith, please." Anders pleaded at her back.

She stormed down the steps, her case at her side, her small body tilted in the opposite direction to compensate for the weight. She threw the case in the back seat.

She rolled down the driver side window, calling to him where he stood on the porch.

"Anders, you need to figure out what you want. I love you, but I'm not sure you love me. I don't want to be second best. I deserve to be someone's first choice. If I can't be that for you—" She stopped, shaking her head sadly. Then she turned the car and drove off.

Anders stood watching her. The sunset that was so beautiful a few moments earlier becoming just a sad metaphor for his life. Was everything just going down, like the sun? Was he about to find himself in the dark, all alone?

* * * *

The next morning, he got up early and decided to go back to the city. He needed to be away from the allure of the country. The fresh air, the wide spaces, big sky, and the wonderful woman who was making his heart wander from the wonderful woman whom he was supposed to be marrying.

Is Meredith wonderful? He asked himself over and over. In many ways, yes. She is beautiful, smart, career oriented. She is kind. She can make appropriate conversation when necessary. But the more he thought about her, he realized, she was also cold, not overly affectionate, and he wasn't sure if she could even cook. Being appropriate when necessary really didn't seem to be the best reason to marry someone. *Huh. And when exactly did Jane say something inappropriate?* he asked himself. *Never. You're just afraid of what people might say about Ellie, or Jane, because she isn't fancy.* "Eww." Anders didn't like this about himself, not one bit. *I'm the one who has a problem. I need to let these unfounded thoughts go.*

For three days, Anders stayed in his apartment, just thinking. He went over all the time he'd spent with Meredith, and all the time he'd spent with Jane. With Jane, he felt more like himself, he admitted to his reflection while he shaved one morning. But Meredith was the kind of woman that made a good Brookstone. But why wouldn't Jane make a good Brookstone woman? There wasn't a clear reason. She just wasn't from his world. Is that why he couldn't get his head on straight? Was his world changing? Was he realizing that all the things he thought he wanted, the things he thought his father wanted for him, weren't really what he wanted after all?

There was a knock on the door. He figured it was Meredith. When he opened the door, he was surprised to see his mother standing there.

"Mom, what are you doing here?" he asked, opening the door wider so she could come in. She carried a grocery bag.

"I heard you were sick, so I brought you some soup," she said as she went to the kitchen and pulled out a container.

"I'm not sick," Anders replied.

"Oh, well, your brother said you were sick, so here I am." She looked at him.

"Why did he think I was sick?" Anders wondered aloud.

"I don't know, you disappeared, he just assumed." Mrs. Brookstone busied herself looking for a pot. "Where do you keep your pots? I'll heat this up." He found her a pot. "So, if you're not sick, what's going on?"

His mother stirred the soup while she looked at him. He had a flashback of when he was little, staying home from school when he had the flu.

"Oh, well, I think Meredith and I are breaking up," he said, matter of fact.

"I see." His mother replied in a calm way that made Anders think she wasn't surprised.

"You don't sound like this is a big shock to you." He sat on a stool at the kitchen counter.

"Well, no," she replied, still stirring. "I saw you and Meredith, and you and Jane, and I figured — Jane's the one for you. The way you two looked at each other. Her little girl. You and Meredith never looked like that. No passion." She reached for a bowl, put in two heaping ladles full of her traditional chicken noodle, and placed it in front of him. Then she made one for herself, then passed out two spoons.

"Passion," Anders repeated.

"Exactly. You and Jane," his mother said, waving her spoon a little for emphasis. "I think you have the passion."

"But I thought you and Dad wanted me to marry someone like Meredith." Anders ate some of his soup. It was good. He felt some comfort spreading through his body. He hadn't felt comfortable in a long time, he realized suddenly.

"Listen." His mother put down her spoon. "Your father pushes this image, of success, wealth, and importance. But don't believe for one second that he doesn't want you and your brother to fall in love and be happy. Building a life where you can be happy is the most important thing in the world. And it doesn't matter what the person you build it with looks like or does for a living. That is the greatest measure of success. It is okay if your successful life looks nothing like the one your father and I have built. You choose with your heart, honey."

She patted his hand and went back to eating her soup.

After his mother left, Anders went back to thinking. If he wanted a life of happiness, then he wanted a life with Jane. A life that he would build with Meredith would be fine, maybe even some people might be jealous of that life, because from the outside it would look perfect. On the inside, however, Anders knew it would not have passion. With Jane, he could have passion.

From the outside it would look difficult and messy. Some people might even pity them because they weren't wealthy, and they had a child with special needs in their life. But none of that really mattered. With Jane he could have space, air, Ellie. And love. With Jane, he would be happy. He wondered if Jane would be happy with him too.

* * * *

Meredith phoned the next day. "We need to talk," she said.

"Yes." Anders agreed.

The break up was respectably amicable. She brought over a box of his things, and he had already packed up some things for her as well. She handed him the ring they had chosen together.

"This is yours," she said, stone faced. He tried to hug her. As usual, she pulled away from him, cold. "Look," she said, her voice quivering a little, "I don't want to fight."

"Neither do I," Anders replied.

"Was any of it real?" she asked.

"Yes, in the beginning," Anders said. "Then I was just trying to do what a Brookstone would do. I'm sorry you got caught in the middle."

"That was a selfish thing to do, Anders," Meredith said. "But, I guess I understand."

"I'm sorry," Anders said once more, taking the box from her that she held, and replacing it with the box he packed for her to take.

"Me too," she said, frowning. "See you around, I suppose." She started to leave.

"Meredith," Anders called after her.

"Yes." She turned to face him.

"I wish you a life of passion and happiness," he said. She looked him over.

"I'd say the same to you, Anders, but I think you've already found it." She turned away, walking toward the elevator with her box of things. He shut the door to the hallway.
Bye, Meredith.

* * * *

When Anders returned to Millvale, he felt a lightness in his heart that hadn't been there for some time. He had screwed up again. He lost his fiancée, he might lose his job, he had sold his home, and he didn't even know if Jane would be interested in having him. But at least he was starting to make decisions that would, hopefully, lead him to what he wanted in life. This was a new opportunity, to be the kind of man his father said he could be. A man who stuck to his principals, made his own decisions, and got the job done. Inventive, confident, and capable. Anders wasn't sure he was any of those things, but he was willing to try. It was a new day for him. A day where he stopped being the reliable one for other people and started to be reliable to his own heart.

46

Anders had been sitting on the front porch in a rocking chair, contemplating his new life. About an hour later Alec and Valentina arrived in the driveway, their truck kicking up gravel along the way.

"We have great news." Valentina hailed Anders who still sat on the porch, deep in thought.

"We do indeed," Alec sauntered out of the truck and placed his arm around his wife's waist.

"What?" Anders looked up at them completely surprised they were there. The couple exchanged a concerned look.

"What is the matter?" Valentina came to sit next to Anders. He played with the ring that was returned to him. "What is that?" Valentina reached out her hand. Anders deposited the ring in her palm. "Ah," she nodded to Alec, handed the ring back to her brother-in-law and then went inside leaving the brothers to chat.

"She dumped you," Alec said, not unkindly.

"She did." Anders admitted.

"Good." Alec took a seat in the neighbouring rocker. The anger that had been lingering between the brothers, dissipated.

"Yes, I think it is too," Anders replied.

"I never understood what you saw in her anyway," Alec said.

"Yeah, okay, so maybe I made the wrong choice." Anders admitted.

"You did?" Alec teased.

"Yes," Anders replied.

"Okay." Alec gave up his argument. "But, she wasn't right for you."

"No," agreed Anders. "But she was right to be a Brookstone."

"That's stupid, you know." Alec sighed. "I don't understand where you got this idea from that someone has to be a particular type of person to be a Brookstone. It's just a name." Alec propped his legs up on the porch rail and leaned back.

"Right, well, that's because you've been gone and haven't really seen how hard Dad worked to establish the name," Anders said bitterly.

"Okay, yes, I was gone," Alec admitted. "But even with how hard Dad worked, it doesn't make us royalty or something. Dad is just a person. A person made of stone, but a person nonetheless. Any woman you love would be good enough to be a Brookstone, you dummy."

"Ha." Anders' bitterness grew in his throat. "You know, I went to see Dad the other day, and he said he hoped I would be more like you. Take risks, be independent."

"Really?" Alec lifted his head up a little. "That's funny, the last time I saw him he told me to be more reliable and dependable, like you."

"Of course." Anders laughed wryly. The men were quiet for a while. A warm autumn breeze blew around their shoulders and faces turning Alec's cheeks pink. Leaves fluttered to the ground in the garden. A crow flew past. "I asked him for money." Anders broke the silence.

Alec rocked quietly, waiting for the rest. Valentina returned with a tray and three glasses of whisky on the rocks. She passed them around then leaned her hip on the porch rail and took a sip.

"I told him about the changes I wanted to make to the project. He told me no, to forget it. He threatened to fire me. Said I was just doing it to get Jane's attention." Anders took a drink.

"Aren't you?" Valentina said.

"Yeah, aren't you?" Alec piled on. Anders attempted to be incredulous but couldn't do it.

"Yes, partly," he admitted. "But I truly was inspired by the visit I took to the hospital with them. The changes I suggested would be an asset to the inn and the area."

"We agree," said Alec.

"You do?" Anders said, feeling somewhat brightened.

"We do," Valentina reiterated. "And, the money problem is easy," she said gaily. "I will give you five million dollars. That should be enough to finish your project and to do something with afterward."

"What, five million, what?" Anders tried to wrap his head around what he just heard. Alec laughed and laughed at his brother.

"Yes, five million. Is that not enough?" Valentina took a sip from her whisky, her eyes shining.

"You have five million dollars to spare?" Anders was confused, looking to his brother who just continued to laugh at him. Valentina joined in the fun. "Guys come on," Anders felt he was being made a fool. "What's going on?"

"Okay, okay." Alec wiped a tear. "I tried to tell you this before, but you wouldn't listen to me, so bullheaded to be responsible and dependable and not get help from your baby brother." He placed air quotes around responsible and dependable. "Valentina is a descendant of Princess Giovanna of Italy. She's royalty, and very rich."
Anders turned his attention to his lovely sister-in-law, disbelieving.

"This is true?" He couldn't even imagine it.

"It is." Valentina held her glass up in a toast to her wealth. "I will be your angel investor."

Anders tried to absorb what had just happened. A weight lifted from his chest.

"Thank you." He leapt up and embraced her, then his brother. "Enough money to finish the inn and to do something else. But what else should I do?"

"What do you want to do?" Alec said.

"I don't know." Anders sat down again, bewildered. "I never really thought about it."

"You haven't?" Alec took a sip from his glass. "Well I have." He sat up. "Can I tell you my good news now?" He took another drink.

"Yes, of course." Anders tried to focus. A five followed by six zeros floated behind his eyes. Five. Million. Dollars. He was elated. He shook his head and looked his brother in the face.

"Well, remember how you connected me to the man, Michael, at the hospital?" Alec went on not sure if Anders was following, though his dark-haired brother nodded. "Well, I showed him the support frame I made for Ellie and he wanted me to patent it and start making them at the hospital. He suggested I go into business, building special things to help people who need a little something extra to make their lives easier. So that's what I'm going to do. I'm going into business, making accessibility accessories."

"Wow." Anders was happy for his brother, but not surprised. He always did just what he wanted. "That's great, Alec." He shook his brother's hand.

"Well, there's more. I was wondering if you might want to come with me. You could handle the business side of things and I can do the building." Alec waited to see what his big brother would say.

"Oh," Anders said. "I don't know."

"Well, what are you hoping for in your life, Anders?" Valentina said, "I just gave you the gift of freedom. What are you going to do with it?"

Anders spoke aloud what he had been secretly thinking, and trying to make work, despite the ill-fitting piece of the puzzle — Meredith.

"I want to live here, in Millvale. I want to leave the city, stop working for Dad, and I want to be with Jane."

"Well that last part isn't so surprising." Valentina laughed. "But the rest is. Right, Alec?"

"Yeah, I didn't know you wanted to leave the city." Alec nodded his approval.

"Actually, I want to buy this house." Anders admitted his secret wish aloud.

"Well, now you can." Valentina laughed again, her happiness like music.

"And you can do whatever you want Anders, you don't have to have Dad's approval." Alec stood, leaning down to his brother to meet his eyes. Blue eyes matched brown and looked meaningfully into one another. "You have been doing what you've been wanting to anyway, now you don't have to make yourself feel guilty about it."

"You're right." A new light dawned in Anders eyes.

"If you want, we could start something together. Valentina and I were going to move to Millvale too." Alec held out his hand waiting to shake on it.

"Jane offered me a job working at the new restaurant," Valentina said. "I'm excited." Anders eyebrows shot up in surprise, then lowered because Valentina would be perfect to work at the inn. She was a wonderful cook.

"Deal." Anders shook his hand.

"Best part is we can go in and quit together. I can't wait to see Dad's face." Alec raised a glass to that. The sound of clinking glasses carried on the wind.

"Let's not be too hasty," Anders said. "Why not see if Dad wants to be partners? He has lots of great knowledge. Just because he is annoying doesn't mean we don't love him."

"True," Alec replied, then rolled his eyes. "We can work out the details of our new business idea later. I can't wait to see how Dad reacts to us asking him to join in on *our* business. We will be his bosses." Alec looked proud for a moment. "Oh yeah, I also thought that maybe we could bring Simon Chan in to consult." Alec suggested.

"Ugh, Simon," Anders scrunched up his face. "I hate that guy."

"You do?" Alec was surprised. "You loved him a couple weeks ago when you unveiled your extravagant blueprints."

"Yes, well, that was before he took Jane out on a date a couple nights ago," Anders said. "I saw them when he dropped her off. At least there was no kiss."

"You are just jealous. You do not hate him, Anders." Valentina pointed out. "Wait, you saw them when he dropped her off?" Valentina repeated. "How was that exactly?"

"Damn," Anders cursed himself for having a big mouth. "Okay, fine. I don't hate the guy. He's a very talented architect and someone who I would like to be friends with. And, well, I was spying on her. I parked down the street from her house and used my binoculars to watch when he dropped her off at the end of the night." He flushed a deep red.

"Oh, Anders," Valentina scolded.

"What were you thinking?" Alec said, shaking his head.

"I don't know. I just wanted to see if they hit it off."

"Whether they did or didn't is none of your business," Valentina said, in a disappointed tone.

"Right." Alec chimed in.
Anders sagged under the team effort to make him feel ashamed.

"You were engaged," Valentina continued. "What did you expect her to do?"

"I don't know." Anders pouted. "I just didn't want her to go out with anyone else until I figured things out."

"That's not how it works," Alec replied.

"I know." Anders ran his hands through his hair.

"Well, you aren't engaged anymore," Valentina offered, a sneaky smirk spreading across her mouth.

"Exactly." Alec nodded.

"Right, but I'm probably too late." Anders moped.

"Maybe, but maybe not," Valentina said, her voice sparkling. "I know she likes you," she continued. "You should be brave, take a risk. Go for what you want Anders. You only get to live once."

"She's right," Alec said, reaching out his hand to his wife. "And who knows what might happen." Valentina came to him and sat in his lap, wrapping her arms around his neck, planting a lovingly enthusiastic kiss on his lips.

"Okay, okay." Anders shielded his eyes from their P.D.A. "You've convinced me. But how do I convince her to go out with me when I've been such a tool."

"You have been a tool," Alec echoed.

"Thanks." Anders rolled his eyes.

"I don't think it will be as hard as you think it will be," Valentina said, her face giving away a look that said she was formulating a plan. "Tomorrow you will go to her. But tonight, we make a plan to win her heart."

It is a damn good plan, Anders thought. But Valentina was his angel investor, and maybe not just monetarily. Perhaps his sister-in-law could sprinkle some of her angel dust on his heart as well.

47

The next afternoon, Jane sat on the porch of her home enjoying the warm sunshine on her face. She had spent a busy morning of menu planning with Iris. They had done a month's worth of breakfast menus, along with a dozen lunches, and a week of dinners. The menu for "snack times" as they liked to call them, the times of day like mid-morning tea or afternoon coffee breaks when people were looking for something sweet would have a rotating offering of fifteen items. New treats would be added whenever the mood struck. There would also be Ellie's cookie creation menu available, provided that was something Ellie wanted. The drink menu was still left to tackle, along with a few more dinner ideas because Jane wanted to be over prepared for the opening whenever it came. She knew it would be soon. She just wasn't sure when exactly. Perhaps by the end of November, hopefully before the snow.

She took a break after Iris left for work, hugging a mug of hot cider and carrying some snickerdoodles. Ellie wouldn't be home for a couple of hours and her mother was out with Ed for lunch before his afternoon route, for which she'd undoubtedly join him, and get off the bus when Ellie was dropped off. Jane was planning on enjoying the quiet and continuing her menu planning, only this time she intended to brainstorm some ideas for Meredith and Anders.

Next to her on the table was a cute notebook, something she picked up at the Dollar Store that reminded her of something "wedding-ish." It was bound in cream coloured satin with tiny, blue, embroidered flowers on the cover. She thought her clients might appreciate presenting their menu options in a themed book such as this.

"Okay," she said aloud to herself. "Firstly, I wonder how many guests they will have." Judging by the snootiness factor of the Brookstones, she'd estimated at least two hundred, maybe even three. She'd need to hire help. She wrote *Staffing Requirements* at the top of one of the pages, and, *Estimated Number of Guests* on the line below.

On the next page she scrawled *Appetizers*. Some passed nibbles were always a hit with hungry guests. Something to distract women wearing uncomfortable shoes. Maybe something fun like coconut shrimp or grilled pineapple wrapped in bacon. Something easy to hold or stick a tooth pick in. She wrote down the ideas.

The next page was dedicated to the salad or soup. She wondered if it would be a buffet or plated dinner. She assumed plated, as that was fancier. Gingered squash soup or a fennel and pear slaw served in a hollowed-out pear bottom. That was a good start.

She took a sip of her cider, ate a cookie, and rested her head on the back of the chair. There was a lovely breeze brushing her cheeks and she found herself drifting. She dreamed of bulldozers, sand castles, Ellie diving through the waves. Waking with a start when she heard a car door slam, she found her notebook had fallen from her lap and Anders standing in her driveway.

"Hi," she said, somewhat unsure if she was still dreaming. "Did we have an appointment today?" She stood, picked up the book and placed it next to her mug and cookies, then smoothed her hands over her hair.

"No, no." Anders stood awkwardly in the driveway.

"Come on up." She gestured to him. She watched him move with ease up the drive, the sun highlighting some auburn in his hair she'd never noticed before. He looked handsome as the sun lit up his brown eyes making them look amber. She mentally shook it off. "I was just working on your wedding menu."

"Oh." Anders now stood awkwardly on the porch.

"Have a seat." Jane had the feeling she wasn't going to like whatever conversation Anders had come to her house to have. Was he going to fire her? Tell her the kitchen was a no go? A burning settled in her throat. He placed a package he was holding on the ground next to his chair.

"I heard you were over at the restaurant for an inspection yesterday." Anders began, somewhat laboriously.

"Yes." Jane looked at him. He avoided her gaze. "Is something wrong?"

"Oh, no, no," he said, too brightly. "I just wanted to check to see that everything was to your liking. For instance, is the kitchen missing anything you need or wanted, or, were hoping to have?" He looked at her straight in the face, this time unflinchingly.

"Oh, well, um, I've always wanted one of those really fancy Italian espresso machines. You know the kind where you put the freshly ground beans in and pat it down and then you can steam the milk." Jane spoke excitedly, opening up. The moments of awkwardness must have just been in her mind.

"Done," Anders said. "I'll order you one tomorrow."

"What?" Jane was confused. "You'll order one tomorrow? I don't think it's in the budget."

"Of course, it is," Anders said. "What colour would you like?"

"Red." Jane scoffed, thinking this was a joke. "We really can't afford one, Anders? What's going on with you?"

"Well, Valentina, you remember her." Anders eyes looked playfully at her.

"Um, well yes, I do." Jane scrunched her forehead in confusion.

"She's rich." Anders clapped his hands together. "And she gave me more than enough money to finish the build. And with any money left over, Alec and I are going to start our own business."

"Wow." Jane let this information sink in. "What kind of business?" She asked first, then, "Wait, Valentina's rich?"

"Oh yes." Anders laughed. "A descendant of Italian Princess Giovanna, or something."

"Okay," Jane said again. "Hey, I just hired her to be one of my kitchen staff. Well, I hope she doesn't think I'm going to go easy on her, or, pay her more or something." Jane took a drink out of her now cold cider. It was bitter. She stood. "You want a drink?"

"Yes, sure. But, in a minute." Anders gestured for her to sit again. "There's more,"

"Oh, alright." Jane was surprised.

"So, the business Alec and I want to start will be to build accessible accessories, like the frame he made for Ellie, on a client-by-client basis. Whatever special thing they need, Alec will make. I'll deal with finding the clients. The best part? I'm going to be moving to Millvale." Anders excitement for this idea was evident.

"That sounds like a really great idea," Jane said. Inside her heart did a jig at the idea of Anders being here, permanently.
"Congratulations." She shook his hand, actively ignoring the spark she felt when she touched

him. She saw in his face he felt it too. His hand lingered. To try and change the subject she added, "You should ask Simon to consult on your projects. He'd enjoy that kind of work, I think."

"Oh, no, I don't think that would work," Anders said.

"Why?" Jane became wary and withdrew her hand from his welcoming grasp.

"Because, you're dating him, and I think that might be a conflict of interest." Anders tried to hide a grin growing on his lips.

"I'm not dating him," Jane replied immediately. "I dated, once, past tense. We decided to just be friends."

"Any particular reason?" Anders pried.

"Not that are any of your concern," she shot at him.

"I see." Anders' smirk turned at the corners of his lips.

"I really don't see how it would be a conflict of interest for you even if we were dating." Jane was becoming annoyed.

"Oh, well that's easy," Anders said. "That's because I want to date you."

"You want to date me." Jane stood up and faced him. This was too much. "You can't date me. You're getting married to Meredith. And if you think I'm the kind of woman who would help you cheat on your fiancée, you are sadly mistaken." She grabbed her cup and plate and stormed into the house.

"Jane, wait." Anders went after her. He cursed himself for getting too cocky. He called out to her quickly, "Meredith broke it off with me."
Jane stopped in her tracks midway to the kitchen sink. "She did?" Her back was to him.

"Yes," he replied. This time there was no smirk on his face. "Why?" she asked, still not turning around.

"Because, she said I'm in love with you," he practically thundered the words at her, so happy to finally be able to admit his true feelings. She finished walking to the kitchen sink, placing her cup and plate inside. Then, she turned slowly to face him.

"You are?" she asked as her mouth struggled not to break out into a grin.

"Yes, I am. I'm in love with you and Ellie." Anders threw open his arms.
She came running to him, burying her head in his shoulder and practically cackling with laughter and relief, for she had been holding onto some shred of hope he might feel the same way she was so scared to admit.

"You're in love with me and Ellie," she mashed the words into his shirt. This was all she could ever hope for after Tom died. She had never told anyone this, but every birthday, she wished on her candles that there would be a man out there that would love her and her daughter. Anders didn't know it, but he had just made all her birthday wishes come true. He laughed into her hair.

"Yes," he whispered. Then he tilted her face up away from his shoulder. "May I kiss you now? Please?" Jane nodded. Anders placed his lips softly on hers. All their fears melted away in that kiss. They knew they were perfect for each other and that they were finally on the same page.

When the kiss eventually broke, Anders was the first to speak. "I brought you something," he said. "Sit," he commanded, and Jane did without argument because her knees were too weak from once again kissing the man she had loved for so long. Anders went to the porch and returned with the package he had been carrying.

"I was going to buy you some flowers," he said. "But then I decided that flowers die, and since I wanted our love to live, I bought you something else." He handed her a package. She carefully unwrapped the cellophane cover from the box. Inside was a small oak tree sapling.

"It's lovely," she said. "But I don't have anywhere to plant it here." She frowned. He knew her yard was small and would never be able to support a fully-grown oak tree.

"That's okay," he offered, sitting next to her to hold her hand. "You can plant it at my house. I'm going to buy the place where I've been staying. And maybe one day, when you and Ellie are ready, you would like to come and live there too, so you can see your tree grow every day."

"Wow," Jane replied. She really didn't know what to say.

"It's okay if you're not sure what to say." Anders offered, stroking the back of her knuckles with his thumb. Little electric pulses radiated up her arm from the spot. Jane chuckled.

"I'll have to talk to Ellie about all of this you know," she said happily, but also serious.

"Okay." He nodded.

"But we will for sure be planting this tree at your new house." Jane kissed him again, this time more playfully than the last. They were so happy that their love practically bust out the windows. She would wait to tell Ellie that Anders was here to stay, and so were Alec and Valentina, whom the girl had come to love. And maybe, if they wished on a few more birthday candles, Anders would soon be Ellie's stepdad.

48

Anders and Jane dated for a month, keeping it a secret from Ellie. They wanted to tell her when they were sure. That moment came when they decided this thing was really for real. They sat by the creek behind the inn, lights in the windows of each room. The build was nearly complete, just the final touches remained. They had been looking at Ellie's kitchen, with its bright white tiles, interspersed with purples and orange, her two favourite colours, she had told Anders. There were painted signs reading *Yum!* and *Bake!* in bubble letters written in a dark purple. Another hand-painted sign designed and made by Alec read *Baking with Ellie and Sally* which would act as the backdrop to their videos. The shiny stainless-steel counters looked great, and the place was set up with colourful bowls and utensils. The tables could be used at standing height or when Ellie used her wheelchair as they were on adjustable legs. The place was perfect for her, and for anyone who might be interested in taking classes there when Ellie and Sally weren't using the kitchen.

"The kitchen is wonderful," Jane said as she leaned against Anders' chest where he was propped up against a tree. "She is going to love it."

"I'm glad." He held her tight around her waist. "What about your kitchen?"

"My kitchen is perfect too." She turned to kiss him. "Especially that Italian espresso machine, courtesy of Princess Valentina." She laughed and kissed him again. "The inn and restaurant are going to be brilliant."

"I think so too." Their lips met once more.

"One thing is missing though." She turned to look at him. "The inn hasn't got a name."

"You're right." He was quiet for a moment. "What do you think of Oak Leaf Inn on the Creek?"

"Hmm, it's a bit wordy," Jane said. She thought for a second.

"Millvale Oak Leaf Inn?" she suggested.

"Yes, I like it." Anders hugged her. Jane laughed. "Millvale Oak Leaf Inn," he repeated. "You can tell everyone that you got engaged to the man of your dreams at the Millvale Oak Leaf Inn." Anders pulled a ring box from his pocket.

"Got engaged?" Jane turned to face him, confused. Then she saw the box. Anders shifted positions so that he was on one knee. He opened the box. Inside was a white gold ring with a bright green diamond in the centre. On either side was a white diamond. One for him, and one for Ellie, he would later tell her. The green diamond was for her, bright, shining, amazing to behold.

"Jane, since the moment I met you, I have been under your spell," Anders began. Jane's eyes sparkled with joy. "Will you do me the honor of bewitching me for the rest of my days?"

"Yes," Jane said, without hesitation. They embraced and kissed. The evening was turning from dusk to dark and the stars had just begun to twinkle. They didn't shine nearly as brightly as the ones in the couple's eyes, or the diamonds in Jane's new ring.

"You know what we should name the restaurant?" Jane said as she admired her new band.

"I have no clue," Anders said, smitten with his new fiancée.

"The Acorn." A hopeful look spreading across her face as she said it. "Or, is that too cheesy?" She looked at him with a furrowed brow.

"No, it's perfect," he said. The place where they fell in love, planted just like the tree in his yard, growing up into new and exciting possibilities.

They held each other and watched the stars come out, and then the moon. "I guess we'd better fill Ellie in now, don't you think?" Anders ventured. He knew Jane was feeling apprehensive about telling her daughter about their relationship, just in case.

"Yes, we absolutely should," Jane said, happily. "Tomorrow. We could show her the kitchen and tell her our news. It'll be a big, exciting, day.

* * * *

The next afternoon, Jane and Anders picked Ellie up from school.
"We have a surprise to show you," Jane said, practically giddy. Her fears of Ellie feeling pressured into a life of cooking had subsided after her talk with Simon, and then another talk with Anders where she made it clear they weren't to be disappointed if Ellie didn't want to have the kitchen. They would find other uses for the space, great, wonderful uses.
Ellie chatted all about her day at school throughout the drive. When they arrived at the inn, Jane gave Ellie a snack. Then they pushed her wheelchair past some lingering piles of debris. First, they stopped in the garden. Ellie really liked the meandering pathway that was smooth and wide enough for her wheelchair. In the spring there would be a riot of colours. Right now, there were some mums here and there to add some hints of colour.
Next, they stopped by one of the accessible guest rooms. It was met with rousing enthusiasm.
"Can I stay here some time, Mom?" Ellie asked, turning on her best puppy-dog eyes.
"We'll see," Jane said. Then Anders whispered in the girl's ear.

"We can for sure arrange that." Then the two made a pinky promise.

They visited the restaurant last. The dining room was getting set up by some waitstaff. Creams and cool blues were the colour scheme in here, something to remind diners of the water, which they could see running through the creek from the large picture window.

"Pretty." Ellie gave her stamp of approval.

Next, they examined her mom's new kitchen. It was shiny and clean. Painted with scrubbable paint and decked out with as much stainless steel as was possible, it was ready to roll. A machine waiting to be fired up.

"Very nice, Mom. You're going to cook lots of great stuff in here." Ellie gave her mom a hug. "The big windows are cool too."
Diners were able to look in not just from the parking lot, but also from the dining room.
"Interactive." Ellie's new word she'd learned at school this week, was perfectly applicable to this scenario.

"Okay," Anders said. "I want you to close your eyes."
Ellie's kitchen was tarped off anyway, but this added to the drama.

"Alright, my eyes are closed." Ellie giggled with excitement. Jane and Anders laughed at her contagious happiness. They pushed her through the tarped doorway.

"Okay, open your eyes," Anders said.

Ellie's eyes popped open. She looked around. Her mouth hung agape as she examined each nook and cranny. She took off and inspected the room. Tried out the counter top. Looked at the open shelves with all the colourful bakeware, even looked over the spot where the video camera could go.

"What is this place?" she asked, wide eyed.

"This is your kitchen, sweetie," Jane said through a happy but watery grin.

"My kitchen, my very own kitchen?" Ellie sounded like she couldn't believe it.

"We built it just for you, so you could make your videos with Sally and bake your cookies, and not have to worry about space or if you can use something." Anders had happy tears too.

"Really? Wow!" Ellie took another tour of the space. "This is so awesome, and it even has my favourite colours." She high fived Anders. Then she spotted something on the shelf she hadn't noticed before. A book, with her picture and some cookies on the cover. "What's this?"

"It's a prototype," Jane said. "Anders made it."

"I thought that maybe we could turn all your recipes into a cookbook and sell them here, along with your cookie creations, at the restaurant. That is if you want to." Anders was quick to add the last part.

"Right," Jane reiterated. "Only if you want to, no pressure. You could make money for yourself to buy things you want or save for school. But no pressure. This kitchen is built for you to use whenever you want. And if you don't want to use it, that's okay too."

Ellie looked through her cookbook, ran her finger over her name on the cover. "Cookies by Ellie Michaels-Jenkins," she read aloud. "This is really great, Anders, Mom. I love it. And I bet Sally would like to make our videos here." She looked at them excitedly. "Do you really think people will want to buy my cookies?" She suddenly looked overwhelmed and like a tiny little girl.

"Absolutely they will." Anders cheered, reassuring her.

"Yes, I'm sure of it too, sweetie," Jane added. "We can have a special's board, just like we had at the café."

"Well, okay," Ellie said thoughtfully. "There's one thing missing though." A mischievous look spread across her cheeks. "We need a Cutie Pie's Bake Shoppe sign, for old time's sake. We could hang it up on the wall with the others."

"Great idea," Jane said. "It's always good to remember where we came from, right?"

"Right," Ellie said then came over to give hugs to her mother and Anders.

"While we are hugging, there's one more thing I wanted to ask you," Anders said.

"Okay," Ellie said, a grin on her face.

"I was wondering if you would like me to be your stepdad?" His grin spread to match the magnitude of the little girl's.

"Are you serious?" she said, sounding again like a teen.

"Super serious," Jane replied and held out her hand, so Ellie could see her engagement ring. "Anders asked me to marry him, and I said yes. I hope you'll say yes too." Jane held her breath.

Ellie whooped. "It's about time," she replied, joyfully. "I would love to have you as my stepdad. I thought you two would never figure this out!" Ellie laughed.
Jane and Anders looked at each other in surprise.
So, I guess kids know more than they let on.

"I suppose that means you're staying in Millvale?" Ellie asked, obviously hopeful that she wouldn't have to move.

"Yes, but I hope you'll like your new room, Anders replied.

"My new room?" Ellie looked at him skeptically.

"I've bought the house where I've been staying, and when your mom and I get married I hoped we would all live there together." Anders ventured cautiously.

"Amazing," Ellie said. "I love that back yard! Could this day get any more incredible?" She was so excited. She clapped and whooped and hugged her mom and stepdad-to-be in a tight squeeze. "Wait," she said, suddenly concerned. "Where will Alec and Valentina live?" The little girl's brows bent toward each other.

"Don't you mean Uncle Alec and Aunt Valentina," Jane teased.

"Oh yeah, I guess so." Ellie giggled.

"They are buying another house in town, so don't worry, they will be around as much as you can stand them." Anders teased then hugged his new daughter.

"Awesome, I'm so happy. We are going to be the best family." Ellie grinned.

"I think you're right," Jane agreed.

* * * *

That night, when Ellie went to bed, Anders helped tuck her in. Jane and Anders kissed the girl on the forehead and wished her sweet dreams. And Ellie had very sweet dreams indeed, about her Mom, and her new stepdad, and some special new cookie recipes she could whip up in her brand-new kitchen.

Epilogue

The Announcements

When Jane and Anders told Fae about their engagement, it couldn't have gone better. Jane's mother was so pleased, having known about the feelings Jane was harbouring inside her heart for Anders all along. She wanted nothing more than for her daughter to be happy. As a bonus, she really liked Anders and could see how he would be able to build a wonderful life with her daughter and she knew that he would make a great father for Ellie. Though Ellie didn't talk much about it, she knew her granddaughter missed having a father in her life. Even though she didn't really remember Tom, she remembered his love somewhere in her heart. It was an odd thing that she couldn't put her finger on but would sometimes talk about when she went to bed. Many nights over the years Fae listened as Ellie described a warm sensation on her shoulders or how at some point during the day, it had seemed someone had pulled her hair, but when she went to look around there would be no one there.

"Maybe it was your dad, just saying hello?" Fae would suggest. Ellie would be comforted by this explanation. Chances were that it was just some kind of neurological misfiring inside her due to her medical condition, but it might be her dad giving her a squeeze from heaven. Who was to say differently?

Ed was also thrilled with the news of the newly betrothed couple. He gave Anders a big hug and an even bigger one to Jane. Ellie got a high five. Fae loved to see everyone together and hoped one day soon she and Ed might be headed down the aisle as well. Bonus, Ellie was getting an aunt and uncle as part of the package, as well as two new grandparents. Fae was unsure about the Brookstones but knew that Alec and Valentina were already some of her granddaughter's favorites. If Ellie had her way, she would charm the senior Brookstones soon enough. Having only one child was one of Fae's regrets in life, but it seemed now that things were evening out and her family was growing. More hearts to love. More hands to hold. More smiles to count.

On the flip side, announcing the happy news to the Brookstones had not gone as smoothly. To cushion the blow of telling his parents that the engagement with Meredith had been called off and one month later he had proposed to another woman, he and Alec decided to also announce their leaving Brookstone Holdings to start their own company and their move out of the city to Millvale.

"Just rip off that bandage," Valentina said with a flourish on the drive into the city. Her accent made it sound like having adhesive cloth stuck to your skin and tiny hairs ripped off would be a pleasure.

Dinner was served in the formal dining room. When Mrs. Brookstone came to the door, she was only somewhat surprised to see Jane standing on the other side.

"Oh, where is Meredith this evening?" Ever polite, her surprise was cleverly masked in courteous speech.

"She couldn't make it tonight, Mom." Was all Anders offered as an explanation while they removed their coats and shoes. Blair and Mrs. Brookstone, in fact, were not at all surprised to see Jane.

"Drink?" she asked as Jane sat on a mushroom coloured chenille couch that probably cost more than her first car.

"Please, white wine if you have it," she said, placing her palms on her thighs. Her skirt had begun to develop static cling and she was silently trying to perform a magic spell to release the fabric from her nylons. Mrs. Brookstone delivered the drink on a silver tray lined with a hand crocheted doily.

"Where is Meredith this evening?" Mrs. Brookstone pressed Anders once more when all the drinks had been served.

"Well." Anders cleared his throat. He looked to his brother for support, who nodded to him. On his brother's left Valentina laughed and stuck up her thumb. With this encouragement he pressed on. "Meredith and I broke up, actually."

"You what?" Mrs. Brookstone pretended to be shocked. Blair just drank from his glass of scotch.

"Yes," Anders continued. "We decided we weren't right for each other, Mom, I'm sorry if you're disappointed."

"Oh, well dear," Mrs. Brookstone tutted. "What matters most is that you're happy."

"I'm so glad to hear you say that." Anders took Jane's hand. "Because, Jane and I are getting married, Mom, Dad." He looked to both his parents. His parents turned to each other, stunned into momentary silence.

When his mother found her tongue, "Well, that's rather sudden." Was all she said.

"Yes, I suppose it is." Anders raised Jane's hand and kissed it. "But when you're in love, you just know."

"Dear," Blair shushed his wife, "surely you remember what it was like when we fell in love?" At this, Mrs. Brookstone cheeks reddened, looking like a shy school girl.

"I certainly do," she said. "Well, it seems our little talk helped."

"You had a talk with him too?" Blair added.

"We all did," said Alec.

"Yes," added Valentina.

"Okay, fine." Anders jumped in, trying to stop the pile on. "I had no idea what I was doing, but now, luckily, because of all of your advice, I do!" Everyone laughed.

"We are so happy you two are happy." Mrs. Brookstone raised her glass. They toasted the new couple.

"I'm so glad to hear you say that," Anders continued. "Because, Dad, thanks to an angel investor…" Anders was careful not to give away Valentina's secret. "The inn project is coming to the finish line on budget."

Blair stopped as his glass hit his lips, then continued to drink as if this news didn't faze him.

"And what's more," Anders said, gesturing to his brother, "Alec," he said to make sure the ball kept rolling.

"Anders and I are leaving Brookstone Holdings to start our own business."

"Accessible accessories," Valentina added proudly as she took Alec's arm.

"And, we both bought houses in Millvale," Alec said, the final bit of news.

"But we still want to work with you, but as business associates and team members, instead of working for you any longer," Anders said.

There, the bandage was off.

With all the surprises delivered while they were still having drinks, understandably dinner was filled with lectures, questions, more lectures, and more questions from both the Brookstone elders.

Anders held his own, not once caving to the pressure to go back to his old habits. He could still be a responsible and reliable fellow, while following his dreams, which is exactly what he told his father.

Blair expressed his disappointment, but Jane couldn't help noticing a gleam of pride in the man's eye, and when it was time for them to leave, he patted his sons on the back and gave them each a hug, something that was evidently a rare occurrence. He also slipped an envelope into Anders hand saying, "For your wedding." Inside, was a cheque for five thousand dollars, a gesture left unexpressed when Anders was going to marry Meredith.

The Preparations

Trying to decide where to hold their wedding, Anders and Jane sat at her kitchen table one Saturday afternoon. Fae was making sandwiches at the counter and Ellie was on the couch reading a book with her headphones on. Two requests to turn down her music had already been given out.

"Ellie, turn it down," Jane hollered. Ellie rolled her eyes but did as was requested.

"I don't know," Jane said. "Should we go somewhere out of town? Maybe cottage country? Or would you prefer somewhere in the city?"

"Cottage country sounds nice," Anders said. "But I feel like it's too far." Anders was still wrapping things up in the city and the commute was starting to wear on him.

"Okay." Jane picked up a salmon sandwich from the platter Fae put down in the centre of the table.

"Lunch, dear," Fae called to Ellie who joined the party momentarily.

"Let's come back to that." Jane picked up a pickle and bit down with a loud crunch. "Maybe we should start with a wedding date?" The crunching was loud enough to hear outside her cheeks.

"Next summer?" Anders asked as he bit into his sandwich.

"Too hot, I don't want to sweat in my dress," Jane said scrunching her face. The group was quiet while they ate their lunches. Suddenly, Ellie piped up,

"What about getting married at the inn?" She spoke with a mouth full of salmon salad.

"At the inn? But it's not open yet." Jane patted Ellie's arm. "Don't talk with your mouth full, sweetie, especially when it's filled with salmon salad."

Ellie's response was to say that they all liked seafood and opened her mouth, so they could *see* hers.

"Gross," Anders said laughing. "But hey." He turned his attention to Jane. "It's not open yet, but the staff are having trial runs of services and guests etc. We could help train them on a real event."

"But the inn opens in December. That would only leave you a month to plan." Fae grabbed a cucumber spear and dunked it in some ranch dressing on the side of her plate.

"A late fall wedding," Jane said, looking wistful.

"Not too hot for your dress," Anders offered.

"Should we?" Jane asked, a twinkle in her eye.

"I don't want to wait until next year, do you?" Anders said.

"I know I don't," Ellie chimed in.

"Okay," Jane said. "Let's do it."

After the decision was made the rest of the plans fell into place. First, they set a date for the last weekend of November, one week before the inn was set to open. That meant they could get away for a "mini moon" for a couple nights before Jane would need to be back to finalize the kitchen prep.

Ellie and Sally oversaw the invitations. Anders and Jane settled on a fall colour palette of deep burgundy and gold. The girls took the script they gave them and created beautiful handmade invitations. The guest list was small, only forty people.

"Just friends and family," Anders had said. Jane agreed. Since this was her second wedding, she didn't need all the stress a fancy big party brought. Instead they would have a beautiful, intimate ceremony, and a fun-filled reception.

Anders took Alec, Ed and his father to pick out tuxes. They chose a handsome slate colour with burgundy waistcoats. The colour brought out Anders' dark features.

Jane's dress was something vintage she found in a shop in Bellfield. The bodice was a luscious cream colour with long sleeves and a lace overlay. The neckline was in a boatneck style which highlighted Jane's face. The colour set off her chestnut hair and freckles. The bodice cinched in at a natural waist that complimented Jane's figure and the skirt transitioned to satin in the same creamy shade. Jane chose a gold headpiece with an oakleaf motif she found online. She would tuck this into her upswept hair to recall the day she and Anders declared their affection for one another. Her earrings would be small golden heart studs. To complete her ensemble her mother fashioned her a cloak with a long train out of velvet of the deepest red.

    Ellie would wear a burgundy dress with a cream peacoat embroidered in gold. As a surprise, Jane bought her a locket which she planned to give to her daughter before the ceremony. Inside, she'd place two pictures. One of Ellie with her father, and the other of Jane and Anders with Ellie, so she could carry all her parents with her always.

Fae chose a long gown in brown with embroidery and crystal accents. She even found a fascinator to wear in her hair. Mrs. Brookstone chose a red dress with a sensible black taffeta jacket featuring black pearls and beading.

Iris and Valentina would be her bridesmaids. They would wear burgundy dresses with cream and gold capes to match Ellie's attire. With Jane's blessing, the ladies handled the décor for the ceremony and reception. They wanted to surprise the happy couple with the design, so they didn't let on any of the details.

Next, Jane hired a cellist for the ceremony, a minister to marry them, and a band for the party. She also hired caterers, because there was no way she was going to cook for her own wedding.

Anders and Jane picked out rings. Jane's was a white gold band with a filigree design. Anders was also white gold with beveled edges and tungsten accent.

They were ready. All the plans were in motion.

The Ceremony

The day of the Michaels-Brookstone wedding it was crisp and clear. The ceremony began just as the sun set and the stars began to arrive for their nighttime journey across the sky.

Valentina and Iris had outdone themselves, decorating the courtyard of the inn with a hundred cream pillar candles in varying heights. Along the stone walls they hung strings and strings of white lights. The aisle was strewn with red rose petals. The altar was made from white muslin draped over the grapevine archway, pinned back with burgundy and dark purple mums accented with white roses.

Rows of gold café chairs filled with guests, who found their way by lantern light and the warm glow of candles. Despite the hoar frost sparkling on the rooftop, it was warm in the courtyard.

Anders stood at the front, awaiting his bride's arrival. More excited than nervous he laughed with his brother and the minister, who had selected white robes for such a beautiful occasion.

The cellist played Pachelbel's *Cannon in D* to signal the start of the ceremony. Ellie came down the aisle in her motorized chair which had been bedecked with white tulle and red roses, with a hand lettered sign hung on the front reading "Here Comes the Bride."
Next the bridesmaids were escorted by Alec who seemed more than happy to have a beautiful woman on each arm.

Lastly, the bride accompanied by her mother, made her way toward her betrothed. They did not take their eyes off each other for a second. Anders took in the beautiful sight of his wife to be as she approached their forever life waiting for them at the end of the rose petal path. She held a bouquet of white roses and mums wrapped in gold ribbon. On her face, she wore a grin more brilliant than she'd ever worn before.

The vows went in a traditional way, with the "will you take this man, and will you take this woman," heartfelt "I do's" and promises to be faithful and true. The one departure was when Anders stepped away from his new wife and knelt before Ellie. He presented her with a white gold band, a small green diamond in the centre.

"Will you be my daughter?" he asked her, for he knew that he was marrying both Jane and Ellie and promising to love and care for her as her father from now on, just as much as he promised to love and care for Jane. Ellie was of course thrilled at being included. She placed the ring on her finger. Then she joined Jane and Anders at the altar where the minster had them all vow to love and cherish one another as a family.

Everyone in attendance had tears in their eyes as the powers that be announced Anders and Jane were now husband and wife. A grand kiss was met with whoops and hollers as hearty applause followed them back down the aisle and into the reception hall.

The Reception

The hall was decked out in a party style, courtesy of the bridesmaids' happy spirit. Streamers dangled from the ceiling as balloons acted as centrepieces. A disco ball awaited party time at the centre of the dance floor ceiling. Round tables were set with gold tablecloths and fancy china. The stemware sparkled in candle light. At each place setting sat a small oak sapling in a terracotta pot wrapped in burlap and burgundy ribbons as a thank you for attending. The gift table was piled high with presents.

    At the head table, the freshly minted Michaels-Brookstones could barely get in a morsel to eat for all the clinking of glasses. The food was delicious and hearty, which served the guests well for all the champagne being consumed. Classic flavours of comfort food delighted the guests including a Caesar salad to start, chicken pot pie for main, and rich carrot cake with cream cheese frosting for dessert.

    Blair Brookstone delivered a heartfelt speech, much to the surprise of his son Anders. Mrs. Brookstone cried the entire time as Blair described his pride for Anders and how happy he was that Jane was joining the family. He even requested a dance with Ellie, which was a good sign of things to come.

    Despite his standoffish nature, Jane had hoped the curt man would learn to love her daughter as much as everyone else did. Ellie had a wonderful time dancing with Blair and the two of them laughed and sang along to songs late into the night together. Jane did however, catch Ellie examining her locket from time to time.

When she had a moment alone with her, Jane asked how Ellie was feeling.

"I feel excited, nervous, happy, and different somehow." Was her answer.

"Me too," Jane said.

"I also feel a lot of love," Ellie added.

"Me too," Jane said, holding her wonderful, smart, beautiful, resourceful daughter tightly.

Fae read a beautiful little poem about love by Rilke:

Understand, I'll slip quietly
away from the noisy crowd
when I see the pale stars rising, blooming, over the oaks.
I'll pursue solitary pathways
through the pale twilit meadows,
with only this one dream:
You come too.

"Always remember to include one another in your thoughts and daily life," she added when she finished.

Then, the party got started in earnest. The band was hot as Sally and Ellie cut a rug with Valentina and Alec. Jane's new kitchen staff started a limbo competition with a broom from the back. The bartenders invented a signature cocktail featuring coffee liqueur which was going down a hit.

In attendance was Simon, whom Jane greeted warmly. Anders, who had long since buried his jealousy over their one date, shook hands heartily with the architect, talking business ideas with him until Jane pulled him away. Before Simon got lost in the crowd, she made sure to introduce him to Iris. He went with her over to the bar where Jane was pretty sure she could now see sparks flying between them.

When they cut the classically decorated three-tiered wedding cake, covered in white fondant and decorated in red buttercream roses and gold piping, they made a wish to a long life filled with health, love and happiness, then fed each other careful bites of rich chocolate cake.

After some time, when no one was looking, Ed and Fae snuck off to a secluded corner of the inn. A fire roared in the fireplace. They sat together holding hands on a large leather chesterfield, watching the flames flickering. In the distance, they heard the young people celebrating, laughing, and cheering. The music thumped through the lobby and down the hall.

"Fae." Ed pulled a small red velvet box from his pocket. "I would get down on one knee if I thought I'd ever get up."

Fae laughed at this, knowing what was coming. She'd hoped for some time that Ed would ask her to marry him. Oh, she had been so afraid to date him for so long. Afraid she would have her heart broken like when she lost her first husband. What a fool she had been to not see that love is never something we should fear but should always be something toward which we run.

Love is a place of peace, of shelter. Ed had become that for her. He was also funny, which she liked. He kept her on her toes, matched her in wit, and was kind to a fault. Plus, he loved her daughter and granddaughter. What more could she ask for?

"So, what do you say?" he continued. "Do you want to get married like the young ones did?" Ed opened the box. Inside was a yellow gold ring, old fashioned in style, just something that Fae would like. It held a solitary diamond, and an inscription inside reading *Forever*. "It might not be a long time, but it will be a good time," Ed promised.

"Yes, I will marry you," Fae said as she let Ed slip the ring on her finger.

After some time alone, the newly engaged couple rejoined the party to celebrate their pending nuptials and the union of the new Brookstone couple. Their wedding wouldn't be as wild as this one, but it would be as beautiful.

The End.

Coming Soon in 2021

Inn the Oven

Chapter 1

Valentina handed a glass of water to Jane, who looked quite green, as she sat on the kitchen floor of the inn restaurant The Acorn with her back against the stainless-steel fridges below the prep counter. She held the glass to her forehead, closing her eyes when the cool hit her skin.

"You look real bad," Gerald, one of the lunch time waiters said, as he leaned over the passthrough to get a better look at her.

"Thanks," Jane said, not opening her eyes.

"Get outta here, Gerald," Iris shooed him away after giving him a plate of chicken Cesar salad to deliver to a table overlooking the gardens. Gerald turned on his heel, disappearing beyond a white tiled wall. "You do look pretty peaky," Iris said, and pated her friend's hair.

"I'm fine," Jane fanned herself with her hand, breathing slowly.

"No, you are not," Valentina spoke sternly, but lovingly to her sister-in-law. "You are sick. You cannot be sick in a restaurant. Absolutely, it is against the rules."

"Are you going to hurl?" Gerald was back.

"No," Jane said, grabbing some of the lunch rush chits to fashion a fan. She needed more air.

"You look like you're going to hurl," Gerald offered. "Your lips are all white and thin and you're sweating."

"Gerald," Iris huffed, looking worriedly down at her friend. A chit printed, and

Valentina returned to the stove to prepare a plate of pasta. "Why don't you do something helpful, like, I don't know," she paused.

"I could phone Anders," Gerald miraculously managed to say something useful.

"Yes, you could phone Anders to come pick Jane up and take her to see a doctor," Iris shook his hand, impressed his brain worked some of the time.

"No," Jane said, attempting to sip some water, her eyes still closed. She moved her arm slowly toward her face, glass in hand. "I'm fine." she swallowed carefully.

"Alright," Iris placed a hand on her hip, "if you're fine, stand up. The next order that comes in is yours."

"Deal," Jane said, putting the glass on the counter above her head using a reverse arm maneuver. She carefully moved her feet into position, heaving her body up, grabbing her stomach and head simultaneously as she became upright. "Whoa," her head spun, her stomach flipped. "I'm fine," she stuck her hands out for some balance, knocking over her water. "Uh, shoot." She closed her eyes again and appeared to be praying.

"Call Anders, now, please," Iris said, grabbing Jane's arm that flailed nearest to her. "And a chair for Jane. Chair first." She called after the kid. Gerald returned promptly with the chair. They set Jane up in a corner away from the action and near the staff washroom, just in case. Then Gerald made the call to Jane's husband.

"Brookstone Adaptive, Anders speaking" he answered his cellphone on the third ring.

"Mr. Brookstone, this is Gerald, a waiter at The Acorn," Gerald tried to sound professional.

"Yes," Anders was looking over some orders in his email, stopping to listen.

"Uh, you need to come to the inn, Jane is sick," Gerald said, matter-of-factly.

"I'm not sick," Jane bellowed in the background, followed by a groan.

"Well, she is uh, all pale and sweaty. I think she's sick," Gerald said helpfully.

"She's sick, come get her out of here," Valentina piped up her voice lilting with an Italian accent into the receiver.

"I'll be right there," Anders hung up the phone. "Jane's not feeling well, I'm going to pick her up."

"Okay," Alec, Anders' brother nodded as Anders rushed past. Alec resumed sanding a special-order footstool for one of their clients. Next, he'd be painting it red.

When Anders arrived at the back-kitchen entrance of The Acorn, Jane was sitting outside on a garden wall. "What are you doing out here?"

"They kicked me out," she held a bunch of damp paper towels to the back of her neck.

"I see," Anders said, taking her arm. "It was probably for the best." He ushered her to his Jeep, depositing her in the passenger seat.

"I'm fine," Jane buckled in as Anders shut the door and went around to climb into the driver's seat. They drove out the driveway.

"What's wrong?" Anders asked, taking a sideways look at his wife. She was looking pasty.

"Nothing, I'm just," Jane held her stomach as they turned out onto the road. "Just a bit queasy, and dizzy."

"Okay," Anders glanced at her again. "I think we should go to the doctor's office, see if he can take a look at you."

"I'm still in my chef's whites," Jane whined.

"I'm sure he won't care," Anders hit the gas, perhaps a bit too hard.

"Huh," Jane heaved, "pull over." Anders did, and Jane proved just how fine she was.

At the doctor's office, Jane sat on the examining table, clutching a plastic bed pan. She has seen the nurse and given blood, a urine sample, and had her pulse, temperature, and blood pressure taken.

"Hello Jane," Dr. John entered the room after a quick knock on the door. "I see you are not feeling to well.

"No," Jane admitted.

"Well," he looked at his computer screen. "Everything seems to be in order, the only thing out of the ordinary is that you are pregnant." The doctor smiled.

"What?" Jane said, shock evident on her face.

"She's pregnant?" Anders balked, then grinned. "Pregnant!" He jumped up and grabbed his wife's hand.

"I'm pregnant," Jane shook her head. "No," she shook it more.

"Let's take a look and see how far along you are," Dr. John wheeled an ultrasound machine from the corner next to the table. "Lie back." Jane did as he said, instinctively lifting her chef's jacket to expose her stomach. Anders watched quietly as the doctor squirted clear goo onto her freckled skin. The machine whirred, then made a rhythmic whooshing sound.

"There's your baby's heartbeat. I'd say you're about two months along," the doctor examined the image on the screen. "It looks healthy so far," he smiled. Anders examined the blob on the screen. His baby. He closed his eyes, so he could remember the sound of its little heartbeat.

"Would two months be possible?" Dr. John asked, fingers poised over a keyboard to take notes.

"Um, yes," Jane blushed, turning to look at Anders. "Very possible." Anders smiled back an squeezed her hand.

"Well, congratulations," The doctor shook the hands of the father and mother to be.

"Thank you," Jane said, a little stunned. The doctor handed her a prescription for prenatal vitamins. "You take her home now, Anders. Jane, get some rest today. Hopefully your morning sickness subsides. Do the usual things, crackers, decaffeinated tea. My wife, well she found some warm milk helped her. You can go back to work tomorrow but come back in for another visit if your morning sickness gets worse. Congratulations, once more," he left the room.

"Pregnant," Jane said again, as Anders helped her sit up. She clutched the prescription in her hand.

"Pregnant," Anders grinned. They looked at one another and hugged.

"Pregnant," they both said together.

Upon returning home, Jane changed out of her work clothes into something comfortable, taking up residence on the couch, her fuzzy socked feet propped up on the chesterfield arm.

"I told Valentina you have a stomach bug," Anders said, as he put his cell phone in his shirt pocket.

"Our baby is a stomach bug, is it?" Jane chuckled, then groaned a little as another wave of nausea hit her.

"I don't know, we could nick name it 'little bug', seems like a pretty cute nick name," Anders took Jane's hand as he sat under her legs which she had moved only to deposit back into his lap.

"Pregnant," Jane shook her head in disbelief. "I'm too old to be pregnant."

"Evidently not," Anders patted her hip, smiling.

"I have a half-grown daughter, I'm thirty-five years old," she shook her head again.

"Thirty-five isn't old honey, some women are only starting their families at that age," Anders reassured her with a kiss on her palm.

"But we haven't even really talked about having more kids," Jane worried as she held her forehead, her chestnut hair spread out around her freckled face as she placed all her weight on her mind into the pillow below her skull. "I mean, I know you love Ellie."

"I do," Anders interjected.

"and, I guess I just assumed you would probably want more kids one day, but, not yet.

We've only been married for a few months," Jane lifted her head, looked at Anders, then flopped down again.

"A few wonderful months," Anders rubbed her hip again.

"Yes," Jane smiled. "But a baby, now? The restaurant is only just starting to hit its stride, the inn is too, and Ellie's cooking videos and books are doing well. I'm just not sure we have time for a baby. Not to mention your new business." She let out a heavy sigh.

"Look at me," Anders said, and Jane lifted herself up on her elbows. "Adding another member to our family, whenever it happens, is never going to be a bad thing. It is a joyous, wonderful thing, and I am so happy. I hope you'll be happy too, once it all sinks in." Jane considered her husband, tracing the outline of his handsome face with her gaze. A baby that was part him and part her would be lovely. He was right.

"Okay," Jane smiled. "You know me, I like to worry, plan."

"I know," Anders nodded.

"A baby," Jane said in awe.

"A baby," Anders echoed. They sat in silence for a moment. Then Jane leapt up and ran to the bathroom to deal with another bout of morning sickness.

Chapter 2

"I am telling you, she is pregnant," Valentina hissed over the water she sprayed into a scorched pot of pastry cream she'd just made. Iris fanned the steam away from her face.

"Really? I don't know," she frowned, placing her hands into the pocket of her apron.

"Think about it," Valentina dumped the first spray's worth of water into the sink drain. "Sorry Marcus, I did not whisk hard enough." She passed the pot to their dishwasher who looked doubtfully down at the blackish brown lumps at the bottom of the heavy bottomed aluminum pot.

"It's okay," he sighed.

"I will have you and Demetri over for supper if you can get the bottom of that pot to look silver again," Valentina offered to have Marcus and his husband over for a special meal, in hopes of it being an incentive for him to forgive her clumsiness. Marcus paused considering.

"Only if you make your famous risotto, with chicken parmesan on the side," Marcus countered her offer. Valentina rolled her eyes. Risotto was so time consuming. She really needed to pay better attention when she made pasty cream. This was the third time this month she burnt the pot. Marcus was going to get too used to her cooking at this rate.

Valentina sighed, "Deal," and shook hands with Marcus.

"You're mine, pot!" Marcus yelled, brandishing a silver scrubbing pad like a sword.

"What am I thinking about?" Iris tilted her head as the women moved back to the meal prep area. She started in on a bag of potatoes, peeling them carefully into the compost.

"Well," Valentina started in on another batch of pastry cream to fill the choux pastry puffs she'd just removed from the oven. She separated eggs as she spoke. "First, Jane complained about being tired, then she was dizzy that one day in the walk-in fridge."

"True," Iris grabbed another potato, scratching her nose with her forearm so her hands stayed clean. "Oh, and I saw her eating chocolate chip cookies with a dill pickle on the side. What is that about?"

"Right," Valentina waved a white eggshell in her friend's direction. "I'm telling you, after today, she is for sure pregnant."

"But they've only been married for six months, do you really think," Iris was cut off by Valentina.

"Absolutely," she laughed and flung a bowl of shells into the compost.

"Ladies," Francis, the front desk manager appeared at the pass-through window.

"Oh, hi," Iris rolled her eyes before turning around. "What can we help you with Frank?" Iris knew that he preferred being called by his full name. He cleared his throat and straightened his tie. His red hair was cropped short on the sides, but long enough on top to be slicked back into what could only be described as the epitome of a Brill Cream commercial look. His squinty eyes were brown and beady.

"I was hoping to talk to Jane, I have a," he cleared his throat," special, party waiting to see her. They and I want to discuss a," he cleared it again, "special menu."

"Jane has gone home for the day," Iris broke the news. "She's not feeling well."

"Oh," he reached for the bottle of hand sanitizer they kept on the counter near the pass for the servers. "I hope it's nothing catching." He cleared his throat and fixed his tie again.

"No, I don't think so," Valentina said, then winked at Iris. Iris flopped her head, her dark, curly hair bobbing behind her.

"Good, good," Francis whined. "Well, I'll be back tomorrow to talk to her.

"You do that," Iris smiled painfully at his back as he walked away. "What were Anders and Jane thinking when they hired that guy?"

"A friend of Anders' and Alec's father's son, or something," Valentina waved her whisk in the air, preparing to add the milk and cornstarch to her mixture.

"Well, if Jane is pregnant, I certainly don't want to be dealing with him while she's on maternity leave. We'd better get some feelers out for possible replacements, and fast." Iris' brown skin was glowing from the sweat the heat, and possibly the frustration, that Francis had caused in the kitchen.

"Good thinking," Valentina agreed. "I'll make some calls this evening when I get home." Just then, Marcus strode into the prep area.

"Ah, ha!" He waved a sparkling pot around, then high fived two servers and Iris.

"Dinner this Wednesday evening work for you," Valentina sighed.

"Let me ask my husband and I'll get back to you," Marcus said as he sauntered back to the dish pit.

Chapter Three

At a quarter after four that afternoon, Ellie arrived home from school. She came roaring through the front door, singing a song she'd learned in choir at the top of her lungs. Fae, her grandmother and Jane's mom, and Ed, Fae's fiancé and Ellie's bus driver, brought up the rear.

"Hey kiddo," Anders cut her off at the hallway. "Could you keep it down a bit please, your mom isn't feeling too great today." He took her backpack from her, removing her lunch box, then hung it on the back of her motorized wheelchair. Ellie zipped her lip and zoomed herself into the living room.

"Hey Mom," she deposited a kiss into her palm and then pressed it onto Jane's forehead because she couldn't reach to bend down to kiss her from her chair. Jane kissed Ellie's palm back, smiling, albeit weakly. Ellie mushed the kiss into her cheek. "What's the matter?" Ellie looked concerned.

"Oh, it's nothing sweetheart, just an upset stomach," she smiled at her daughter, trying not to feel guilty about the small lie she just told. Anders and Jane had agreed to tell Ellie the big news over dessert this evening.

"Do you need anything?" Ellie asked, continuing to look worried.

"No, no, I'm fine, Anders has been looking after me," Jane closed her eyes.

"Okay," Ellie said. "I'm going to go do my homework now?" She said it as a question.

"Yes, that's fine honey," Jane smiled at her daughter again, "I'll call you for dinner soon." Anders had already started making some chicken soup, using her recipe, of course. Ellie left to go do her homework, shutting her bedroom door behind her. Anders asked Ed to lend a hand in the kitchen, while Fae sat at her daughter's feet.

"You okay?" Fae rubbed the top of one of Jane's feet.

"Oh, yes, I'm fine. It's just," Jane paused as a wave of nausea washed over her. "Morning sickness." Jane opened her eyes to watch her mother's expression.

"Morning sickness?" Fae clapped. "Oh honey! What exciting news," she launched herself across the chesterfield to smother her daughter in hugs.

"Whoa, take it easy mom," Jane laughed. "Also, you have to keep it down. We are going to tell Ellie tonight after dinner. And tell Anders' parents next time we see them."

"Okay, alright," Fae wiped tears from her cheeks. "Oh, this is so exciting." Just then they heard the men laughing in the kitchen. Evidently, Anders couldn't keep it a secret any more either. They laughed and Jane heard Ed slapping Anders on the back. Then Ed ducked his head around the doorway and smiled at

Jane, giving her a wink. Jane smiled back. Then, leapt up, to beat it to the bathroom once more.

"She's been doing that all day," Anders said to Fae and Ed when he heard her closing the bathroom door.

"Morning sickness," Fae nodded. She had it pretty badly with Ellie, and she's older now, so maybe this time it might be harder on her." Anders nodded, looking worried.

"I'll do everything I can to help her," he said.

"I know," Fae smiled.

'You'll do a fine job, son," Ed chimed in, giving his son-in-law to be a few more slaps on the back.

When Jane returned, she sat gingerly on the couch and carefully sipped from a glass of ice water. "Was there a reason you stopped by today?" She looked quizzically to her mother who'd taken a seat in an overstuffed arm chair.

"Actually, yes," she propped her feet up on the coffee table. The room wasn't much changed from when Anders first rented the house, except for the fact they'd changed the furniture and done some painting when Ellie and Jane moved in. The once mostly brown living room was now a soft cream colour. Anders comfortable leather sofa and tartan patterned easy chairs flanked the room, which was bright because of a bay window that looked over the wide front yard with its circular drive. Jane had added some photographs of cheerful things like flowers or her little family, done in black and white with red frames that complimented the furniture. The windows were curtained in a red and cream stripe. Overall, it was a comfortable and welcoming space. Fae went on, "we stopped by the inn today, we wanted to book an appointment for a tasting, for the wedding." Ed came over and propped himself on the arm of her chair. Anders took a seat at the end of the chesterfield next to Jane.

"You don't need an appointment, Mom," Jane sipped again from her glass.

"No, no. I don't want special favours. You're a busy person," she patted her daughter's knee. "Anyway, that Francis from the front desk said you were away today, which I thought was odd, so we stopped by to make sure everything was alright. But we made an appointment for next week. "

"Okay," Jane sighed a little. "Does this mean you've settled on a date?"

"It does," Ed smiled. "October 10th, it's a Friday. Do you think you'll have that date available?"

"I think so, most of our weddings are during the summer so far, and all of them are on weekends," Jane smiled. "October 10th. That sound just lovely."

"We thought so too," Fae squeezed Ed's hand. "Right, well, we will get out of your hair," Fae patted her beau on the back. "Mister," she said to him. Evidently, this was a clue for him to get moving.

"Congratulations again," Ed offered as he was hurried out the door. Fae shut it behind them. Jane watched them walk hand in hand back to Ed's accessible bus.

"They're pretty cute," Anders said, taking Jane's hand in his.

"They are," Jane smiled, somewhat sadly.

"What's wrong?" Anders asked.

"Oh, just missing my Dad a bit, but I'm also really happy to see Mom so happy," she sighed.

"I'm sure your Dad misses you too, but he'd probably want your Mom to be happy," Anders tried, hoping to be helpful.

"You're right," Jane's father had passed almost fifteen years ago. He wouldn't have wanted her Mom to be alone forever.

"Soup," Anders leapt up, hearing the pot boiling over, that certain sizzle of hot liquid evaporating from the stove travelling to their ears.

"I'm just going to rest," Jane said, sliding into a curled position, pulling a red checked blanket over her.

"Alright," Anders shouted, then cursed under his breath.

Some time later, Jane wasn't sure when, Anders woke her by stroking her hair. It was dark out and Ellie chatted happily at the table, telling Anders about her day.

"Dinner," he said to her, planting a kiss on her cheek. Jane sleepily rose, feeling somewhat better. Maybe the morning sickness had subsided now that it was night? She ate two bowls of soup, and some bread with butter. Then, when dessert came, slices of apple pie she'd brought home from The Acorn, they told Ellie the news.

"Ellie," Anders began.

"You know we love you," Jane continued.

"Of course," she looked them over. She was almost thirteen now and too smart for her own good. "What is it, you're acting weird?" She put down her fork and held her bad hand in her good.

"Well," Jane smiled at Anders, "we have exciting news."

"We are expecting," Anders said.

"Expecting what?" Ellie half thought they were getting something from some online shopping. Maybe they bought her a present.

"A baby," Jane finished, making things clear.

"A baby?" Ellie repeated. "You're pregnant?" She was both excited and grossed out, since she just had been in health class earlier today and understood too much about how babies came into the world. "Wow," she was stunned.

"I'm two months along," Jane offered.

"Wow," Ellie said, feeling sad somehow. Jane stood and kissed her daughter on the head. "Is that why you were sick today?" Ellie asked. "And why I saw you eating chocolate ice cream with olives the other day," she made a gagging noise.

"Yes," Anders laughed. "Your mom might be eating some weird things for a bit, while the baby grows."

"Okay," she took up her fork again, stabbing some apple slices, depositing them in her mouth. Anders stood and gave her a kiss on the head too.

"You alright, kiddo?" He looked worriedly over Ellie's wavy brown hair to catch Jane's eye. Jane raised her brows as if to say, *let it lie*.

"Yep," Ellie said in a teen tone that warned them to back off. She was going to be a big sister. Weird.

About the Author

Whitney Sweet is a poet, writer, and artist. Her work has been included in *A&U Magazine*, as well as *Mentor Me: Instruction and Advice for Aspiring Writers* anthology. She is the winner of the 2014 Judith Eve Gewurtz Memorial Poetry Award. Her poetry is included in *Another Dysfunctional Cancer Poem Anthology* and essays can be read in the *Far Villages: Welcome Essays for New and Beginner Poets*. She is the creator and editor of T.R.O.U. Lit. Mag, a literary magazine dedicated to love and diversity. Whitney holds an MA in Communication and Culture from York University, as well as a BA in Creative Writing and English. When she isn't writing you might find her laughing with her husband, napping, knitting, cooking, or petting her dog.

Photo by Kevin Walsh

Look for these titles also by Whitney Sweet

The Weight of Nectar

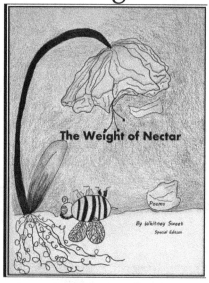

From the author's heart to yours. The Weight of Nectar is a confessional journey through mental illness recovery. With emphasis on experiences related through nature imagery, these primarily free verse poems shine an honest light on struggle it takes to feel well when under the weights of depression and anxiety.

Warrior Woman Wildflower

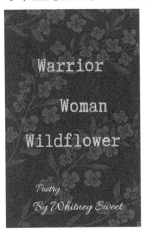

Exploring the world from a woman's perspective, these poems take an honest look at self love, bodies, romance, femininity, strength, and living in a patriarchal world.

Connect with Whitney. She would love to hear from you.

Website: www.whitneysweetwrites.com

Twitter: @CreatesWrites

Facebook: @whitneysweetwrites

Instagram: @WhitneySweet_Writes

You can find prints of her art: www.fineartamerica.com Just search for her name.

Thank you so much to my readers. I feel honoured you have chosen to spend some time with my story.

CPSIA information can be obtained
at www.ICGtesting.com
Printed in the USA
BVHW032339121020
590880BV00001B/8